BODYGUARDS
IN BED

BODYGUARDS IN BED

Lucy Monroe
Jamie Denton
Elisabeth Naughton

BRAVA

KENSINGTON PUBLISHING CORP.

www.kensingtonbooks.com

BRAVA BOOKS are published by

Kensington Publishing Corp.
119 West 40th Street
New York, NY 10018

All Kensington titles, imprints, and distributed lines are available at
special quantity discounts for bulk purchases for sales promotion,
premiums, fund-raising, educational, or institutional use.

Special book excerpts or customized printings can also be created
to fit specific needs. For details, write or phone the office of the
Kensington Special Sales Manager: Kensington Publishing Corp.,
119 West 40th Street, New York, NY 10018, Attn: Special Sales
Department. Phone: 1-800-221-2647.

ISBN-13: 978-0-7582-1033-3
ISBN-10: 0-7582-1033-7

First Kensington Trade Paperback Printing: June 2011

10 9 8 7 6 5 4 3 2 1

Printed in the United States of America

Contents

Who's Been Sleeping in My Brother's Bed?

LUCY
MONROE

For the boys—Travis, Zach and my own superhero, Tom.
You inspire and bring joy to my life.

CHAPTER 1

Danusia wiggled the key in the lock on her brother's apartment door. Darn thing always stuck, but he wouldn't make her another one. Said she didn't come to stay often enough for it to matter.

Yeah, and he wasn't particularly keen for that to change either, obviously. He'd probably gotten the wonky key on purpose. Just like the rest of her older siblings, Roman Chernichenko kept Danusia at a distance.

She knew why he did it, at least, though she was pretty sure the others didn't.

Knowing didn't make her feel any better. Even in her family of brainiacs, she was definitely the odd one out. They loved her, just like she loved them, but they were separated by more than the gap in their ages. She was seven years younger than her next youngest sibling. An unexpected baby, though never unwanted—at least according to her mom.

Still, her sister and brothers might love her, but they didn't get her and didn't particularly want her to get them.

Which was why she was coming to stay in Roman's empty apartment rather than go visit one of the others, or Heaven forbid, her parents. She did not need another round of lectures on her single status by her *baba* and mom.

The lock finally gave and Danusia pressed the door open, dragging her rolling suitcase full of books and papers behind her. The fact the alarm wasn't armed registered at the same time as a cold cylinder pressed to her temple.

"Roman, I swear on Opa's grave that if you don't get that gun away from me, I'm going to drop it in a vat of sulfuric acid and then pour the whole mess all over the new sofa Mom insisted you get the last time she visited. If it's loaded, I'm going to do it anyway."

The gun moved away from her temple and she spun around, ready to lecture her brother into an early grave, and help him along the way. "*It is so not okay to pull a gun on your sister. . . .*" Her tirade petered off to a choked breath. "*You!*"

The man standing in front of her was a whole lot sexier than her brother and scarier, which was saying something. Not that she was afraid of him, but *she* wouldn't want him for an enemy.

The rest of the family believed that Roman was a scientist for the military. She knew better. She was a nosy baby sister, after all, but this man? Definitely worked with Roman and carried an aura of barely leashed violence. Maxwell Baker was a true warrior.

She shouldn't, absolutely *should not*, find that arousing, but she did.

"You're not my brother," she said stupidly.

Which was not her usual mode, but the six-foot-five black man, who would make Jesse Jackson Jr. look like the ugly stepbrother if they were related, turned Danusia's brain to serious mush.

His brows rose in mocking acknowledgment of her obvious words.

"Um . . ."

"What are you doing here, Danusia?" Warm as a really good aged whiskey, his voice made her panties wet.

How embarrassing was that? "You know my name?"

Put another mark on the chalkboard for idiocy.

"The wedding wasn't so long ago that I would have forgotten already." He almost cracked a smile.

She almost swooned.

Max and several of Roman's *associates* had done the security at her sister Elle's wedding, which might have been overkill. Or not. Danusia suspected stuff had been going on that neither she nor her parents had known about.

It hadn't helped that she'd been focused on her final project for her master's and that Elle's wedding had been planned faster than Danusia could solve a quadratic equation. She'd figured out that something was going on, but that was about it. This time her siblings had managed to keep their baby sister almost completely in the dark.

A place she really hated being.

Not that her irritation had stopped her from noticing the most freaking gorgeous man she'd ever met. Maxwell Baker. A tall, dark dish of absolute yum.

Once she had seen Max with his strong jaw, defined cheekbones, big and muscular body, not much else at the wedding had even registered. Which might help explain why she hadn't figured out why all the security.

"It's nice to see you again." There, that sounded somewhat adult. Full points for polite conversation, right?

"What are you doing here?" he asked again, apparently not caring if he got any points for being polite.

She shrugged, shifting her backpack. "My super is doing some repairs on the apartment."

"What kind of repairs?"

"Man, you're as bad as my brother." They hadn't even

made it out of the entry and she was getting the third degree.

Really as bad as her brother and maybe taking it up a notch. Roman might have let her get her stuff put out of the way before he started asking the probing questions. Then again, maybe not.

"I'll take that as a compliment." Then Max just paused, like he had all the time in the world to wait for her answer.

Like it never even occurred to him she might refuse to respond.

Knowing there was no use in attempted prevarication, she sighed. "They're replacing the front door."

"Why?"

"Does it matter?" Sheesh.

He leaned back against the wall, crossing his arms, muscles bulging everywhere. "I won't know until you tell me."

"Someone broke it." She was proud of herself for getting the words out, considering how difficult she was finding the simple process of breathing right now.

This man? Was lethal.

"Who?" he demanded, frown firmly in place.

Oh, crud, even his not-so-happy face was sexy, yummy, heart-palpitatingly delicious. "I don't know."

"A break-in?" he asked in that tone her brother got sometimes, the one she secretly called his *work* voice.

"An attempted one, yes. Whoever it was didn't expect the crazy loud alarm Elle installed the last time she visited."

Neither had she. It had woken Danusia from an exhausted sleep after too many hours going over research data. If her heart wasn't so healthy, it would have stopped.

She only hoped whoever had tried breaking in and disturbed her sleep hadn't been so lucky.

"You don't talk like a professor."

"That's because I'm a student." Sort of. She was an adjunct professor during the school year, but it was summer and she was firmly in researching student mode.

"Roman said you're getting your Ph.D."

She shrugged. Playing down her academic accomplishments was a long-held habit for her.

He looked her up and down. "You're pretty young to be going for your doctorate, aren't you?"

"Not if you consider I started college when most of my peers were starting high school." When even being reminded of how out of step with her peer group she was didn't dampen his effect on her libido, she was in serious trouble.

"That's my point."

"Point?"

"Don't play dumb, Professor. We both know you're smarter than that."

"Don't call me Professor."

He just gave her a look.

"Being younger than my peers is bad enough. I don't need to talk like a total geek on top of it." The normal college student speak was something she worked diligently on. It was too easy to let five-syllable words slip into the conversation when she wasn't thinking about it.

"Why not? You should be proud to be so intelligent."

"I am more than my brain." Not that other people seemed to realize that.

Sometimes, even her family, as wonderful as they were, tended to treat her like an extension of her I.Q. They were all highly intelligent, but the fact that she'd outdone every one of them academically put her inside a bubble that could get really lonely.

Not that she ever complained. She wouldn't disappoint her family for the world. And being anything less than grateful for the opportunity of the amazing education she'd had would do that.

"Why didn't you just stay in a hotel overnight?" Max asked, apparently dismissing the subject of her smarts.

Thank goodness.

"The super wasn't sure he'd get to the door right away." And she hadn't wanted to stay in her apartment alone right now.

Her roommate wouldn't be back until a few days before fall term started and that was weeks away. Rebekah had gone home for the summer, while Danusia had opted to stay on and work on the research for her doctoral thesis.

The attempted break-in had shaken her; not that she'd admit that to anyone else.

"Bullshit. A new door for you is his top priority."

"Now you really sound like my brother." And she didn't feel sisterly toward Max. Not even a little.

"Do you want me to talk to your super?"

"I'm perfectly capable of handling this on my own," she gritted out. She was not his little sister and even if she had been, Danusia was twenty-four. "I'm an adult, or hadn't you noticed?"

Something flared in his gaze that sent butterflies on suicide bombing missions in her stomach. "I noticed."

"I don't need anyone talking to my super for me, not you, not my brother. Understood?"

Amusement curved his lips and he saluted, way too precisely for him to be anything but true military. "Understood, ma'am."

She laughed. "Oh, knock it off."

"You've got Roman's temper."

"Most people think my brother doesn't have a temper." He was too cold to be considered temperamental.

"I've known him a long time."

"You haven't known me very long, but you've already sussed out one of my secrets."

He shrugged, those big, muscled shoulders rolling and pulling his dark T-shirt taut across his perfectly defined pecs. "What can I say? I'm good."

"No arguments here." She gave him a look, doing her best to let him know she didn't just mean his interrogation techniques.

His eyes widened and then narrowed. "Save that for your college boyfriends."

"I don't have any."

"You don't have any male friends?"

She didn't have very many friends at all, but that wasn't what she meant. "I don't have a boyfriend."

"So, get one."

That had her laughing out loud. "Right, like that's going to happen."

"Shouldn't be too hard. You're wicked smart. You're sexy." He did that shrug thing again.

She wasn't sure if it was the shrug, or his words, but her heart felt like it had started practicing for the Grand Prix. "You think I'm sexy?"

"Don't let it go to your head. I'm sure a lot of guys do."

"Now I know you're just being nice. Guys do not think geeky Ph.D. students are sexy."

He reached for the handle on her rolling case. "If you say so. You'll have to sleep in Roman's room. I'm in the guest room."

He started walking down the hall toward the bedrooms, tugging the overloaded case like it was filled with nothing more than air.

"Why are you staying here?"

"I gave up the lease on my apartment, but the condo I bought and was supposed to move into won't be ready for another two weeks."

"The builder is running behind?" she asked, wondering

who in their right mind didn't keep their commitments to a man like Maxwell Baker.

"Yeah, but we negotiated a twenty-thousand-dollar drop in my condo price because of it. It's all good."

She'd just bet they'd negotiated.

He deposited her suitcase at the end of Roman's king-size bed. She dropped her backpack with her clothes in it on the corner of the mattress closest to her.

He looked at the backpack and then at her suitcase. "Let me guess, clothes in the pack and books in the heavy-as-hell case."

"I told you. Geek."

"Serious student, anyway. How close are you on your thesis?"

"I've still got some research to go through, but I should be ready to present and defend by the end of October."

"That's still a few months out."

"It's a doctoral thesis, not a term paper, or so my adviser keeps saying."

"Sounds like a hardass."

"I'm sure Dr. Shay would appreciate you saying so. I'm convinced she works on her scary factor in front of the mirror at night."

"So, what's this thesis on?"

"The use of nanotechnology in pharmaceuticals." Which was something that fascinated and delighted her, but usually caused glazed eyes and yawns in other people.

"I didn't think we were there yet."

"We're closer than a lot of people realize."

"You and Spazz would have fun talking this technical shit."

"You mean Lieutenant Kennedy?"

"That's the one."

"He's really . . . um . . . hyper."

"On coffee? He's all sorts of scary."

"So, the nickname, Spazz?"

"Yes."

"What do they call you?"

"Luke."

"Luke?" What kind of nickname was that? Then she thought for a second. Unable to believe she hadn't gotten it right away, she asked, "Like in Luke Cage, the superhero, super strong, with skin impervious to almost any weapon?"

"Yep."

She looked him up and down, making no effort to hide her perusal, but doubting it had the same effect on him as his in the hall had had on her. "I can see it, but why not call you 'Power Man'?"

"You know your superheroes."

She felt a blush climb her cheeks. "I like comic books."

"You've got to more than *like* them to know the details of Luke Cage."

"Born Carl Lucas, came by his powers in a military experiment gone wrong and first appeared in *Luke Cage, Hero for Hire*. One of only a handful of black superheroes in either the Marvel or DC comic universes."

Max was grinning by the time she was done reciting the basic facts of one of her favorite superheroes. "Like I said, sexy, professor. Very sexy."

Not only was his nickname from Power Man, but he thought her closet superhero obsession was sexy? Oh, this man was perfect for her. Now she just had to convince him of that fact.

Not that she had a clue how to go about doing that. Her dating record was sketchy at best. She'd had blind date disasters instigated by her family and Rebekah, but that wasn't the same as participating in the mating dance with a man that she had the hots for.

But Danusia had never even kissed a man she was attracted to. Oh, she'd been kissed. She'd even had sex. Disasters didn't get that designation lightly, after all.

But this was different. When she'd met Max at the wedding, Danusia had been sure he was way out of her league. That a geek like her wouldn't even register on his radar. Now he was telling her that she wasn't just a blip, but she was a sexy one.

Oh, wow. Oh, wow. Oh, wow.

Would fainting prompt him to give her the kiss of life and would that start something she'd only be too happy to finish?

"What are you thinking about?" he asked suspiciously. "You've got a strange look in your eye and your brother warned me about you."

That was the second time he'd admitted to talking to her brother about her. That had to mean something, right? That he was at least interested enough to mention her in passing to Roman.

"What did he warn you about?"

"That you have an unbalanced sense of humor."

"Unbalanced? That's harsh." Though Roman had said worse when she'd switched salt for sugar in his canister and he'd added it to his morning coffee.

It was an old trick and she shouldn't have gotten away with it, which was what she'd told him. Sugar and salt didn't look alike to a person with a background in chemistry, not to mention the different smell, texture and melting rate in hot water.

He'd told her she needed to get a life. Of course, it was his effort to see she had one that had prompted the salt in his coffee. He'd fixed her up the night before with the most boring, obnoxiously intelligent man she'd ever met. To make matters worse, they'd gone on a double date and

WHO'S BEEN SLEEPING IN MY BROTHER'S BED? 13

while her brother was having fun with his not-so-brainy arm candy, Danusia had spent the evening arguing quantum physical theory. Not discussing, but arguing.

Her blind date had been an opinionated cretin.

"Do I have to worry you're going to sabotage the kitchen?" Max asked, proving Roman *had* been telling tales.

"I don't know. Are you going to try to fix me up with the most obnoxious man on the Eastern Seaboard?"

"Is that what Roman did?"

"Yes. And when you're contemplating murder, salt in the coffee doesn't seem like such a harsh retaliation."

Max laughed out loud. "I can promise you, I've got no plans to fix you up with anyone while you're here."

"Good." She had her own plans and they all revolved around the gorgeous black man whose laugh made her thighs clench.

Weird. Was that a primal reaction, she wondered, or an evolutionary one? Whatever it was, there was an ache between her legs that would not go away.

"You're doing it again."

"What?"

"Thinking about something that puts that alarming expression in your eyes."

"Do I worry you?" she asked in disbelief.

"More than you know." With that, he spun on his heel and headed out of the room, stopping at the doorway. "I'll make dinner tonight."

"You don't trust me to cook?"

"Let's just say I'll be sure what goes into it if I make it."

"I'll have you know I'm a very good cook." It was basic organic chemistry and she'd had that particular subject down before she'd been out of training bras.

"When you aren't switching ingredients on the unsuspecting."

"I told you, he deserved it."

"And I don't."

"Not yet," she couldn't resist saying.

He laughed again and she decided that sound could become more addictive than McDonald's French fries.

CHAPTER 2

Max julienne sliced the carrots while he reminded himself of all the reasons why the sexy little doctoral student currently studying in the living room was off limits.

One—despite her advanced education, she was six years younger than he. Two—that education disparity was just another reason that nothing between them could work. After barely graduating high school, he'd gone directly into the Marines and learned how to kill people. No amount of reading and online courses since then could bridge the gap between the two of them.

And hell, why bridge a gap for a casual fling?

Which was the next biggest reason he needed to keep his hands to himself. Three—Max didn't do serious and Danusia Chernichenko deserved more than a casual roll in the sack, no matter how hot it was. And it would be desert at high noon hot too.

He wanted to undo the dark brown hair she always wore in either a long ponytail or braid down her back and bury his fingers in the silky strands. Damn if it didn't make him some kind of walking cliché, but he wanted to see that long dark hair spread out under her while he drove into her small but curvy body over and over again.

While she shared the rest of her family's pale coloring with almost black hair, unlike the rest of them, Danusia wasn't more than average in height. She couldn't be more than five and a half feet tall with bones like a sparrow.

Too fragile for a man like him, but that didn't stop him wanting her.

Hell, if she didn't deserve more than he could ever give, though.

The biggest reason she was off limits? Four—she was his friend and team leader's baby sister. A smart man did not play with that kind of fire. It was likely to burn him to ashes for his trouble.

And five—if he needed a five—they didn't even live in the same state. Not that he spent a lot of time here, but it was home.

Which again implied he was thinking long term, which he wasn't. Because he never did. He'd lived his whole life watching his mom struggle with what amounted to single parenthood while his daddy spent weeks on the road as a long-haul trucker.

Max's job not only took him away for weeks at a time, but there was no guarantee he'd come back. His missions were dangerous, though necessary.

He wasn't putting a woman through that kind of pain, or himself through the struggle between his job and his family. His daddy's weeks on the road had taken their toll on him as well and he'd died young from a heart attack.

Max wasn't following that path, no way, no how.

But, damn, he wanted Danusia. Had wanted her at Elle's wedding, and the hot need had only grown since. He might not have seen Danusia in the intervening time, but he'd dreamt about her. A lot.

Which was just plain crazy.

Even crazier, he'd pictured her face on more than one woman's body as he was screwing a one-night stand. It didn't make him proud either. He might not do serious, but he respected the women he had sex with and knew it was wrong to bury his cock in one woman's body while thinking of another one.

Which went a long way toward explaining why he'd gone without sex for longer than he had since his first time with the divorcée who lived across the hall when he was fifteen.

His agitated thoughts did not stop him from noticing the muted sounds the moment she stood up and started moving around in the other room. He knew she'd come into the kitchen before her sweet, floral scent told him she'd moved into his personal space.

She leaned around him. "Looks good. Can I help with anything?"

"I've got it."

"I really am a decent cook."

"You're a Chernichenko. I doubt there's anything you don't do well."

She laughed, but the sound was more sad than humorous. "Isn't it obvious? I'm not like the others."

Sliding the carrots into the steamer, he fought the urge to turn around. And lost. He put the lid on the cooking vegetables and then turned to face Danusia.

She was mere inches away and it was all he could do not to reach out and pull her the remaining distance so their bodies connected. "What do you mean?"

She rolled her eyes and stepped back. "You don't have to pretend to be nice. I know my limitations."

What the hell? "Don't you know how proud of you Roman is?"

"Sure. I'm the freak among freaks, right? My siblings are so smart, they scare people and I'm even smarter. That's really something great, isn't it?"

"I guess it depends on what you do with that big brain of yours." But he didn't like her sad, almost weary tone.

"My cranium capacity is no larger than average for a woman of my height."

He shook his head. "That's not what I meant."

The amusement now lurking in her grey gaze said she knew that and was teasing him. She didn't dwell on whatever bothered her and while he found that admirable, he didn't like the idea that she carried a burden like that about herself.

"You are something special, Danusia."

"I'm a freak." She shrugged. "But we take the bad with the good, right? If I can be like Matej and develop something to make the world a better, or safer, or healthier place, then it's worth it to be such a bad fit with other people."

"You fit just fine with me."

"And you are a good friend to my brother."

"He's not here now and I still like spending time with you."

"So, give me something to do."

"Tired of studying?"

"You could say that. The latest batch of research I downloaded from Luminescent Pharmaceuticals isn't making sense. I think I've been staring at the printouts too long."

"Are they one of the companies experimenting with the use of nanotechnology in medical treatments?"

"Yes. They've had some breakthroughs too, or so some of their research would suggest. But the reports I've been looking at today don't back it up. I'm not sure exactly what they do say, to be honest."

"If anyone can figure it out, it's you."

"Right. I'd rather slice vegetables."

"All done, but if you're intent on manual labor, you can start on the dishes."

She looked over to the nearly empty sink. "You're a clean-as-you-go kind of cook, aren't you?"

He shrugged. He liked order. Nothing wrong with that.

She grinned, as if she knew a joke she wasn't telling, but headed over to start on the dishes.

He put the red snapper covered in Cajun spices into the melted butter in the cast-iron frying pan. The fish started to sizzle immediately, the scent of chili powder and crushed red pepper seeds filling the kitchen.

"Smells delicious," she said as she washed the pan he'd used for the sauce. "You're a really good cook, aren't you?"

"It's a hobby."

"A pretty serious hobby, by the look of things."

"It relaxes me." Cooking blackened red snapper with mango-lime sauce was a far cry from MRE rations and helped him to distance his home time from that in the field.

"I like to cook too, but my roommate says I'm too keen on experimentation for my own good."

"How can you help it?"

"That's what I tell Rebekah."

"A fully stocked kitchen's an irresistible temptation to someone with an intimate working knowledge of chemistry. Or so Roman says."

"Roman experiments in the kitchen too?" Danusia sounded shocked by the idea. "Rebekah is more into physics than chemistry, but she is happy to just follow a recipe, you know? I like to try different things. And Roman does that?"

Max nodded, all serious. "They don't all turn out either."

She laughed and this time the sound was pure joy. His cock throbbed in response and he would have given it a good thump if she wasn't looking right at him.

He settled on turning back to the stove and finishing dinner, tossing the now cooked carrots in a chicken stock and butter sauce and plating everything while it was still hot.

She was drying her hands when he finished. "Where do you want to eat?"

He didn't really care and said so.

She blushed and looked off to the side. "Um, there's a

new show about a superhero family I've been wanting to watch. The dad is one of my favorite actors."

"So, we'll watch it."

"Really? You don't mind, after all the work you put into dinner?"

"Nope, don't mind a bit."

It was so worth the grin that entirely lit her pixyish face. And the show wasn't bad. Even better, though, was her reaction to it.

"You've really got a thing for superheroes, don't you?"

She blushed. "With my family, can you blame me?"

"I'd say they'd all consider you more the superhero than them."

"Superbrain maybe, but Elle got the whole package. She's beautiful, smart and she can kick ass too, just like Electra. Then there's Matej. He's not a secret agent like the others, but he's doing such important work, he might as well be Dr. David Banner without the whole Hulk side-effects thing. Mykola has got the superspy thing going on too and then there's Roman."

"A scientist for the Army."

"Tchya." The look she gave him told Max Danusia didn't buy the long-held cover story for a minute.

"Let me guess. You think being a military scientist has some superhero quality to it too?"

"Maybe, maybe not, but you and I both know Roman doesn't work for the Army—at least not as a scientist. Nope, he's no more a scientist than I am a cover model."

"Why not a scientist? He's got the degree and the brains."

"And he carries himself like a soldier, a real soldier, not a lab rat. Roman's too tanned to spend his days in the lab. And he's got this scary aura, almost as scary as yours."

"You think I'm scarier than Roman?" That would be a first.

"Yes, but maybe that's because I see him through the eyes

of a baby sister. I know he'd never willingly or knowingly hurt me." The way she said it made Max wonder if Roman had unknowingly hurt his little sister.

"Who do you think he works for?" The Chief was going to shit kittens when he found out his baby sister wasn't taken in by his cover.

Not one little tiny bit.

"He told my parents he was speaking at a symposium on polymer sciences in Europe. Funny thing, he's not listed as a speaker."

"Maybe they didn't get his name up in time."

"Maybe he's on assignment somewhere else. My guess is out of country, or he would have told them he was going to be somewhere in the States. And he's not in Europe, because he would never give his real destination."

Hell, she should be working for the Atrati. "Maybe you've got an overactive imagination."

Hurt flared in her eyes. "Maybe I'm not as dumb as my family seems to think. I realized Elle was some kind of government agent before her first husband died. I didn't tell anyone else. Little sisters find secrets, they don't share them. I knew when Mykola was working undercover on that drug case. I even knew where he was living, but I'm not about to tell him that. When he couldn't save everybody, I knew he'd be broken up and when he showed up at Elle's company, it was obvious there was more going on than anyone wanted to admit."

"What the hell?"

"I use my brain for more than studying."

"I think maybe *you're* the scary one."

She shook her head. "I'm just a little sister who wants to know more about her siblings than they're willing to tell her."

There was pain in Danusia's voice he understood all too well. He'd heard it often enough in his mother's tone when his daddy had refused to talk about his weeks on the road, saying that when he was home he didn't want to think about his time in the truck.

"They all love you." He knew that much from things Roman had said.

"They keep secrets. They share with each other, but think I'm too young to know, or something."

"They're just protecting you."

"They think I'm a security risk."

"You *are* telling me stuff I doubt they want others to know." Not that he considered her a risk, but she needed to be more circumspect, especially when it came to Roman.

Who was in Africa right now on a black-ops mission commissioned by the Army. But Danusia was right, neither Roman nor Max worked for the military anymore. They were agents for the Atrati, a paramilitary organization that did a lot of work for the government, but was not under the government's official aegis.

"You're one of them, if not a spook, something super secret." He opened his mouth, but she put up her hand. "Don't. Don't lie to me. Just don't say anything if all you're going to do is deny it."

He had an insane urge to tell her the truth, which was absolutely not going to happen. "You sure this isn't your superhero obsession playing tricks with your brain?" he asked instead.

She stood up, grabbing her plate and his. "Never mind. I shouldn't have said anything."

"But you did."

"Right. So, I guess I *am* a security risk."

Well, shit.

CHAPTER 3

Danusia adjusted the hand towel on the rack after wiping down her brother's marble countertops.

She'd insisted on cleaning the kitchen on her own, telling Max that it was only fair since he'd cooked. He'd seemed like he was about to argue and she'd given him the look, the one she used on her big brothers and sister when she was absolutely adamant about getting her way.

Max took the hint and left.

Thank goodness for small favors. She couldn't believe she'd set herself up for disappointment like that. He'd been right about one thing—she'd let her imagination run away with her.

Oh, not about her sibs, but about the connection she'd thought she'd made with Max. He might find her sexy; he didn't have a reason to lie about it anyway. But they weren't friends and even if they had sex, they weren't about to become lovers.

Men like him did not have full-on relationships with women like her. The fact was she knew *most* people didn't want to. No matter how hard she tried to fit in, her intelligence made most people give her a wide berth. It was hard to make friends, even in the academic community. She was lucky her roommate had stuck with her through college. Even though Rebekah was four years older than Danusia, she'd never let that get in the way of being the younger woman's friend.

Rebekah was the only person in Danusia's life who didn't push her away or treat her like she was different or a freak. In fact, she treated Danusia more like a little sister than her own siblings. The main reason for not going to Rebekah when Danusia realized she didn't want to stay in the apartment alone had been her fear of finally wearing out her welcome with the other woman.

So, she'd come to what she'd believed to be Roman's empty apartment and ended up sharing with Max. The one man she found more interesting than even her doctoral thesis.

Max was no more interested in being real with Danusia than her brothers and sister. So what? She was used to being lied to and kept at a distance, wasn't she?

If they weren't smothering her with protectiveness, her family kept her as far away as possible. Even her parents and *baba* had insisted she attend a university too far away from them for her to live at home.

For her own benefit of course—the physics and chemistry departments were second to none. Thank God she'd been placed in a room with Rebekah her first semester. Homesick and terrified by the campus living, Danusia had glommed onto a kind and extremely patient Rebekah, who helped the younger girl navigate her strange new world.

Rebekah had steered Danusia toward the lab when she was feeling out of place and taught her that no matter her age, sex, or circumstance, this was somewhere she would always belong.

So, Max wasn't going to be her boyfriend? That wasn't some big surprise, was it? And it didn't mean Danusia had to abandon all the plans she'd been making since showing up in Roman's apartment and discovering it wasn't as empty as she'd expected it to be.

She'd never had good sex, much less any in the amazing category. She just knew Max would be amazing. Even if she wasn't all that great at it. She could learn and a man like him, he could teach her.

She was tired of fantasies and loneliness. She didn't know how long she had in the apartment with Max, but she was going to take advantage of whatever she did have.

With that in mind, she went looking for her brother's liquor supply. Not that he'd ever offered her a drink, though she'd been legal for more than three years now. Everyone in the family except her mom and *baba* treated Danusia like she was still a teenager. Mom and Baba? Wanted her married.

A harsh laugh sounded. Right.

She was better off married to her studies and one day to her own research.

She found Roman's alcohol supply in a cabinet in the living room. She supposed it was considered a mini-bar, but all she knew was that he had a truly impressive array of alcohol from all over the world.

Even some good old-fashioned Ukrainian potato vodka, distilled and bottled by an official distillery. She was sure there was a bottle of her papa's efforts in there somewhere too, but that was too special to drink on a whim. Or without permission. She pulled the vodka with the black label out of the cabinet and poured a finger each in two highball glasses.

"Indulging in a nightcap, Professor?" Max asked from behind her.

She hadn't heard him come in, but this just meant she didn't have to go looking for him. Turning, with a glass in each hand, she extended one toward him. "Join me."

"I don't know if that's such a good idea." He eyed the drink like it was a snake set to strike.

Interesting. What did he have to be wary about?

"Sure it is. How can you turn down vodka distilled in the Ukraine?"

"Do you swear in Ukrainian like your brother?" he asked instead of answering.

"Sometimes." Worried, she asked, "Do you not drink? Should I have not offered this to you?"

"I can hold my liquor just fine, but every soldier knows better than to drink when he needs to keep his head."

"Why do you need to keep your head?" Was he planning on going out?

"I've got five good reasons."

"Care to share them?"

"Not really."

She looked at her drink, then back to him, trying to understand his reticence, but respecting it. It might be time to go to Plan B, getting herself tipsy enough she wouldn't care if he was slightly lubricated or not.

Then without warning, Max took the glass and slammed it back like a shot. He held his breath for a second and then let it out slowly. "Those Ukrainian moonshiners know their stuff."

She giggled. Which she never did, and she hadn't even had a drink yet, but she followed his example, swallowing against the burn of the strong grain alcohol. "Papa says his grandfather made some of the best potato vodka in the world. Good for your liver."

Max gave that ultra-sexy laugh again. "Right. Does your father distill his own?"

"I'll never tell."

"You can tell me, I'll keep your secrets." He gave her a serious look, like he was making a promise.

But she wasn't going to read anything into the words. She was done wearing those fantasy-inspired, rose-colored glasses.

She took his glass and turned back to the cabinet. "Like another?"

"I think one is enough. For both of us."

"You do what you like, but I'm having another. If you don't mind being outdrunk by five-feet-six inches of academia, that's on you."

She poured again, this time two fingers of the clear liquid, and then slammed it back.

Max made a sound that was suspiciously close to a growl and then he grabbed the bottle and poured his own double shot.

He grinned wildly at her. "Here's to Ukrainian brainiacs and Marine grunts."

She didn't call him on the fact that he admitted to being a Marine and her brother was supposedly Army and yet they worked together. She simply nodded and gave him her own crazy smile. The alcohol was already hitting her.

He shook his head afterward. "If I didn't know better, I'd think you were trying to get me drunk to have your way with me."

Smart man. "Is it working?"

"Doesn't matter."

"You don't think?"

"No matter how much I want you, or how drunk you get me, I've got enough control to stop myself screwing my friend's baby sister."

She didn't lie and say Roman wouldn't care. They both knew he would. He wanted her settled down with another brainiac, off in a lab somewhere where she wouldn't worry her family, hence the blind dates from hell.

He didn't want her getting more embroiled in his life, through his *associates*, or any other way. "Don't worry . . . I won't share your secrets," she said, repeating Max's words.

He shook his head. "Not going to happen."

"That's what I said. You don't have to worry about me telling tales." She wasn't a blabbermouth.

"We're not having sex." Well, that was blunt.

But she could be blunt too. "You want me."

"*Yes.*" That single word held a wealth of meaning.

He really wanted her, like seriously, really. Of course the growing and quite impressive bulge in his jeans said so even more than his affirmative.

"I'm right here." She pulled her T-shirt over her head and dropped it on the floor. Blunt was good. Action was better.

He made a strangled sound in his throat and stepped back. "Ain't going to happen." But his eyes ate her up.

And that was so hot, she couldn't help posing a little. She might have felt stupid but for the alcohol and the way he watched her, like he was a sailor on leave and she was the first woman he'd seen after getting off the ship. No, even hotter . . . so hot, her skin burned.

Her jeans came off almost as easily as her top. She stepped out of them. "Really?"

She thought maybe it was going to happen. Max's body for sure wanted it, no matter what his mouth said. She stretched and did a little turn. "All yours for the night."

"*Shit. Piss. Damn.* You shouldn't have done that." He spun away and practically sprinted for the guest bedroom.

"Where are you going?" she demanded, even the warmth from the alcohol not equal to the chill of his blatant rejection.

"Bed, where you should go too . . . in the other room, not mine." He was babbling and it would be cute except for what he was saying. "Good night, Danusia," he called over his shoulder as he disappeared down the hall.

Danusia stared down at her nearly naked body. Okay, she wasn't a nearly six-foot-tall supermodel like her sister, Elle, but she wasn't horrific either. And they hadn't done anything yet, so he couldn't know she wasn't a perfect sex kitten between the sheets.

Oh, she'd be happy to try, but no amount of reading

made up for practical experience and hers had been pretty dismal.

Her alcohol-muddled mind couldn't decide what she'd done to send Max running. He'd said he wanted her. His body had shown it. Oh, how it had shown it.

But he'd also said he had five reasons. *Five reasons for not having sex with her.*

She needed to find out what those were.

Because she wasn't about to give up on the first man that could hold her attention when there was new data to decipher.

CHAPTER 4

Max woke to the smell of coffee and frying ham.

So, the little professor was up and around already.

His stomach growled, reminding him it had been a long time since dinner and he'd slept later than normal. He'd been awake half the night fighting the urge to go find Danusia and finish what she'd started with her impromptu striptease.

He couldn't get the image of her sexy, pale curves out of his mind and it'd haunted him right into his dreams too.

She might be average in height, but her legs looked long enough to wrap around his hips just right.

The matching sheer blue bra and panties she'd been wearing hadn't left anything to the imagination either. Who would have thought the serious student would wear such sexy lingerie?

He knew her nipples were a deep raspberry red when excited and that while her breasts would be a generous handful, her nipples weren't overly large. He would have so much fun teasing them to swollen hardness though.

Knowing her pubic curls were the exact same chocolate-brown shade as the hair on her head only made him want to play down there and see how much darker they looked when wet with her excitement.

His morning hard-on liked the image so much it went from semi-hard to locked, loaded and ready. Shit.

Not what he needed right now.

And she wasn't just sexy, she was sweet and hella smart.

And she'd made coffee. And ham. Which usually meant some kind of eggs as well. His stomach growled again at the thought. Of course there was no saying she'd made enough for him, not after the way he'd rejected her the night before. Running away like the scared little boy Maxwell Baker had never been.

Piss and damn.

She was sitting at the table, drinking a mug of that delicious-smelling coffee when he made his way into the kitchen a few minutes later. She looked up and smiled, her expression nothing like what he expected from a woman he'd turned down the night before.

She nodded at a covered plate on the other side of the table. "Your breakfast. It's a good thing you got up when you did. Eggs Benedict are just nasty cold."

"You made Eggs Benedict? *For me?*" Where was hers?

"Yep. I prefer fruit and yogurt for breakfast."

He looked pointedly at the empty spot in front of her at the table. She had only a cup of coffee.

She shrugged. "I ate earlier. I never sleep very late when I drink the night before."

"Really?" He, as a rule, slept later and if he wasn't careful, woke with a headache—even if he hadn't drunk enough to get a hangover.

"Yeah, just another way my brain doesn't work like other people's."

He sat down, pulling the cover off his breakfast. "Looks perfect."

"I followed the recipe."

He caught himself on a chuckle. "That's good, I guess."

She nodded.

He pulled his napkin from under the silverware to put in his lap and noticed a piece of paper beneath. It was blank except for the numbers one through five.

He looked up at Danusia. She had that look in her eyes again, the one that made him wary. "What's this?"

"You said you had five reasons. I want to know what they are."

"Does it really matter?"

"It does to me."

"Telling you what they are isn't going to change the fact that they exist."

"Refusing to tell me what they are isn't going to change the fact I want you and that you want me."

Well, hell. "Roman didn't tell me you were so stubborn."

"It sounds like he told you plenty, even if he didn't tell you that, which he knows by the way. In case you were wondering." She sipped her coffee. "But, you know, it sounds like you and Roman have talked an awful lot about me."

"I guess." He went for casual, but he knew he'd been caught.

He could see it in her eyes.

She confirmed it with her next words. "I wouldn't think my brother would talk about me much, not without prompting, anyway."

"He's proud of you."

"Still . . ." She gave him a look that dared him to deny asking about her.

He shrugged. "I was curious."

"Because you wanted me."

"You're blunt."

"It's the scientist in me. You're changing the subject."

"Yes." To both. He did want her and he really wanted to change the subject.

His control had never been so close to the edge, which scared the hell out of him and excited him beyond reason too. It was almost a better adrenaline rush than going on assignment.

Something in her grey gaze said she knew exactly what he'd meant by the yes. She nodded toward the paper with the numbers on it. "So, tell me why you can't have me."

"I'm not writing it down."

"Afraid my brother will find it in the trash after you're gone?"

It was a serious consideration. "Look, if you can't live without knowing, I'll tell you."

"Okay, so talk, but don't let your breakfast get cold."

He started eating and thought about how to approach telling her his reasons. Should he start with the biggest one and try to circumvent the need for the conversation?

The stubborn tilt to her jaw said that wouldn't work.

He decided to start with the reason he figured she'd consider the most valid. She'd already shown she didn't consider the fact she was Roman's baby sister any kind of roadblock. "I'm not in the market for a relationship."

"So?"

What the hell did she mean, so? "You're a forever kind of woman."

"Tell that to the other men I've had sex with." She shook her head, her expression nonplussed. "I don't think they got the memo."

"You've had sex?" Of course she'd had sex. She was twenty-four, but other than the striptease the night before, she came off as Pure Grade A innocent.

"My family might have sent me away from home when I was thirteen, but they didn't send me to a nunnery."

"You had sex back then?" he asked, feeling queasy.

She grimaced. "No, of course not. I was still a kid, but I've been an adult for six years."

"So, you've had sex." He was still having trouble wrapping his mind around it.

"Yes. Not mind-blowing sex, or even good sex actually, but I have copulated with members of the opposite sex."

"How many?" Oh, shit. "Forget I asked that."

"Why? You wouldn't want me to ask you the same thing?" she guessed.

He winced. "Something like that."

"You're not a man-whore. If you were, you would have taken me up on my offer last night. Regardless of your reasons."

"You have a lot of faith in a man you barely know."

"You think you're the only one who has asked Roman a few subtle questions?"

He wasn't touching that one. "So, the stupid assholes you've had sex with aside, you still deserve more than a night rolling in the sheets."

"You won't have sex with me because I deserve a relationship?" she asked, sounding really confused and more than a little irritated.

And if that wasn't too damn adorable, he didn't know what was. Which was not the way he was supposed to be thinking.

"That's one of the reasons, yes."

"Since I'm not expecting anything other than that mind-blowing sex I've only ever read about, that particular excuse is voided." She spoke with a firm certainty that showed she knew how to argue for what she needed.

More than that, she expected him to blow her mind?

Who was he kidding? *Blow her mind?* If he got his hands on her, he wasn't going to stop until she was past coherent and right into passing-out-from-pleasure mode.

"You can't just void a reason because you don't like it." He wished he was as sure as he sounded.

"I can void an excuse that is directly linked to me and *my* feelings. You don't get to make choices for me in that regard. No one does."

He could argue that he got to make choices about his own feelings, but that would be admitting he was experiencing emotions he didn't usually. He'd rather drop the F-bomb during Sunday dinner at his mother's when she had the pastor over.

"We don't even live in the same state," he reminded her.

"It's only a six-hour drive from upstate New York to Boston, but I don't even see how that excuse has any relevance since we both agree you aren't looking for a relationship."

"You should be looking for a relationship."

"Who are you to tell me what I should be looking for?" There was that temper again, flaring in her voice and snapping like molten metal in her grey eyes. "If I want a break in the monotony of my own company, whatever the cost, don't tell me not to go for it. Because *what I deserve* is a few lousy hours of not being alone."

She should have sounded desperate. Another woman saying it would have, but damned if he didn't find himself agreeing with her instead of pitying her. The fact he was panting to touch her colored his view, he was sure.

Still, he shook his head. "I know you don't think it matters, but Roman is your older brother and he's not only my boss, but he's my friend."

"He's your boss?"

Shit. He never let stuff slip. "Yes."

"Don't look so discombobulated. I told you, I'm good at finding out what I want to."

"Is that what this is about? You're trying to use me to find out more about your brother's life?"

"I wouldn't do that." She jumped up from the table and started wiping down the already clean countertops. "I don't use people."

He knew that. He did. It just wasn't in her nature. She was a sacrifice-not-to-upset-others kind of person.

He got up and went to her, laying one hand on her shoulder. "I believe you."

It wasn't an apology, but he wasn't great at those. Would it be enough?

She turned to face him, her grey eyes swirling with things he couldn't decipher and some that he could. Desire. Pain. Loneliness.

"Your family has no clue, do they?" he asked her before he could stop himself.

She didn't ask what about; she just shook her head.

"They think they did the best for you, sending you off to university at thirteen."

"I was mature for my age. It came from having a really facile brain and siblings that were so much older than me. I told them I didn't need my mom to come with me. It wouldn't have been fair to take her away from my dad. Baba would have come, but she didn't move over from the old country until I'd been at university for two years already."

And her parents had believed Danusia when she told them she didn't need them. She'd let them off the hook and they'd swum on happily in their local pond while she tried to find a place for herself in unfamiliar waters.

Unable to keep himself from touching her, he brushed her hair behind her ear. "You deserve so much more than I can give you."

"I'll take what I can get." Again the words could have been desperate, but she said them with a calm certainty that blew him away.

He let his hands drop to her waist, his long fingers almost touching behind her back. "You're so tiny."

"Please tell me that's not one of the five excuses."

"*Reasons.* And no, it's not." Though maybe it should be. "Good."

"I joined the Marines right out of high school."

She tilted her head back so their gazes were locked. "If that's one of your five, you're going to have to explain why."

"I didn't go to college."

"Right. So, no fancy degrees for you, huh?"

"Not a one."

"At the risk of sounding like a CD with a skip in it, does that really matter if you're not looking for a long-term relationship?"

"I guess not." It felt like it did with her though.

"But it bothers you."

"Some."

"Not everyone gets their education at a university."

"True."

"You've got life experience I can't begin to match. Does that make you think less of me?"

"No."

"Good."

"It's not the same."

"Oh, I think it is. You read a lot too, don't you?"

"Roman tell you that?"

"I guessed, but he confirmed it. I already know you've taught yourself to cook like a chef. Degree, or no degree, you're a renaissance man, Max. And for the record? I've known more academics than most people. A university degree does not decree instant compatibility, nor does the lack of one mean two people cannot find and maintain common ground. You may not have my brain, but you're a long way from stupid." She smiled up at him. "Unless you really refuse to take me up on my offer. Then I'm going to revise my opinion of your I.Q."

"Brat."

"Matej calls me that sometimes, but it sounds different coming from you."

"I sure as hell hope so." The temptation to kiss her was so strong, he had to step back.

Only his hands refused to let go, so the distance between them was limited and not real effective.

"Five," she said in a breathy voice that revealed he wasn't the only one affected by their nearness. "You said there were five reasons and you've only given me four so far."

"You're six years younger than me."

She gave him a considering look. "You know, for a man not in the market for a relationship, an awful lot of your excuses are based on your perception of long-term compatibility."

He didn't have an answer for that, or at least one that would make sense—to either of them.

"But six years? Really?" she went on, when he didn't say anything to her observation. "Sixteen *might* worry me, twenty-six would give me some doubt, but six? Please. When we were teenagers, those six years would have mattered, but we're both adults now and they just don't."

"I'm thirty and I should have enough self-control to keep my hands off you."

"But you don't?" she asked hopefully.

He found himself grinning as the inevitability of what was going to happen between them washed over him. "I don't."

And if she wasn't convinced by his reasons, he wasn't going to hang on to them like a sulky child. She was right, this was just sex and if she wasn't pushing for more, who *was* he to insist she should?

"Seriously?" she asked.

"Oh, yeah."

"Now?"

He shook his head. "You have work to do today."

"It's the weekend, I can take some time off," she said suggestively.

"I'm teaching a class this morning. Advanced techniques in hand-to-hand combat. I need to be there in forty minutes, but I'll be done by three," he said quickly when her face fell.

He could call in and cancel class, but he wanted her to have some time without him around to think about what he'd said and change her mind if she was going to.

"Hmm . . . not feeling like working. Maybe I'll get a massage."

"I guarantee you'll get plenty of touching when I come back."

"That's what I'm hoping, but to maximize the experience, I should work on getting relaxed." He couldn't tell if she was joking or not.

Scientists didn't think like normal people. Roman might be more soldier than scientist now, but the man still proved the rule.

Then he realized why she was so tense. "The break-in threw you, didn't it?"

"It scared me, yes."

He should have realized, but she'd done that thing with him that she clearly did with her family. Pretended to be okay when she was frightened and facing the unknown. He wasn't going to fall for it again. "Why didn't you go stay with family?"

"Everyone but Roman is in a fairly new relationship. They don't need me horning in on their privacy."

"And your parents."

"Would you go stay with *your parents?*"

"Point taken." He loved his mom, but he preferred to get a hotel room when he went to visit her.

"So, three o'clock?"

"I'll be here by three-thirty."

"Yum."

Laughing, he shook his head. "You're sweet."

"You think?" She fluttered her lashes outrageously and he laughed again.

Giving in to the urge that had been riding him since walking into the kitchen, he leaned down and gave her a brief but thorough kiss.

He ran his tongue along her lips to savor her flavor before pulling back. "A little taste of what's to come."

She just nodded, her expression dazed.

Sex between them was definitely going to be mind-blowing.

He was whistling when he got in his car.

CHAPTER 5

Danusia rolled the pencil between her teeth, the faint taste of wood comforting in its familiarity.

Her roommate, Rebekah, teased Danusia for using the old-fashioned, yellow No. 2 pencils that had to be sharpened every morning before she started work. Danusia firmly maintained a mechanical pencil was not the same. She grabbed the No. 2 and put a check beside another anomaly in the research.

These results simply did not make sense in the face of the company's claims of a breakthrough in nanotechnology for medical treatment.

She put the pencil back in her mouth and flipped to the next paper in the stack. This one listed results exactly as she'd expected them to be. Her brows drawn together, she put the two printouts side by side.

A big warm hand landed on her shoulder and she gasped, spitting the pencil out. It clattered as it rolled across her brother's glass tabletop.

Her heart galloping, she jumped up and spun, knowing on one level that it had to be Max and another not so sure.

It was Max and he was smiling. "You know, after this morning, I expected a little different reaction to my return."

She looked around frantically for her cell phone, the only

"watch" she ever wore, but it was probably buried under the papers she'd been reading. "Um, is it that late already?"

"Later."

Then she noticed his black hair was damp and he was wearing PT shorts that exposed the full length of his dark, muscular legs. No shoes, and no shirt. Oh, man.

Her legs wobbled.

The man had a to-die-for chest. "You took a shower."

Without her, darn it!

"I did." He tugged her ponytail. "No massage?"

"Oh, I was going to call and then got to thinking about something I wanted to check in my research. . . ." She trailed off, embarrassed. "Um, how long have you been here?"

"A while. When you didn't respond to my initial greeting, I found you studying in here." He looked around the dining room she'd taken over for her work area.

"Roman's desk isn't big enough to spread out on." She bit her lip. Like Max cared where she studied.

"You get really lost when you're working, don't you?"

No use denying it. "Yes."

"That could be dangerous."

"I don't study away from my apartment at night." When all of her older siblings kept harping on it, she'd finally promised them she would do her library work earlier in the day.

"It's cute."

"Seriously, you're not irritated?"

"Nope." And he didn't look mad either. Not even a little annoyed.

"Oh." Cool.

"You looked pretty intent when I first got here, and not very happy."

"It's these results." She indicated the printouts on the

table. "They're supposed to show Luminescent Pharmaceuticals' breakthroughs, but they're pretty much the opposite."

"You think Luminescent is making false claims for their research?"

"They could be. Maybe this data is older, but they're really sloppy about some stuff. It's hard to tell."

"What do you mean?"

"They keep meticulous records of results, but there are no dates anywhere on three of these reports, or names for the projects. It's odd."

"It sounds suspicious, if you ask me."

"Yeah, that's what worries me. Luminescent is a major supplier for pharmaceuticals for third-world countries and the Middle East. If they're supplying products that don't work, but make things worse, that's . . ." Words failed her.

"Dangerous."

"Right." Not to mention, unethical. Despicable. Just plain rotten.

"I mean, dangerous for you."

"What? Why for me?"

"You've got to wonder if you were supposed to be given this set of data."

He had a point. "The woman helping me get the downloads was a little ditzy." Then it was like Danusia's brain finally switched on and she shook her head. "What are we doing talking about my research?"

"Just discussing our days, right?"

He wanted to do the how-was-your-day thing? It was her own fault, so she backed up and asked how his was.

He laughed. "If you could see your face, Professor. My class was a wash. I nearly sent two of the participants to the infirmary."

"That doesn't happen very often?"

"Try never."

"Why today?" she prompted, wanting him to say it.

"Wasn't paying enough attention to pull my punches properly."

"Oh." She liked hearing that. A lot.

"Yes, *oh*. Want to take a guess what I was thinking about?"

"Your best friend's Bar Mitzvah?" she couldn't help teasing. She was feeling giddy.

"Not Jewish and neither is he."

"The government cover-up of alien visitations?"

"Not a conspiracy nut."

She was grinning as he reeled her into his body. "How best to utilize your retirement fund?"

"Brat." Then he kissed her and all desire to tease fled, along with coherent thought.

His mouth fit perfectly over hers, his lips using just the right pressure to send tingles of awareness radiating outward until she could feel this one perfect kiss in her toes. She responded, letting her tongue dart out to taste. He groaned and suddenly their tongues were sliding against each other and his arms were around her, pressing their bodies together.

His skin was so warm and soft under her hands, his muscles so hard.

She caressed along his sides, around his back and over his chest, loving the feel of his curly chest hair under her fingers. Her hands could not stay still though. They sought out one treasure after another. Hard male nipples, well-defined pecs, biceps that bulged under her fingertips, inviting her to grip them tight and hard.

She mapped his every bulge and valley of muscle with the investigative fervency of an obsessed topographer.

This man could so easily become her obsession, probably was already, if she was honest with herself. And she did try to be.

She couldn't believe she could touch and feel to her heart's content. Was there such a thing? She didn't think she would ever grow tired of caressing this man, her desire to touch never completely sated.

His hair was cut Marine short, the high and tight even more compact than on other men because of Max's tight nap. It felt amazingly sexy against her palms and she writhed against him, her hands on his head, pulling him closer, moaning into the kiss.

His arm made a shelf under her buttocks and then he lifted. They were moving, his hold on her strong, his mouth masterful.

Both their eyes were open, but while his were watching where he carried her, hers were fixed on him. He was just so incredibly gorgeous and even more so with that look of desire in his sherry-brown eyes.

She landed on the guest room bed with him on top of her. And wasn't that just perfect?

He thrust his hips against her, his hard-on pressing, teasing, making her whimper. "You're wearing too many clothes, Professor."

She'd heard that word tens of thousands of times in her academic career, sometimes directed at others, sometimes at herself. Never before had it sounded like a synonym for sweetheart.

"So're you." Naked would be good. Oh, yes. Really, really good.

He gave that delicious laugh even as he started unbuttoning her blouse. He pulled it open and then gave a low whistle. "Nice."

She wiggled out of the top. "Nice would be naked."

He nodded, moving so he could get her jeans too. She didn't like wearing shoes or socks, if she could get away with it, so he didn't have any hindrance to pulling the jeans right off. Other than the fact that they were the tightest pair she owned, but that didn't seem to hamper his efforts even a little.

She'd never gotten this particular pair of pants off as fast. When they were gone, he stopped and just shook his head. "*Damn.*"

It sounded more like *damn fine* than a curse so she let him look his fill without worrying what he was thinking.

"I like the panties." She was wearing a fire-engine red thong. "But you're missing your bra today, professor."

"I thought it might help my cause." That and her tight jeans. She could admit she'd brought them along on the extremely off chance she somehow saw Max while she was in Boston.

"You really are a brat."

"Determined."

"Calculating."

"A scientist knows to take the right tools into the lab."

"You consider your breasts tools?"

"In attracting you, I sure hope so."

"You're so damn refreshing."

"That's better than irritating."

"Not the same at all."

"I'm glad."

"I'm horny."

She burst out laughing. "Then, I guess you'd better do something about it."

"You take off those tiny little panties and I just might."

"Might?" she asked with a teasing look as she hooked her thumbs in the waistband and started pushing down.

"Will."

"Better."

She tossed her thong away and then waited for him to do the same to his shorts. Only he hadn't moved a muscle and his gaze was fixed on her nudity. "You're exactly like I dreamed."

"You had dreams about me?"

"I did."

"I had dreams about you too. That means something, don't you think?"

"It means we should have made it like bunnies at your sister's wedding."

She found herself laughing again as he pushed his shorts off. Her laughter ended on a choked gasp as she got her first glimpse of his hard penis.

Okay, so her previous two encounters had been with much smaller men overall, but Max wasn't just big. He was huge.

"You got a license for that thing?" she asked on another choked laugh.

He prowled toward her. "It'd have to be a Class OIC #3 for large weapons."

"You've got that right." Was he even going to fit?

She was going to try. Really, really hard. And like she'd told him, she was very determined.

He climbed up onto the bed, slinking over her until his body completely dwarfed hers, his hardened flesh a hot brand against the apex of her thighs and up her stomach.

Definitely big. Really, really.

"You okay, Professor?"

"Oh, yes." More than. Really.

"You sure?"

"Why do you ask?"

"You keep saying *really* over and over again."

"Oh, um . . . it's just a word." And she'd been thinking out loud again. *Aargh.*

"And you are just adorable."

Again, huge improvement over how her other sex partners had seen her—as irritating.

She leaned up to kiss him for that. He responded immediately, his mouth molding to hers in that way that felt so, so perfect. This time, he didn't stop at her lips though.

He kissed down her neck, paying close attention to where it joined her shoulder, sending chills of pleasure along her nerve endings. Then he moved down to her collarbone, using his tongue tip to trace along each clavicle bone before lapping between her breasts. She'd never realized she was sensitive there, but he showed her she was and so much more.

He avoided her breasts and the small bit of flesh pulsing with a hungry need between the folds of her labia.

Only when she was breathlessly begging for, "More, more, more, please, more, just more, please, Max!" did he move to take one nipple between his lips.

He nipped it gently and then laved it with his tongue. She gasped out a sound more animal than woman; it was certainly one she'd never heard herself make before.

He started suckling, while bringing his hand up to cup her other breast and roll that nipple between his fingers.

It was an overload of pleasure and she felt tremors she only recognized as a different kind of orgasm as they crested and she found herself shouting his name and several Ukrainian naughty words.

Oh, wow. *Wow. Wow. Wow!*

Suddenly long, thick, masculine fingers were delving into the wet flesh between her legs. He pressed one into her vagina and crooked it, curving upward. He rubbed and hit a spot that she'd read about but never discovered on her own.

She screamed again, this time a wordless sound of pure need.

He reared back. "You ready for me?"

"More than."

He nodded, leaning over her to grab stuff from the bedside table. When he kneeled up again, he had a condom in his hand. "Want to put it on me?"

"Yes."

She sat up and put her hand out for the condom packet. She fumbled, but managed to get it open and the condom out intact. Then she stopped. "I want to touch you."

"Later," he growled out as he tugged her hand toward him.

She nodded. Later. Yes. Lots of touching later, but now? He was going to be inside her.

First though? She needed to taste, just a little. She touched his weeping slit, and then brought her finger to her mouth. Salty. Sweet. All man.

He groaned.

She moaned.

"Put it on me," he demanded.

She nodded again, this time frantically. Yes, yes, yes. Hands shaking, she rolled the condom down his big erection, squeezing a little as she went. Oh, man. Her fingertips didn't quite touch as they circled him at the base.

She whimpered. "Want you."

"Lie back, sweetheart. I'm all yours."

Falling back, she spread her legs, bending her knees to make all the room he needed between her thighs.

"Damn, you are one sexy brainiac." His dark gaze burned through her.

"Uh-huh." Whatever. She just wanted him inside. Now.

He laughed, even as he moved into position, his head right at her entrance. "You're thinking out loud again."

"I do that sometimes." She arched up, trying to get him to come inside.

"I've noticed." He pushed forward, just a little. "It's cute."

"Max! Come on."

That dark chuckle sounded again and then he was pushing inside, stretching tender intimate tissue to capacity.

"Feels so good," she gasped out.

"Oh, yeah."

He made little rocking motions with his hips, pushing deeper with each small thrust.

She felt like she was going to fly apart and he wasn't even all the way inside.

"Me too," he ground out, making her realize she'd done it again.

Good thing he didn't find her habits irritating.

"Not irritating. Sexy. Oh, shit." His big body shuddered as he bottomed out inside her.

Their eyes locked, neither of them moved. The moment felt too profound. It was supposed to be just sex, but there was something going on here, something she didn't even know could happen. But she felt that in this moment, they were one being.

The look of intense concentration on his face said he felt the same, or at least something close to it.

She opened her mouth to say something, she didn't know what, but he shook his head. And started to move.

His strong hand gripped her buttocks, tilting her pelvis just so and that tingle-inducing spot inside her vagina got stimulated on the long, slow glide out and then in again.

He didn't speak. She couldn't. He moved in and out, one slow thrust after another.

She'd thought she'd wanted hot, hard and fast, but this was so good. *So perfect.* The pleasure built, and built, and built, and she never wanted it to end.

"Gonna do this for hours," he said.

"Next time." Because even with the slow thrusts, she knew she wasn't going to last long.

And he was already so swollen and hard inside her, he had to be close too.

"Next time," he agreed as the thrust of his hips increased in tempo.

Unable to do much, the way he had her tilted, she strained against him. "Want it. Want it. Want it," she chanted over and over again, knowing that blissful release was just over the next rise.

Then he locked her knees over his arms and pressed her legs farther apart while thrusting deeper than he'd done yet.

She felt her climax explode through her, taking her in wave after wave of drowning bliss. She screamed. She cried. And she came. And she came again.

Her body wasn't even hers anymore; it belonged to pleasure.

A hoarse, masculine shout sounded above her and his body went rigid. She was so sensitive, she could feel the pulse of his erection as he came too.

She wondered what it would be like without the condom, without any barrier between them.

"Dangerous, Professor, damn dangerous."

Oh, man. She *had* to stop thinking out loud, or she was going to tell him she was falling for him . . . *had fallen for him* and in a way that was anything but casual.

CHAPTER 6

They were cuddling together in his bed after a delicious bout of shower sex when her cell phone rang.

She flung her arm out toward the sound, but the rest of her body didn't follow. "You broke me."

"You complaining?" He stroked his hand along her flank, leaving shivers of sensation in his wake despite her total satiation.

"No."

"Didn't think so."

"I should get that."

"Later." He didn't make a move to initiate more sex though, but pulled her closer into the curve of his body. "We need a nap."

And that? Was really dangerous.

Danusia listened to the message her apartment manager had left on her phone for the second time, trying to convince herself it said what she'd thought she'd heard. But it was just so wild.

Max sauntered in from the kitchen. He'd insisted on making dinner again, saying cornbread crust pizza was a no-brainer and she could work on her thesis while he threw it together.

He'd made it pretty clear he didn't want her help, so she'd come into the dining room. The research wasn't making any more sense than it had earlier, and she'd remembered the phone call. Listening to her messages seemed like a legitimate reason to procrastinate.

Only the message didn't make any more sense than the printouts littering the table.

"What's the matter?" he asked.

"What? Oh . . ." She closed her phone and stared at the opposite wall, wondering if she should head back to her place tonight, or wait for morning.

Ever since they'd woken from their nap, Max had been putting distance between them. She got that. The sex between them had been too intense and he'd made it clear he wasn't looking for a relationship.

It still hurt.

"Danusia?" he asked, sounding wary.

She turned to look at him. "I need to get back to my apartment."

He didn't look disappointed, or happy, or well *anything*. Max had his game face on and she had no hope of reading it.

"The super get the door fixed?" he asked.

She filtered the message her manager had left through her brain for an answer to that question. "Yes, with a fancy deadbolt and an interior security flip bar."

"Sounds like they're taking your safety seriously."

They should. Her apartment had been broken into a second time, but left totally trashed on this occasion. The thieves, vandals . . . whatever . . . had disabled the security alarm this time. Elle was going to be pissed.

All Danusia said was, "Yes."

"When are you going?"

"I was thinking about heading back tonight." The police

wanted to talk to her and needed her to go through her place and see what had been taken.

His head jerked, his game face gone in the wake of dark emotion. "Tonight? What's the rush?"

"There's no reason to put it off."

He frowned and then got that sexy look she found so irresistible. "I can think of a few."

"Really?"

"If you leave now, you'll be driving into the wee hours. That's not safe. Don't even pretend to think that's a good idea for a woman alone."

That was so not where she'd expected him to go. And he was right, but she was feeling reckless. She just shrugged.

His eyes narrowed, but all he said was, "You don't want to miss my pizza."

"It's that good, huh?"

"It is."

She sighed, knowing his first argument was a valid one, especially in light of what had happened at her apartment. "I guess."

"Do you really want to give up one more night of this?" he asked, indicating himself.

Finally, he went with what she'd thought he was going to begin with, but maybe it was good he hadn't started out with the sex, which was so much more than just sex. At least for her.

And she would have said for him too.

But she was the first to admit her ability to read men was nothing like her skills in the lab.

"Conceited," she accused.

"You saying I don't have reason?"

"No."

"So?"

She wasn't sure her heart could handle more of the kind of sex they had together. And what came after.

Her leaving. And his letting her go.

He stepped toward her, his expression predatory. "You don't look convinced."

"I might need a little persuasion." Her heart might not survive this intact, but it was already cracking around the edges.

At least one more night in his arms was one more night before she had to let the pain in. Before the loneliness took over.

And it wasn't as if she didn't know how to deal with being alone.

"I think I can do that." He pulled her gently up from the chair, taking her phone and laying it on the table before wrapping her in his arms.

He lowered his head. "The pizza's got fifteen more minutes. I can do a lot of convincing in that amount of time."

"You'd better get to it then."

"Oh, I plan to."

Then he did. The kiss was incendiary and her worries about her heart melted in its heat. She reached up and locked her hands behind his neck and threw herself into it. Maybe it was that she'd never kissed a man she found so attractive, or maybe it was simply kissing this man, but every time their lips locked, she lost herself.

He lifted her against him, pressing that impressive hardon into the apex of her thighs. It wasn't enough.

She wrapped her legs around his hips and rubbed against him, unable to stifle the sounds of frustration when that just made the ache worse.

He broke his mouth away from hers. "Shhh, sexy, I'll take care of you."

Then he sat down in the chair she'd been using, standing

her up between his thighs. He unsnapped her jeans and lowered the zipper. "Let's get rid of these."

"Yes." She shoved the denim down her legs and kicked it away.

He grasped her hips, his hands so big that his thumbs easily reached her clitoris through the nylon of her panties. He brushed over the aching nub first with one thumb and then the other, teasing and satisfying with the same touch.

"Touch me, Max."

"I am touching you, Professor."

"You know . . ." Her voice failed as he rubbed a little circle over that spot.

"I do, yes."

Suddenly, her panties were gone and then she was sitting astride his lap, facing away from him. He tilted her head up so he could kiss her while his other hand moved between her thighs.

He brushed his fingers up the sensitive skin of her inner thighs before delving into her most intimate flesh. He slid one long finger inside her while the heel of his hand pressed against her swollen clitoris.

She moaned into the kiss, her body arching toward that touch, her brain losing touch with reality in a maelstrom of pleasure. She didn't know how long he touched her like that, but the faint sound of a buzzer sounded from the kitchen just as her body and mind exploded like nanobots in a microwave. Sparkly lights danced behind her eyelids while she cried out against his lips.

Dinner was delicious, but what happened after was mind destroying. He yelled her name when he came and held her throughout the night. She woke before dawn, knowing she needed to get going before she did something really stupid, like ask him to come with her. Or if she could come back.

She was in the shower when she heard her phone ring. It stopped by the time she'd turned off the water and reached for a towel.

She was still drying herself off when Max walked into the bathroom looking pissed off and too darn sexy for this early in the morning.

"You want to explain to me why I just got off the phone with a police detective who wants to know when you'll be back in town?"

She wrapped the towel around herself and tried sidling toward the door, but Max wasn't moving. She stopped in front of him. "It's about the break-in."

"Like hell. The police don't follow up like this on an attempted break-in when the perp didn't even make it inside the apartment."

"Not the first time."

"What the hell happened?"

"Do you think I could go to Roman's room and get some clothes?" Her backpack was still in the master bedroom.

Max leaned against the doorjamb. "Talk."

"You're bossier than all my older siblings combined."

"You think?"

"They never grill me naked."

"You're wearing a towel and I'm your lover. That comes with certain privileges."

"You're my current sex partner. That's not the same thing."

"I'm not done with you yet."

"Right. I'd say we're done. I'm going back to my apartment and I don't see you making a six-hour drive for a booty call."

"You plan to go back to an apartment that's been broken into twice now, *alone?*" His volume rose with each word until he was as loud as her dad watching the Super Bowl.

She made a show of shaking her finger in her ear. "Loud, much?"

"Tell me what is going on." He bit each word out with a jaw like granite.

So, she told him.

He didn't look any happier once she'd explained than when he'd been in the dark. In fact, there was a muscle ticcing in his jaw now and his breathing was even only by force of will. She could tell.

"Man, you really are worse than Roman."

"Like hell you are going back there alone," he said, instead of responding to her accusation.

"I have to go back. The police need to know if anything has been stolen and I don't want them calling Rebekah and upsetting her."

"Your roommate can stay just where she is."

Since Danusia agreed, she didn't say anything.

"I'll go with you."

"What? No. No way. I'm an adult, I can take care of this."

"It's either take me, or I call your parents and your sister and two brothers who are in country right now."

"You don't have their numbers."

He held up the phone. "I do now."

"You're being ridiculous."

"Which will it be?"

"You can't just take off from work like that. You've probably got some super-soldier mission to go out on."

He flipped the phone open. "Make your choice."

"Fine. Gosh. If I'd known all it would take to get you to go with me was to get my apartment broken into, I would have done it sooner," she said sarcastically, hoping he couldn't hear the strain of truth in her voice.

He heard something, because he shook his head and

turned with a heartfelt "Shit," as he went back into the guest bedroom.

"You don't have to go with me," she called after him. "I could call my sister."

Because really? Two break-ins? Not normal. Danusia and Rebekah had chosen their apartment partly because of the building security and safe neighborhood.

"Don't start with me, Danusia Lyudmyla Chernichenko," he yelled from the other room.

"You know my middle name?" she asked on a squeak as she hurried into the bedroom, her hand clutched in her towel.

He spun around to face her, a pair of black cargo pants in his hand. "I know a lot about you. Your middle name's the least of it."

"It's not my fault. My grandmother's best friend back in the old country was named Lyudmyla."

He just gave her a look.

"It's embarrassing. So old-fashioned."

"It's cute, like the rest of you. Now, go get dressed."

She would have found it more of a compliment if he wasn't barking at her like a drill sergeant.

She saluted smartly and scurried from the room. He caught up with her halfway down the hall. He spun her around and slammed his mouth down on hers.

He didn't kiss her long, but when he finished, she was gasping and dazed. "Brat."

She nodded before she realized what she was agreeing to and then shrugged. "If you're good at something . . ." She left the rest unsaid.

"I'm good at killing people."

This time she knew exactly why she was nodding.

"I was MARSOC."

"Marines special forces."

"Yes."

"Sniper or assassin?"

"Does it matter? I was and am a human weapon."

"Maybe it's time for a career change."

"Maybe it's not." There was a question in his words, but she wasn't sure he was even aware it was there.

She just leaned up and kissed him softly. "I'll get dressed."

CHAPTER 7

They made the six-hour drive in five and still managed to talk nearly nonstop the whole time. Danusia told Max about what it was like to grow up out of sync with her peers and in a family of such loving, overprotective and yet distant siblings.

Max told her about growing up on the fringe of his middle-class schoolmates with a long-haul trucker for a father. His mother hadn't handled the separations well. When Max told her he'd never heard the woman laugh until several months after his father's death, when she'd started seeing a widowed schoolteacher, Danusia had felt tears burn her eyes.

"You think no woman could handle a relationship filled with absences."

"No woman should have to."

"Military wives do it all the time. Other long-haul truckers have happy marriages."

"The divorce rate in the military, especially any special forces branch, is significantly higher than national averages. Same for long-haul trucking."

"It's still possible."

He'd changed the subject, but she was beginning to see how a man who based most of his excuses for not getting involved on stuff that would only matter in a relationship could say he was only interested in casual sex.

*   *   *

Max looked for anyone or anything out of the ordinary as he walked slightly to the side and behind Danusia into her apartment building. There were security cameras in the parking lot and the entrance.

If the perps hadn't been caught on them, that meant one of two things: lucky or professional. He knew which one he was leaning toward.

Danusia lived on the third floor and her apartment was at the end of the hall. Again, the fact she was the farthest from the elevator and stairwell increased the perps' chances of being seen.

"No news on who broke in?" he asked, pretty sure he knew the answer already.

"None. Two men wearing dark hoodies were seen on the security cameras, but their faces were never visible."

"And no one noticed suspicious persons loitering outside your apartment?"

"The police said they don't have any leads."

He didn't say anything else as they met up with the manager outside Danusia's door.

The woman, wearing a red power suit, let them in. "I don't know what's going on. This is highly irregular," she said, giving Danusia an accusing glare.

"What is irregular was your superintendent's careless attitude about putting a new door in. This second break-in could well have been prevented." Which he actually doubted, but hell if he was going to stand by while the snooty bitch tried to make Danusia feel responsible.

His little professor didn't seem to be paying attention to either of them. Her focus was on the chaos on the other side of the now open door.

Danusia walked slowly inside, her head swiveling to take in what was clearly a very thorough job of turning her apartment upside down. Shit.

This was no robbery. Someone had been looking for something. And they hadn't found it, or the entire place wouldn't be so methodically trashed.

Which was what he said to the detective when he and Danusia stopped by the police station later.

"That was our take as well, Mr. Baker."

Max frowned. "And you didn't warn Danusia? Why the hell not? She could have walked right into something."

The detective gave Danusia what was no doubt supposed to be an intimidating frown. "In our experience, when someone is looking for something with that much determination, the person in possession of that something is already aware of the fact."

"We as in who, detective?" Danusia asked. "Your police department? How many cases of this sort have you investigated? Enough to make an acceptable statistical average?"

"I'll ask the questions here, Miss Chenko."

"It's Chernichenko and you may call me Danusia if that's easier."

"What were the perps looking for?" the detective asked.

"I don't know for sure."

"Look, Danusia, we can't help you if you won't be frank with us. If you're in something over your head, we'll do what we can to help, but you need to tell us what it is."

"Local police are allowed to lie." She turned to Max. "Only federal investigators are required to tell the truth, though that doesn't extend to the CIA, apparently."

Max almost laughed, but he held it in. "Do you think Rebekah is involved in something dangerous?" he forced himself to ask.

"No, but I think I may be."

The detective looked triumphant.

Max should have been surprised, but he wasn't. "The pharmaceutical research?"

"Yes. I realized in the car on the way here what those results could indicate. I mean if you weren't looking for people getting better?"

"What's that?"

"Nanotechnology as a weapon rather than medical treatment."

He cursed. The detective looked confused and he didn't look as if he understood a whole lot better after Danusia's explanation. To give the guy credit—which Max wasn't overly inclined to do considering his negligent attitude toward Danusia's safety—parts of her explanation went right over Max's head as well.

But he had no trouble figuring out that his little professor was in a world of trouble. Or would be if he weren't around to keep her safe. He didn't just know how to kill people, he knew how to stop others from doing it.

He planned to put his knowledge and experience to full use in protecting the sweet and too damn sexy scientist-in-the-making.

And it was a damn good thing, because once the detective did get the gist of what Danusia was trying to tell him, he immediately dismissed her theories as far-fetched and fanciful. "This isn't an episode of *Law & Order*, Miss Chernko."

Max couldn't decide if the man was getting her name wrong on purpose, or really was that dense.

"I'm fully aware that this is real life. It's my apartment that's been ransacked, detective."

"And you want me to believe someone did it trying to get back a bunch of computer data you got for researching your paper?" The man couldn't have come off as more dismissive if he'd called her *little lady* and rolled his eyes.

"Do you have a better theory?" Danusia asked.

But Max didn't need to. The detective had nothing.

"Well, now. It's a lot more likely that you've been turning your knowledge of chemistry to more lucrative endeavors."

The police detective's words were annoying as hell, but expected.

Danusia, though, looked shocked and horrified by the implications. "You think I've been making drugs?" she demanded, proving her brains worked outside the classroom too. "Are you aware that one of my brothers is a former DEA agent?"

"Former?"

"Oh, my gosh, I can't believe what you are implying." She turned to Max. "Is he really saying what I think he's saying?"

"Looks that way to me."

"Now, listen here, Miss Chenkiro."

The detective's misuse of her name yet again was the last straw because she gave him a contemptuous look and got to her feet, marching away from his desk toward the exit without another word.

The detective wasn't so quiet. "Wait a minute, there. You can't go storming off. I'll have you arrested on obstruction of justice."

Danusia ignored the petty threat for the empty hot air it was.

The man jumped up to follow her, but Max got between them. "If you'd found drugs in her apartment, she'd already be under arrest. You've fucked up this investigation and any chance of a promotion you might have gotten out of it."

With that, he left, catching up with Danusia before she was out of the building.

"That man is an idiot," she said.

"He lacks imagination."

"Oh, I'd say he's got plenty of that."

"No, for him, it's same old, same old. He can't wrap his mind around a crime that isn't centered on drugs or domestic violence."

"He thought I was making drugs." She sounded so furious and so hurt.

Max put his arm around her shoulder, even as he maintained easy access to his concealed weapon. "It wasn't personal, sweetheart."

"It felt personal."

"I know."

"Do you?"

"Sure. I've been pulled over for nothing more than DWB."

"What's that?"

"Driving while black."

She didn't laugh like he expected. "That's terrible."

"Hey, it happens to teenagers too. No matter how much they deny it, law enforcement profiles."

She stopped three cars down from where they'd parked and looked up at him, eyes swimming with hurt. "Do I *look* like a drug dealer? Maker? Whatever?"

"Now, *you're* profiling."

"Yeah, I guess. I don't like it and I don't know what to do." Her lower lip jutted out and he felt like a heel because all he wanted to do was nibble on it. "I'll have to call my family," she said in the next breath, her tone about as happy as new recruits' when told they had an extra hour of PT before mealtime.

"No, you don't."

"I don't?"

"I'll call in some friends."

"Like Roman did for Elle's wedding?"

"Something like that." But this situation was going to take official government involvement.

"Why would you do that?"

"You're too smart for stupid questions, sweetheart."

"I was right."

"About what?"

"*Professor* does sound just like *sweetheart* the way you say it."

Danusia lay on the bed and flipped through the complimentary newspaper in their hotel suite an hour later while Max made phone calls in the other room. He'd insisted it wasn't safe to stay in her apartment and she hadn't argued. She'd left their accommodations up to him and wasn't surprised to find herself in a suite at the end of the hall on the seventh floor of a hotel with both a doorman and twenty-four-hour reception desk.

She expected other men like Roman and Max to show up any minute and set up some kind of security plan for her. If it were her family doing this, she knew she'd feel stifled and like somehow she was inconveniencing them. Even if they would deny it. But with Max? She felt protected. Almost cherished.

It was crazy, considering how he insisted they didn't have a future, but the man was way too worried about her feelings and safety for a casual lay.

She idly flipped to the Metro section to see what was going on around the city when a small article in the lower left corner caught her eye. The picture was one of those awful ones used for drivers' licenses and employee identifications. It was of the woman who had given Danusia the data for her thesis at Luminescent Pharmaceuticals.

And she was dead.

She'd been involved in a single-car accident at freeway speeds late at night. No witnesses. The article said the roads had been slick with an unexpected summer rain and it was unclear whether she'd fallen asleep at the wheel or simply lost control of her vehicle.

What were the chances?

Danusia grabbed the Metro section and rushed into the sitting room. "Max."

"Hold on," he said into the phone and looked at her. "What's up, Professor?"

She handed him the paper. "That woman, down at the bottom of the page? She's the one who gave me the data at Luminescent."

Max's eyes narrowed and he read the brief article lead before swearing. "Our timeline just amped up," he barked into the phone. "They're not just trying to get the data back. They're eliminating loose ends."

Danusia couldn't hear what the person on the other end of the call said, and wouldn't have understood if she had. Her brain was going into meltdown. She was definitely not superspy material like her sister.

The thought of someone wanting her dead scared the pee out of her. Well, not literally. But it was close.

Oh, man. She was babbling, even in her head.

Strong arms wrapped around her and Max's body heat broke the chill of terror trying to take hold. "It's going to be okay, sweetheart. I'm not going to let anything happen to you."

She clutched at him. "I'm scared. I shouldn't be scared."

"Who says? This is scary shit."

She almost laughed. "You're not scared."

"You're wrong."

She reared back so she could see the truth in his face and sure enough there was a shadow of worry in his eyes, which was probably as close to really frightened as this man got. "I don't understand."

"I'm damn good at my job. Both of them. Killing and protecting."

"So?"

"So, I've never been personally invested in keeping my client alive."

"I'm not your client. I'm your lover." He'd said it first. He could deal with it.

His head dropped to rest against hers. "I know."

"I think that scares you more than the thought of the bad guys getting past you." She'd meant it as a tease.

But his fierce frown said he didn't get the joke. "Not even close."

"Okay."

"But I've never had one," he said.

"A lover?"

"Yeah."

"You're no virgin."

"Neither are you."

But she'd never had a lover before either. She got it. Sex partners yes, lover no. The difference between them? She *wanted* a relationship. She didn't want to be alone, though she'd proven to herself and anyone else who cared to take note that she did just fine that way.

She'd been raised in a close-knit family with parents who loved each other deeply. She wanted that for herself. She wanted someone to call her own. Not someone. She wanted this man. He wasn't ready to hear that though. She wasn't sure he ever would be.

"It's going to be okay." It was her turn to comfort.

This time he did laugh, though the sound wasn't his usual sexy joy. "A couple of friends are coming in by helicopter. They should be here in an hour."

"I guessed. Should I pretend I don't realize they're some kind of black-ops group?"

"Paramilitary black-ops is the correct term."

Something inside her cracked at this little tidbit of honesty. "Is it?"

"Yes."

"And?"

"They won't tell you their real names. You don't have to pretend you don't realize what they are or why they're here. Our nicknames are used for a reason other than to piss some of us off." He sighed. "Though you'll probably learn who some of them are eventually if you hang around me long enough."

"Am I going to be hanging around?" she asked.

"Long-distance relationships have a pretty bad success rate."

"Is this a relationship?"

"I don't know." He looked so pained, so frustrated, she didn't push.

"We'll focus on the problem at hand right now," she offered.

His game face came over his features like a robot mask. "Right. That's exactly what we should be doing."

She went to step out of his arms, but he didn't let her go, tugging her over to the couch instead. He sat down and pulled her right into his lap.

"This is focusing on our problem?"

"Part of my job is making you feel safe right now."

"I do feel safe."

"You're saying sitting in my lap doesn't make you feel safer?"

"No, I'm not saying that." It didn't make sense, because really it shouldn't make any difference, but she didn't want to move.

"Good."

"What now?"

"The big boss is making some phone calls. They'll need the data and your interpretation of it, but then the spooks will move in on Luminescent Pharmaceuticals."

She snuggled more firmly into his lap. "What's your role in all this?"

"Keeping you safe."

"Don't you want to be in on the takedown?" she asked, as she rubbed her head against his shoulder.

"I want to be your hands-on bodyguard." It sounded like a promise of something else entirely.

She decided to go for the joke, rather than press for him to acknowledge what he was really saying . . . if he was saying what it felt like. "Sounds dirty."

"Sexy maybe."

"Sexy definitely."

"Good."

"Speaking of sex."

"We've got forty-three minutes until the others arrive."

"Let's not waste it."

And they didn't. Though he did insist on taking a few minutes to set up some complicated contraptions on the windows and door before carrying her off to bed and once again blowing her mind with pleasure.

CHAPTER 8

His friends turned out to be a lot like she'd expected. Which meant they reminded her of Roman and Max. Though one of them was a woman. They set up a rotation of guards, but Max stayed with her all the time.

Someone else might have gotten sick of spending so much time in a hotel suite, but she was used to working on her thesis for days at a time. Besides, she had the distraction of Max.

Totally delicious and wonderful, he used sex to help her work off the tension of being cooped up in the same two rooms. She didn't need to go running when he loved her into a puddle of exhausted pleasure. Sex, the perfect cardio.

They kept talking too, about their more recent pasts and their hopes for the future.

"So, you want to be doing this when you're ninety?" she asked him at one point.

He shook his head. "Nah. Can't do what I do when you lose your game."

"So, what does your future look like?"

"There's a pretty high mortality rate in my profession."

"You plan to be dead?"

"Hell, no."

"Then?"

Well, that answered the question of whether a black man could blush. He could. And it was adorable.

"What? With a reaction like that you can't not tell me."

"You know I like to cook."

"You want to be a chef?" She didn't see why that would embarrass him.

"I want to own my own place."

"You want to open a restaurant."

"Nothing big. Not fancy-assed. Something that only serves breakfast and lunch."

"Like a diner."

"More like a deli, but not."

"One of those little food carts?" Maybe he thought former Marines should do something more dangerous, but she thought he'd be really amazing at this.

He loved to feed her. The suite had a mini kitchen and he did most of the cooking.

"That, or a little coffee shop–style place. Though I'm not looking at serving a bunch of fancy-assed coffees either. There are enough places that do that already. Not in Boston, but maybe in California. Mama and her teacher moved there a few years ago and they do enjoy the sunshine."

"Where in California?"

When he named a town only about thirty minutes from the one her parents lived in, Danusia felt the inevitability of destiny shiver across her soul.

Max hung up the phone as Danusia stood up and stretched. She'd been working hunched over the suite's fairly ample desk for the past six hours. He'd never seen anyone get so lost in deskwork for so long. Well, except maybe Spazz, but he was too antsy not to get up every hour or so and work off a little of his extreme extra energy.

Her pretty breasts pressed against her top, her nipples hardening as she moved, probably in response to the now flowing blood in her body. She turned to him and caught him looking.

He grinned. "Nice view."

"I'm glad you're enjoying the perks of babysitting me."

"Professor, I can guarantee I don't see you as a child."

She smiled and sauntered forward, putting a sexy sway in her hips she only did around him. He liked it. And he liked that she did it for him. "I need to go to the library."

"Too dangerous."

"How long are we going to be here?" she asked, though he could tell she wanted to argue about the library.

"The spooks are setting up a sting at your apartment. Making it look like you're moving back in. They want the hit team."

"That tells me what they're doing. Not how long it will take."

"There's no way of telling, but we don't have to stay here, Professor."

"I'm not taking this trouble back to Roman's place. What if they find me there?"

"My condo is ready and the movers delivered my furniture today." He'd been thinking about taking her back to Boston since the threat level escalated with the Luminescent employee's death, but he'd known Danusia wouldn't go for returning to her brother's apartment.

She looked at him, waiting for more.

"Come stay with me."

"I . . ." She looked over his shoulder, though he knew there wasn't a damn thing of interest to see.

"You said you're defending your thesis in October. Does that mean you aren't signed up to help with classes in the fall?" he asked her.

"Yes."

"So, you're just working on your thesis?"

"Yes."

"Does it have to be done here?"

"The university library is here."

"And you still need it?"

"Not exactly."

"Why the trip today then?"

"I want to verify some facts and a couple of resources."

"Sounds like busywork."

"I'm ready to get out of this suite."

She'd lasted longer than a lot of people would have. "I get that."

"So?"

"So, come home with me."

"For how long?"

Shit. He'd known this question was coming and damned if he hadn't decided what his answer was going to be. "For as long as I can get you to stay."

"You mean like in sickness, health and corrupt pharmaceutical companies trying to get to me?" she asked, as her gaze came back to him.

"Yeah, like that."

"I . . ." She was looking at him again, but her eyes were filmed with tears. "I thought you didn't want a relationship."

"I want you."

"Any way you can get me?"

"Pretty much, but damned if I'll settle for casual."

"You sound like a man who knows what he wants." She sounded like a woman who wanted what he did.

"I am."

"And love?" she asked.

"It comes with the package."

"You're not going to say it?"

Damn. He opened his mouth, but closed it again. He hadn't said those words to anyone in his adult life. Last time he'd said it to his mom, he'd been about ten years old. They weren't a kissy-huggy-tell-you-I-love-you-all-the-damn-time family.

Danusia smiled, but shook her head. "We'll go to your place for now. We'll work out the details later."

That was better than he expected after all the times he'd claimed he didn't want a relationship. She didn't ask for explanations. She didn't demand those three words he found so hard to say.

She was perfect for him.

They flew back to Boston in the helicopter. Danusia left her car for the female agent baiting the trap. They settled into a routine. She worked on her thesis during the day and he went into the Atrati headquarters to his job when Stateside.

The hit team took the bait three days after the female agent moved into Danusia's apartment. The threat was over, but nothing was said by either of them about her returning to her apartment. One drawer in his dresser held her clothes, as well as some hangers in the closet.

His spare bedroom had become an office with an oversized desk and overflowing bookshelves.

The spooks wanted Danusia's help building their case against Luminescent. She gave it, though he knew it put her behind on her thesis.

When Roman's team went off the grid in Africa, Max didn't hide the truth from Danusia, trusting her to keep silent about it. Just like she'd managed to not give even a hint of her own involvement in an illegal-weapons case at the federal level, or the fact she'd been the target for a hit team, despite several phone calls with family.

Her mother wanted a visit. He was thinking on that. On what to do about visiting his own family and getting to know Danusia's . . . besides Roman anyway.

Then a team with his name on it got assigned a job in South America and Max had to make a choice.

Danusia was just sending some more support documentation off to the U.S. Attorney General's office for the case against Luminescent Pharmaceuticals when she heard Max arrive. He wasn't due home for three more hours.

With a sinking feeling in the pit of her stomach, she went looking for him. She'd been waiting for this day since returning to Boston with Max. She was sure she knew what was coming. They found each other in the hall outside the room he'd given her to make into an office.

The serious expression in his eyes made her stomach clench. "What's going on, Max?"

"I got an assignment. South America. Fly out oh-four-hundred."

She nodded, her throat tight, her mouth suddenly so dry, she didn't know how she was going to force words out, but she had to. This was where their relationship moved forward or broke forever. "I'll get the rest of my stuff moved in here while you're gone."

Something moved in his dark brown eyes, something like hope and joy. "You didn't ask how long I'd be gone."

"It doesn't matter. I'll be waiting here for you when you come home."

"This is home for you?"

"Wherever you're going to be when you're not working, that's home for me."

"Oh, God." And it was a prayer not a curse the way he said it. He pulled her tight against him, in a way that had become familiar. "I love you, Danusia."

"I love you too, Max, so much." Hot tears ran down her cheeks.

He'd finally said the words and hers had been the right ones. He didn't want to get rid of her. He wanted her to stay. He really *wanted* her.

"I refused the assignment."

"What? You? What?" She couldn't breathe for the happiness blooming inside her. She was scared to trust it, but his dark gaze made promises.

"I'm not leaving you. You're my family. My dad, maybe long-haul trucking was all he knew. Maybe it's all he wanted. But damn, him and my mom? They weren't happy. Maybe they wouldn't have been even if he was home the other twenty-two days of the month, but I want a family with you . . . a life that includes time together."

"I thought you weren't ready to retire from soldiering."

"I thought I wasn't either, until I met you."

He wasn't going to leave her alone. She meant so much to him that he was going to change his life for her. Danusia felt the happiness burst in her chest and she started laughing, even as the tears still tracked wetly down her cheeks.

He picked her up and carried her into the bedroom.

"You really like carrying me."

"Just call me Power Man."

She giggled as he dropped her on the bed. "I'd rather call you Max. You're the man I love."

He leaned down to kiss her, his lips right against hers as he said, "I love you. Always."

After they made love (which was so much more fun than packing him up to leave the country and put his life on the line again), she was snuggled into his side, drowsing when he asked, "Once you finish this Ph.D. thing, how do you feel about moving to California, closer to our families?"

"You're really serious about us, aren't you?"

"I refused any more field assignments. I'd say so, yes."

She grinned against his dark, warm skin. Every time he said it, she loved hearing it—as much as hearing his *I love yous.*

"Matej and Elle's company has already made me an offer of employment. I wasn't sure about it, though it's exactly the kind of place I feel I could make the best income." Maybe she could build closer, more normal relationships with her siblings now that they were all adults and the age gap and the brain gap just wasn't that important anymore.

He squeezed her tight, his hand settling on her hip. "We're going to do it, aren't we, sweetheart?"

"What?"

"Work on that happily-ever-after so many people talk about."

"Yes, yes, I think we are."

Hot Mess

JAMIE
DENTON

To Kristine Bammerlin Thompson,
for being there every day.
I couldn't have done this one without you.

CHAPTER 1

Alyssa Cardellini considered herself a work-in-progress. Unfortunately for her, not everyone agreed. Case in point—the razor-thin woman with mean eyes, glaring at her as if she were nine donuts shy of a dozen.

"Imbecile!"

Flat on her ass in the middle of Los Angeles International Airport and being called names while covered in her favorite flavor of frozen coffee, was *not* how Alyssa had planned to start her day. Hell, she hadn't even dreamed she'd be anywhere near LAX, for that matter. But, she wanted to keep her job at Primo Security Services and therefore had no other choice. Those pesky love/hate relationships she had with food and keeping a roof over her head required constant funding. Just her luck, her savings account was on life support. Besides, the quadruple booking *was* her fault. Since she'd been the only available body left to play watchdog to corporate whistleblower Charles Rolston, here she was, being called an imbecile and wishing she could have a *Groundhog Day* do-over.

Under her breath, the woman muttered a string of curses vile enough to make a truck driver blush. Alyssa narrowed her eyes at the bad-tempered female, dressed in a black micro-skirt and the highest freaking heels she'd ever seen.

Feeling none too charitable herself, she flicked a melting piece of ice from her skirt and said, "What kind of dork wears four-inch spike heels when traveling?"

The woman struggled to stand. "Idiot," she practically snarled as she slipped in the puddle of frozen coffee and landed on her ass again.

Alyssa smothered a giggle. Dressed in much more suitable jewel-studded flip-flops, she easily stood and swiped at the damp spots on her denim capris, without bothering to tell the gangly woman in black to try taking off those skyscraper heels first. Let her figure it out for herself, especially after she flung another murmured f-bomb at Alyssa.

The woman finally managed to get to her feet on her own. "Watch where you're going next time," she snapped, grabbing the handle of her carry-on, then stalking away unsteadily, an angry frown on her pinched face.

Alyssa let out a sigh as she stooped to pick up the placard scrawled with Rolston's name. She shrugged off the woman's bad manners. She'd been called everything from a dingbat to a screwup, and names far worse than what that scrawny witch had called her.

As much as it pained her to admit it, there was some truth to the name-calling. Ever since kindergarten, she'd been trying to find herself, and not doing a very good job of it. All through school, there hadn't been a student activity she hadn't tried. Some she'd done well. Some had bored her to tears. Others were nothing short of a bona fide disaster. If she were a betting woman, she'd lay odds that Melinda Wilcox would still refuse to speak to her. Forget that it'd been ten years since the toppled cheerleader pyramid incident. Was it really *her* fault Sean Bakker had waved to her and she'd waved back?

She let out another long-suffering sigh. From the minute she'd walked into the office this morning, she'd had a bad feeling today was going to be another one of *those* days. The sun in Venice Beach had been playing peek-a-boo behind a heavy marine layer, making for a hazy day. She hated hazy days. They just never felt quite right to her, and something invariably went wrong. Like Mercury was in retrograde *and* on steroids.

Today, apparently, was no exception.

She was supposed to be in the office preparing a bid proposal for security services at an on-location shoot for one of the big movie studios, not standing around LAX with a hand-scrawled placard in her hands. Surrounded by a bevy of professional chauffeurs and other drivers passing time until the passengers of Flight 546 from Charlotte, North Carolina, deplaned hadn't been on today's To Do List. But since she'd been the one to screw up the date, she had to make it right, even if waiting for some geeky pharmaceutical company whistleblower to arrive was so not in her job description.

A Jillian of all trades, but master of few—that was her. She was the go-to girl, the copy girl, the fix-the-website-again girl, the type-up-this-letter girl. She fetched coffee, sorted the mail, fixed the fax machine and ran to the deli for the guys. She was *the* office staff. And, because she'd obtained her commercial driver's license when she was in college so she could make rent by working part-time as a school bus driver, she was also the occasional take-the-limo-for-detailing girl. But her primary nine-to-five responsibility was answering the phones and keeping the schedule for Primo Security Services, a private security firm started by a pair of California surfers looking for a way to make a living and support their passion for hanging ten. In the twenty years Perry Zellner and Craig Newberry had been in business, Primo had been providing security for everyone from Hollywood's A-list to high-powered executives, with a few big-name politicians thrown in for good measure. Whether playing bodyguard for an out-of-towner at a star-spangled media event, or carting some coked-up starlet off in style to the county jail to serve a week out of a ninety-day jail sentence, no job was too big or small for Primo Security Services.

The first wave of passengers arrived, and Alyssa jockeyed for position with the other drivers. Problem was, she had no clue what Charles Rolston, the former accountant for Bastian Pharmaceuticals and the federal prosecutor's star witness, looked like. Once she'd realized her mistake this morning, she'd been in such a rush to get to the airport on time, she hadn't thought to Google the guy to at least see what he looked like. A quick search using her iPhone, while standing in line at Starbucks, hadn't helped because neither Rolston's name or photo had been released to the press. Odd, considering the age of instant information. All she had was a stupid placard with the guy's name scrawled on it in her doctor-worthy penmanship.

And now she was a mess, thanks to the anorexic sky-scraper who'd mowed her over. She looked down at her damp and stained top and capris. Rolston would probably take one look at her and hightail it back to the Carolinas, wondering about the federal prosecutor's seriousness in keeping him safe until it was time for him to testify.

The People of the United States vs. Bastian Pharmaceuticals had been making daily headlines ever since the federal grand jury had returned an indictment. The Justice Department had then filed criminal charges against the top executives of the company. Bastian Pharmaceuticals had developed Tocalis, the first drug appropriate for both sexes for that "total sexual experience," as the television ads had proclaimed. While half of the Tocalis users were busy getting it on, the rest had suffered serious side effects. For those with uncontrolled cholesterol, Tocalis had led to off-the-charts triglycerides, which had resulted in deadly cases of pancreatitis, pancreatic cancer and in some cases, heart failure. And the bitch of it was, the execs had known about the negative side effects for five years and had done nothing to warn the public, earning the company the nickname "Bastard Pharm."

Each night on the nightly news shows, *People v. Bastian Pharmaceuticals* was rarely less than the number three story, commonly with a report of yet another fatality. Despite dire warnings from the Justice Department not to air the special, and threats from both parties of being buried in enough legal paper to kill off an entire forest, NBC's *Dateline* had gone forward with a two-hour investigative report on the case. They had, however, taken Justice's threats into consideration and had kept the identity of the prosecution's star witness a secret.

Still, it wasn't every day the federal government filed criminal charges against one of the country's largest and most prolific pharmaceutical companies. While the plant facilities were located in North Carolina, the company's corporate headquarters was housed on the thirty-fifth floor of the ARCO Towers, thereby allowing the trial to be set in Los Angeles.

Alyssa stood on her toes to peer over the shoulder of an uniformed chauffeur, to no avail. She stepped to the side in time to see the crowd coming toward the drivers, but couldn't find a single guy who resembled what she thought an accountant should look like. It didn't matter. At this rate, buried behind a sea of uniformed drivers, he'd never find her.

With a bit of force and apologies raining from her lips, she pushed her way to the front of the crowd, careful to keep the hurried CHARLES ROLSTON placard she'd made in view. As she elbowed her way around a three-hundred-plus-pound bodyguard, she stumbled. A pair of warm, strong hands reached for her and kept her from falling flat on her face. She murmured a quick "thank you," then looked up and locked gazes with the most gorgeous specimen of male flesh she'd ever seen.

Oh. My. God. He had the greenest eyes on the planet. And a near-perfect face. His thick, sable hair was cropped short in an executive style, just long enough for her to run her fingers through. She would've drooled, but thankfully her mouth went as dry as the sand in Desert Hot Springs. Gracious. She hadn't even dipped her gaze to take in all of him.

Yet.

"I'm sorry," she managed to croak. She regained her balance and straightened. A quick sweep down his body and back up again nearly gave her heart failure. He was tall, easily over six foot, with wide shoulders, like one of her treasured 49er linebackers. And solid muscle. Like a man should be. "Thank you."

Whether she was thanking him again for keeping her on her feet, or for being so freaking drop-dead stunning, she didn't much care. She just wanted another look. And another.

"You looking for Charles Rolston?" he asked.

Her eyes widened. He was the nerd-ball accountant from Bastard Pharm? Not possible. Geeks didn't have voices like melted chocolate poured over silk sheets. They sounded . . . geeky. Nerdy. And certainly not the stuff fantasies were made of—at least her fantasies. Besides, she just didn't have that kind of luck.

Ever.

"I've been waiting for you," she told him.

. . . *my entire life,* she finished silently.

She tossed the placard at a nearby trash can and didn't look to see if it made it in, then slipped her hand around his arm. Struggling not to hyperventilate, she marveled at the feel of his muscles bunching and jumping beneath her fingertips.

She way too easily imagined the rest of him.

Naked.

She cleared her throat, but that did squat to dispel the delicious image of a very naked, well-muscled witness for the prosecution from her dirty mind. "I was worried I might have missed you."

Good God, she'd hit the freaking lottery. Her job was to pick him up and take him to a hotel where she'd have to babysit him until tomorrow morning, when he'd meet with the prosecutor to go over his testimony. Then, back to the hotel with him until he was called to testify at the trial, one or two days max.

Heavens. Her guardian angel had obviously ended her strike and was working overtime to kiss her ass today. Suddenly, she decided she liked hazy days, after all. Well, this one, anyway.

"My car is out front." She talked as they walked, her hand still wrapped around that spectacular muscled arm. "All the town cars were out, so I hope you don't mind. It's small, but runs fine, and the A/C works. Some of the time."

He stopped. "Wait a minute—"

"You have more than a carry-on?"

He shook his head. "No, it's just that—"

"You're hungry," she said, giving his arm a tug as she guided him toward the exit. "I get it. The food in coach sucks."

He looked down at her and frowned. Stopping again, he said, "I think you have—"

"Come on. I'm in a no-parking zone and don't want to get towed."

His frown deepened, and for a split second, she thought he might try to fire her. She understood. What kind of bodyguard parked in a no-parking zone? One who had exactly twelve dollars and thirty-two cents in her wallet and couldn't afford to pay the ridiculously high airport parking fees, that's who, but she kept that bit of information to herself.

"Look, we really do have to hurry."

Something about his demeanor changed, but she didn't know him well enough to decipher his body language. He looked around, and then his body stiffened beside her. He muttered a soft curse, then asked, "Where are you parked, again?"

Before she could answer him, he took her hand and started toward the exit. With her flip-flops slapping loudly, she ran to keep up with him, but decided that was okay. She'd follow this guy just about anywhere if it meant spending more time getting to know him—even if he was essentially, a rat. A gorgeous, make-your-heart-stop rat.

FBI Special Agent Noah Temple had no idea who the two thugs were who'd picked up the name placard that the ditzy blonde following behind him had tossed aside. They weren't the good guys, that much he did know. And neither of them was Charles Rolston.

He snuck one last look over his shoulder before heading for the exit, in time to see the biggest of the two thugs approach the crowd of chauffeurs. When one of the drivers jerked his thumb in their direction, Noah held tightly on to the blonde's hand and pushed through the door, but not before the shorter of the two goons spotted them.

"I'm over there," she said, pointing to a faded blue Honda that looked close to fifteen years old.

He dragged her behind him to the car, praying the vehicle was more reliable than it appeared. "What's your name?" he asked after tossing his bag on the backseat.

She slid behind the wheel and slammed her door shut. "Alyssa Cardellini." She stuck out her hand in his direction. "A pleasure to meet you, Mr. Rolston."

"Mr. Rolston?" No, he wasn't, but he'd straighten that out later. All she needed to know was that two hired guns were barreling toward the exit.

"Charles, then," she said, her hand still extended.

He gave her hand a cursory shake. Otherwise, he had a feeling she'd never start the car and get them the hell out of there. "You need to go. Now."

She gave him a curious look, then flashed a smile at him. If he wasn't worried about the two hired thugs, he would've found her smile appealing, but for the moment, their continued survival outranked an interesting female.

"It's okay," she said. "The reservation is paid for, so there's no late check-in penalty to worry about. We have plenty of time."

He reached over and took the keys from her hand, then shoved them in the ignition. "No, we don't," he said, and turned the key. The faded blue Honda fired up on the first try, for which he was grateful.

"Hey!"

"See those two guys by the exit?"

She turned in her seat to look behind them. "Yeah. So?"

"So, they're after us. Pull out slowly," he said. "Don't draw too much attention."

She nodded briskly and snapped her seatbelt into place. "Got it." She jammed the car into drive, hit the blinker, then pulled away from the curb and snaked her way into traffic.

Noah used the side mirror to keep his eyes on the pair of

muscle. They looked directly at the car. Before he could pull in his next breath, the pair took off at a dead run in the opposite direction.

Shit.

He didn't know who they were, but he suspected they were the muscle of some top-level Bastian Pharmaceuticals exec, hired to silence Charles Rolston. Wherever the hell he might be.

CHAPTER 2

Noah had two questions—who exactly was Alyssa Cardellini and what the hell did she have to do with Rolston or Bastard Pharm? She might have the sweetest ass he'd seen in a while, but he really wanted to know who exactly was this hot mess of blond curls with the skills of an Indy race car driver. Barreling up the North 110 Freeway like a bat out of hell, she dodged cars and wove in and out of traffic like a pro.

He braced his hand on the dash after a particularly sharp lane change. "You do know those speed limit signs are more than just a mere suggestion, right?"

She smiled, but kept her eyes on the roadway. "Just hold on."

He was. For dear life.

Why had he thought letting her believe he was Charles Rolston was a good idea? He hadn't, not really. She'd assumed and he hadn't bothered to correct her. He should say something. Now might be a good time, except they had two seriously dangerous-looking goons on their ass, who might or might not be hired guns from someone high up on the Bastard Pharm food chain. Now didn't quite seem like the right time to bring up the fact that the one person they were both interested in was God knew where.

Despite her valiant efforts to ditch the vermin on their tail, he still needed to find Rolston before those two thugs did. For now, the alleged bad guys were also operating under the assumption that he was Charles Rolston, not FBI Special Agent Noah Temple.

God, how had he gotten into this mess? He'd told his superior he'd prefer to have a partner, but the request had been sharply declined. His assignment was simple—follow Rolston and make sure the guy testified at trial, then bring him in for questioning. The Justice Department had a few questions about some insider trading allegations, an SEC violation that often came with a hefty sentence—if convicted, of course.

Yeah, he'd been given an easy enough assignment, all right. One that even a rookie agent should've been able to accomplish with his eyes closed. Except Rolston had managed to give him the slip during a brief stop in Kansas City. Now Noah was in L.A. and Rolston wasn't. And then he'd gone and complicated matters by becoming involved with a sexy bodyguard who apparently had no clue what Charles Rolston even looked like.

Yeah, that made a lot of sense. Not.

"We probably shouldn't go directly to the hotel," she said abruptly. She looked in the rearview mirror, bit her lower lip, then flipped on the blinker and changed lanes. She stepped harder on the accelerator and buzzed around a Camry filled with blue-haired ladies, then floored it passed a big brown Ford crew cab.

Noah looked back over his shoulder. The black sedan followed at a fast clip, gaining on them. Alyssa glanced in the rearview mirror again, then waited until the sedan was a mere two lengths behind them. Suddenly, she swerved, going two lanes over, then slowed, keeping pace so the brown Ford shielded them from the sedan driver's view. Once the black sedan was ahead of them, she slowed a little more, slipped behind a bread delivery truck, then took the next exit.

She blew out a stream of breath when they reached the traffic light at the end of the off-ramp. "Good grief." She tossed a quick look in his direction. "My heart feels like it's going to explode."

His was doing a nice job of hammering inside his chest, as well. "You did good," he told her. "Exactly where'd you learn to drive like that?" The Bureau would have been proud. While he'd been trained to evade, being in the White-Collar Crimes Unit of the FBI didn't allow for much practice. He was more analyst than field agent. Rarely did his job result in his drawing his weapon, let alone being involved in a high-speed car chase.

The thousand-watt smile she flashed him momentarily blinded his common sense. So did the sharp tug low in his belly that sent his mind wandering down a sexy, dangerous path.

He suddenly realized he was starved. And food was the last thing he was thinking of at the moment.

"Don't laugh," she warned, a hint of humor lacing her voice. "But I was once graveyard shift supervisor for a rent-a-cop outfit. Talk about boring." She shuddered and made a face, pursing her lips as if she'd just sucked on a lemon. "To stay awake, I watched a lot of late-night action flicks on television."

He had no idea what to say to that bit of information. His training with the Bureau no doubt cost thousands of dollars, and he couldn't state with any degree of certainty he'd be anywhere near as effective as she'd just been. He had to hand it to her, she was a cool one. Under the circumstances, he'd half expected hysterical female; instead, he ended up with grace under fire.

"Exactly where are we going?" he asked her. He'd never been to California, so he was completely at her mercy.

Her lips curved into a small smile that was no less appealing than her full-wattage grin had been moments ago. Damn if he didn't feel awareness stirring. Again.

Dammit. What the hell was it about her that kept distracting him?

How about everything?

Yeah, that's kind of what he was afraid of. Enough was enough. He had to stop thinking about the curve of her ass or how her full breasts would feel against his palms. Or how she would feel beneath him with her legs wrapped around his hips.

"Pit stop," she said, derailing his train of thought. "My place."

Noah shifted in his seat and frowned. "I don't think that's a good idea." She might have shaken the goons for now, but they'd been close enough to read her plate number. And there was that whole curve of her ass thing, too. In another situation, he'd probably have welcomed such a tempting distraction, but not when he needed to keep his senses sharp.

"But I need to pick up a couple of things." She stepped on the accelerator as the traffic in her lane finally moved forward. "When I left for work this morning, I didn't exactly know I'd be spending the next two or three days in a hotel room. I need clothes and . . . stuff."

The stuff had him curious as hell. "Better err on the side of caution," he said. "If those two dirtbags managed to get your plate number, it's only a matter of time before they track down your home address and place of employment." Unfortunately, the good guys weren't the only ones with resources at their disposal.

Slowly, she nodded as she pulled into the turn lane that would take them back the way they'd just come. "Dammit," she said, smacking the steering wheel. "What do we do now?"

Good question. Finding Rolston needed to remain his

number-one priority. Instead, he was driving around Los Angeles in a beat-up Honda with a cute, sexy blonde at the wheel, and a pair of hired guns on their tail. He didn't know how to begin to put that information in his field report.

"Never mind." She laughed suddenly, the sound more nervous than joyous. "I don't know why I'm asking you. You're the client."

The client? Not exactly.

"Not even the FBI could get my address that quickly."

Actually, they could, but he kept that truth to himself.

"I live like ten minutes from here," she continued. "If I have to play bodyguard until you testify before the federal grand jury, I at least need clean underwear."

Red lace. That's what he imagined. A dark red lace thong and one of those bras that barely covered her nipples. One he could easily push aside to expose her breasts. His gaze dipped to the anatomy in question, and the view had him pulling in a long, slow breath in an attempt to regain control of the situation.

He cleared his throat.

She shot him a curious glance, then turned her attention back to the freeway on-ramp. She easily merged into traffic, this time driving only a few miles over the speed limit. "You know," she said, "you don't look like a Charles to me."

Probably because he wasn't. "Oh, yeah?" he asked, his tone loaded with enough caution that she cast her gaze in his direction again. "Who do I look like, then?"

She shrugged. "I dunno."

With her attention back on the cars ahead of her, Noah breathed a quiet sigh of relief. God, he was a lousy liar. He'd never have made it as a spy for the CIA. Good thing he'd followed in the footsteps of the Sebastian side of the family and joined the FBI.

"No, you're definitely not a Charles, even with the dark suit," she said. "A Chuck, maybe. Or Charlie."

Not even close. Noah Sebastian Temple, fourth-generation FBI on his mother's side, and named after his great-grandfather, Noah Sebastian, an agent handpicked by J. Edgar Hoover himself in the 1920's. On his father's side, he was third-generation chef. Well, not really, more like a pretend sous chef, since the Bureau forbade moonlighting. But, he did occasionally spend time at Temple's, his father's Washington, D.C., restaurant, just to keep his skills sharp.

"Don't call me Chuck," he said. "Chuck is a cut of beef."

She giggled. "How about Chaz? Or perhaps you prefer the Scottish version, Chay?"

A long look out the back window assured him they weren't being followed. "What are you? A walking dictionary?"

She laughed again, a sound so sweet he'd swear his heart hitched. "I was a document clerk at the hall of records downtown for a while. A lot of names crossed my cubicle."

Document clerk, rent-a-cop night supervisor, bodyguard. Interesting.

The chorus of a Beach Boys song suddenly blared inside the small car. Alyssa reached into the ashtray, filled with loose change and a hands-free device for her cell phone. She quickly slipped on the small unit and pressed the button.

"Hello?"

Noah took another long look out the back window to make sure they still weren't being followed, then fished his BlackBerry from the inside pocket of his jacket. He powered up and within seconds he had notifications of two e-mails, half a dozen text messages and a voice-mail message.

"No, he's here," Alyssa said. She glanced in his direction, then turned her attention back to the freeway.

He zipped through his text messages and answered two from his immediate supervisor, letting S.S.A. Abbott know about the current situation and how he'd lost Rolston before ever setting foot in Los Angeles.

"We were being followed. I lost them, though." A hint of pride crept into her voice.

He saved the other text messages for later since they were personal. Three of them were from his older sister, wanting his opinion on one thing or another, and one from each of his younger brothers. The four of them were in the middle of planning a surprise party for their parents' fortieth wedding anniversary. Well, his event planner sister, Glenna, was really the one doing all the work. His job was to keep his two younger brothers from getting in her way.

"Thanks," Alyssa said, her voice a full octave higher and sounding rather satisfied with herself. "No, change of plans."

More silence. "Just in case," she continued. "I thought I'd take him to the Beach Inn in Manhattan. Yeah, the one right on the beach."

Sounded nice. Too bad he wasn't in town for a vacation. Otherwise, he might actually enjoy being locked up in a beachside hotel with a woman he found more than interesting.

Noah punched in his password when prompted and listened to his voice mail. One of his buddies had called to tell him he'd scored four free tickets to the Nationals' home game the following weekend. Free tickets on the third base line, cold beer and junk food. Since he expected to be home in a matter of days, he typed out a quick text accepting the offer and hit Send.

A tone from his BlackBerry signaled an incoming text message. Noah read the reply from Abbott: MAINTAIN STATUS QUO. BEST FOR CR SAFETY.

"CR" being Charles Rolston, no doubt. Confused, Noah sent a text back: IS CR IN OUR CUSTODY?

The reply was short and sweet: W/B IN TOUCH SOON.

Well, hell, that made zero sense. Who would be in touch? Abbott? Or Rolston?

This assignment had been fubar from the get-go. First

he'd lost Rolston, and no one seemed to be upset by that fact. He'd have thought his ass would've been in a sling by now. But no, now he was supposed to "maintain the status quo"?

"Okay. I'll check in later," Alyssa said to her caller. "Tell Craig I'm sorry about the mix-up, but I've got 'er covered." More silence, then, "All right. 'Bye, Perry."

"Perry?" Noah asked her. He had a sudden intrinsic need to know all the players. Might make it easier to spot the bad guys that way, because right now, he apparently didn't know squat.

Her usual smile faded and was replaced by a frown. "Perry Zellner. I thought you spoke to him when the federal prosecutor put you in touch with our firm."

Shit.

"No, wait. You talked to Craig, didn't you?"

He said nothing and held his breath.

Her smile returned as quickly as it had disappeared. "Yes, it was Craig. I remember because he handed the phone off to me to take your information and confirm the dates. Which I managed to screw up, anyway."

He let out the breath he'd been holding, slowly, hoping she wouldn't notice. "Not a problem," he said.

"That's nice of you to say, but really, it is my fault that none of the guys were available today. I had you on the schedule for next week. Not sure how that happened." She shrugged her slender shoulders. "Must've gotten distracted."

She said that as if distractions happened a lot. He couldn't help noticing she couldn't be more than twenty-five or so. In the hour he'd been in her presence, he'd learned she'd had at least three jobs—night supervisor for a rent-a-cop outfit, a document clerk and a bodyguard. A bodyguard who answered the phone and kept the schedule? That didn't make sense.

"How long has your company been in business?" he

asked. Maybe they were a start-up and perennially short staffed.

She flipped on her blinker and took the next exit. "About twenty-five years or so. Why?"

"How long have you worked there?"

A few blocks away from the freeway, she turned into a well-kept residential area. An older neighborhood, filled with an eclectic mix of pre–World War II architecture, ranging from Mission Revival to Craftsman to Foursquare with the occasional Pueblo Revival thrown in for good measure. Or so he thought he remembered from the art history classes he'd taken in college.

"Almost six months." She turned onto another side street. "Why?"

"Curiosity," he said with a shrug. "You don't look very old."

She chuckled and cast him a sly glance. "Is that some clever way of asking me my age?"

His lips twitched. "I guess so," he admitted.

She shrugged. "No biggie. I'll be twenty-seven in two months."

"And you've had three jobs since college?"

She looked at him, her brows drawn together in a deep frown. "How did you know I went to college?"

He flicked the light-blue-and-gold tassel hanging from the rearview mirror. "Unless this belongs to a boyfriend, I'd say you more than likely graduated from UCLA."

"No," she said, her tone sharp. "No boyfriend."

For some reason, he liked hearing that she had no boyfriend. In fact, it sparked that legs-wrapped-around-his-hips fantasy all over again.

"Actually, it is mine," she admitted. "And I've had more like a dozen different jobs."

"A dozen?" he blurted. And he thought his youngest brother had had trouble finding his niche. Jason had bounced around for a year after college, but he'd eventually settled on law and was now in his second year of law school.

"Or more," she added sheepishly as she turned another corner. "Give or take three or four."

"Such as . . . ?" he asked out of sheer curiosity.

"Well, let's see. I was a baker's assistant, a loan officer, pet sitter, dog walker, document clerk, file clerk, receptionist, paper hanger. I really liked the benefits, so I did that for almost a year, but the summers were miserable. In college I was a school bus driver, cafeteria helper, cashier, fine-dining waitress, cocktail waitress—the tips were phenomenal for both of those."

She slowed the car, made a left into a driveway beside a Pueblo-style duplex and cut the engine. "Oh, and a process server," she added. "But I was shot at once, so I quit."

Noah stared at her, this adorably sexy, resilient woman, and didn't know what to think of her. He'd never known anyone quite like her. "When exactly did you fit in the training to become a personal bodyguard?"

She pulled the keys from the ignition and dropped them into her purse. She looked at him, a curious expression on her lightly tanned face. "Oh, I'm not a bodyguard. I'm the Primo go-to girl."

CHAPTER 3

Alyssa left the kitchen door open for Chas. No sense ditching a couple of tough-looking numbers only to leave them the prize goose sitting in the driveway—should they actually have the ability to track down her home address so quickly. Which she doubted.

She stopped on the threshold and looked back to make sure he was coming. Satisfied once he exited the car, and with his garment bag in tow, she bee-lined a quick trip to the bathroom. By the time she washed her hands, she heard him moving around her living room.

He certainly was a nosy one for an accountant, she thought as she snagged her makeup kit and blow dryer from the cabinet before dashing into her bedroom. The guy might be the new object of her fantasies for, oh, say the next fifty years, but half the time he'd questioned her, she couldn't shake the sensation she was being interrogated.

Oh, well. Maybe it was an accountant thing. Her experience with number crunchers wasn't all that vast. Or pleasant. Most of them were nerdy and didn't possess very good people skills.

She glanced around her bedroom, trying to remember where she'd put her weekender bag. Since she hadn't had much of an opportunity to travel anywhere lately, it took her a few minutes to figure out where she'd last seen the bag.

She stood in front of the closet and frowned. Her duplex was an old Pueblo style built in the thirties with a lot of built-in cabinetry, and the closets were no exception. There were two drawers below and a cabinet above the actual closet space, which was enclosed by two sliding doors that never slid when she wanted them to.

She eyed the closet skeptically. She could attempt to stand on the drawer base, but she was barely tall enough to reach the cabinet. Even with the whole extra foot or so of added height, she'd struggle to open the cabinet doors. For all of three seconds she considered asking the hottest freaking accountant she'd ever encountered to help, but quickly discarded that possibility. No way did she want him anywhere near her bedroom. Or her bed, for that matter. She just might throw herself at him, and God knew he probably already thought she was two shots short of a martini.

"And a bartender," she called out to him, remembering yet another short-lived job. She eyed the inexpensive desk chair with determination. It might work.

Crossing the bedroom to her writing desk, she leaned over it to peek out the window. She breathed a sigh of relief when she spied no sign of a dark sedan lurking outside.

Convinced they were safe for the time being, she rolled the rickety swivel chair to the closet. Carefully, she balanced on the seat and slowly straightened to her full height.

The chair wobbled, then settled. She went up on her tiptoes and gave the built-in cabinet door a yank. The door wouldn't budge.

"Did you say something?"

The sound of a man's voice in her bedroom startled her. The chair started to swivel and she lost her balance. She grabbed the door handle, but the chair shot out from under her. She let out a high-pitched squeal as she landed flat on her ass for the second time that day.

The chair crashed into the dresser. Several perfume and lotion bottles clattered and rolled. Luckily, Chas reached out to keep them from rolling onto the floor, or worse, her head.

"Uh . . . sorry," he said.

Alyssa didn't move, too stunned by the sight of the accountant in her bedroom. He took up all the space, and the oxygen, too, because she struggled to breathe. She rose up on her knees and rubbed at the spot on her rump that had taken the most abuse.

Something in his eyes immediately changed. If she wasn't convinced she was nuts for even thinking along those lines, she'd have sworn she saw the first light of desire sparking in his get-lost-in-me green eyes. "Are you okay?" he asked, his voice husky and low and loaded with sex.

"Of course I'm okay," she answered, annoyed with herself for being turned on by the sound of the man's voice.

He moved around the dresser to extend his hand to help her up. "Are you sure?"

"I'll live." She grabbed hold of his hand and frowned. The most delightful sensation traveled up her arm and down to her breasts to settle right in her nipples. Damn if they didn't stand right up and beg for some intimate attention.

Gently, she tugged her hand free before her entire body ignited into flames. White-hot, searing flames, the kind only hot, raunchy sex could extinguish.

Good grief, he'd only touched her hand. If he actually touched her breast, she'd probably explode.

He let out a long slow breath and dragged a hand through his hair. Maybe he was just as affected as she. Wouldn't that rock her world?

She lost track of that delicious thought when she caught a glimpse of leather beneath his suit jacket. She peered closer, then stared in horror at the shoulder holster she hadn't even known he was wearing.

A shoulder holster? What the . . .

"Where the hell did you get *that*?" she demanded, pointing at the gun tucked neatly inside said shoulder holster. "And how exactly did you even get it on a plane? Do you have a permit for that thing?"

His lips thinned, signaling his annoyance, but that was too damned bad. She wanted answers and his über good looks weren't going to distract her. Much.

"Yes, I have a permit." He looked directly at the offending chair. "Did you need help with something?"

She needed help, all right. Considering they were less than two feet away from her bed, she had a list of the ways he could help her right into a series of orgasms. But the truth was, she was just a teeny bit more interested in how he'd gotten a gun past airport security.

Not wanting to be rude, she took him up on his offer. "Yes, I do. Thank you," she said, rubbing again at the sore spot on her tender bottom. She pointed to the cabinet above the closet. "I need my weekender bag."

He easily retrieved the bag in question and handed it to her. "How did you get it up there?" he asked.

"Hissy fit." She took the bag from him, remembering the third canceled weekend date with a guy who'd turned out to be married scum. "Not to change the subject or anything, but what kind of an accountant carries a firearm?"

He shrugged, then took a seat. On. Her. Bed. "One that's being followed by men who want to keep him from testifying at trial."

"I'll buy that," she said, stunned that her vocal cords continued to function. She was positive they'd been tangled by the sandstorm in her drier than dirt mouth.

He *sat* on her bed.

Her *bed*.

Oh, the fantasies that wouldn't stop running through her head. Her very Southern, very proper Granny Belle would've taken a switch to her behind if she were still around to know the wickedly delicious thoughts her very *im*proper granddaughter was thoroughly enjoying.

With great effort, she turned her attention to packing and started stuffing clothes into the bag. One never knew when an opportunity to spend time on the beach might occur, so she tossed her swimsuit into the bag, just in case. An extra pair of capris, shorts, blue jeans, a few tops, and undergarments followed. She was as ready as she'd ever be to spend the next couple of days alone with a man who had her libido standing up and taking notice.

Not until she had the bag zipped did she dare look over at the sex on a stick lounging casually across the very feminine rose-print comforter she'd gotten for a steal on eBay. Too bad they couldn't stay here. She had very distinct ideas on what to do with his silk patterned tie and the lovely posts of her four-poster bed.

"I'm up for anything now." She realized exactly how that must've sounded the instant her gaze landed on his, which had turned an even more brilliant shade of green.

He coughed, to smother a laugh, no doubt, but couldn't hide the delightfully sexy smile curving his very kissable-looking lips. Damn, but the man just oozed sex appeal.

Heat crept up her neck and settled like little balls of intense fire in her cheeks. "Oh, I . . . I didn't . . ." she stammered. "Oh, hell. Let's get out of here. Please." Good Lord, she needed to get a grip. At this rate every last one of her girl parts would be glowing in the dark before much longer.

The distinct sound of two car doors slamming snagged their attention. She looked at Chas, who put his finger to his lips. Quietly, he slipped off her bed and walked to the window, where he carefully peered through the slats in the mini-blinds. "Dammit," he said, his voice barely above a whisper.

He backed away from the window and came back to her. Everything about him had turned intense and edgy—his body language, the sharpness in his gaze, even his face had changed before her very eyes. He was no less attractive for it, either. In fact, those girl parts she was so concerned with came instantly and vibrantly alive when he slipped his hand around the back of her neck. He urged her forward as if he were about to kiss her.

Anticipation zinged along her nerve endings—until he dipped his head to whisper in her ear. "It's the same two guys that followed us from the airport. Just do what I tell you to, and I'll get us out of here."

Her body was torn between the air of danger swirling around them and the acute sense of intimacy his nearness caused. She needed her head examined. Who got all hot and bothered at a time like this?

Apparently she did.

He slipped his hand over her mouth. "Nod if you understand what I'm saying."

His hot breath against her ear sent a delicious shiver rippling down her spine. Grateful for the silence, she nodded. She couldn't have spoken if she'd wanted to since she had zero moisture in her mouth.

"Is there another way out of here?" he asked her.

Slowly, she nodded her head, then motioned to the bedroom window. She then pointed toward the back of the house. The duplex was a two-bedroom, and the back bedroom served as her anything and everything room. The room's sole purpose these days was to house her various projects, some finished, many not. Unlike her bedroom, the spare room had two windows, one of which opened on her neighbor's driveway.

He dropped his hands and she instantly mourned the loss of his heat as he stepped around her. He snatched her bag from the bed, then motioned for her to follow.

Her heart raced. Whether from the intensity of the situation, or the way he'd gotten all up close and personal with her, she wasn't about to hazard a guess. Or maybe she didn't want to know because then she'd have to face what that said about her.

She crept behind him, wondering exactly when she'd turned into a cat in heat. Maybe it was lack of nooky causing her so much trouble. It had been a while since her last relationship, provided a few late-night booty calls with a friend with benefits even counted as a relationship. Why else would she be seriously lusting after a guy she hardly knew?

Correction—she really didn't know him at all. And what she did know confused the hell out of her. If ever a man existed who was a contradiction in terms, it was Charles Rolston. He didn't behave like a guy with a possible price on his head, all because he'd done the right thing. Sure, he was essentially a rat. Why else would a couple of big scary dudes be after him? But he'd probably saved lives. Thousands of lives. Maybe that explained the air of confidence he carried. He was totally in charge of the situation, and that was sexy as hell.

He paused in the hallway and motioned for her to wait. Crouching low, he rushed into the living room for his own bag. The one where he'd had a gun hidden, she thought, narrowing her eyes. What else did he have in his carry-on garment bag of tricks?

A brusque knock at the door made her flinch and forget about the contents of Chas's garment bag. Her racing heart stuttered and she struggled to remain calm. Hard to do when the sound of her own heartbeat was nothing short of deafening.

Instead of returning to her, he crept to the front door. Dammit. What the hell did he think he was doing? They were supposed to be making their escape out the spare bedroom window, not playing peek-a-boo with the bad guys through the keyhole of her front door.

The doorbell pealed, the dull sound coming from the side kitchen door. Great. They had the place surrounded. She made a strangled sound when Chas looked in her direction. She frantically waved for him to join her, but he held up a finger, telling her to wait a minute. She gave serious consideration to showing him one of her fingers, too, but when he backed away from the door and crept over to her, she decided not to be rude.

"Same guys," he whispered when he rejoined her.

Okay, so he'd been right about their tracking down her home address. Score one for the bean counter.

She heard the back screen door squeak and knew it was being opened. Good thing she hadn't oiled the hinges, like she'd been meaning to do for weeks now.

"Did you lock the back door?" she asked him.

"No."

Oh. My. God. They were coming into her house? Uninvited? She nudged his shoulder, hard, and pointed toward the back bedroom again.

She was filled with such a deep sense of urgency, it was next to impossible for her not to run like the Devil himself were on her tail, but she stuck close to Chas as if she were glued to his back. Just as they cleared the threshold of the spare bedroom, a floorboard creaked, telling her the guy had to be in the small dining area just off the kitchen.

"Move," she whispered as quietly as she could. She motioned toward the window. "He's in the living room."

She was so *not* cut out for this bodyguard business. She'd bet in all the years Craig and Perry had been in business, they hadn't had to sneak out of their own houses to avoid a pair of hired thugs with nefarious intentions.

Chas had the window open and the screen removed in record time. "Go. I'll hand you the bags," he whispered against her ear.

She shook her head and motioned for him to go first. Just who was the bodyguard, here?

His look was stern when he shook his head in opposition. To emphasize his point, he swept her into his arms and started her feet first through the window. With no choice but to comply, she perched her butt on the sill, then jumped to the ground. She landed with a loud slap on the concrete below, courtesy of her flip-flops.

He handed the bags through, then promptly followed— about a second too late. A muffled shot cracked the air, sounding more like the snap of a very large twig than a gun, until she realized the guy had a silencer.

Fear pounded through her. "Hurry," she shouted.

Chas jumped to the ground and shoved her ahead of him, shielding her with his linebacker-wide body. She barely registered the scene, her mind focused on the fact that they'd just been shot at—by a very bad man.

Oh, God.

"Run," Chas ordered roughly.

She didn't argue. She flew up her neighbor's driveway and skirted around a garage, then cleared a three-foot gate like a track star, only to come to a screeching halt in front of her neighbor's elderly Newfoundland, Phoebe. Phoebe was a big, furry sweetheart of a dog, once she got a whiff of you. But with her eyesight not quite what it used to be, the old dog barked if a leaf fluttered in a tree two doors down, like she was doing now.

"Shhh," she hushed when Phoebe wouldn't stop barking.

"This way," Chas called to her from the other side of the fence.

"No," she called back. "I know this neighborhood. You don't. And neither do they."

She hoped.

He must've agreed with her, because he was over the fence in seconds flat. He eyed the dog suspiciously. "We have to hurry," he said.

She led him to a shed in the far corner of her neighbor's yard. Behind the shed were stacked wooden crates, which she climbed in order to scale the cinderblock fence. She went first, caught the bags as he tossed them over, then he followed her.

For the next twenty minutes, she led him through a maze of backyards; they scaled fences and alleyways. She was hot and sweaty, and her feet were killing her by the time they finally emerged on a busy street, half a block from a bus stop.

"I think we lost them," she said as she plopped down on the bench to wait for the bus that would take them to Hawthorne. From there they could catch another bus through Lawndale to Manhattan Beach.

Barely winded, he sat next to her and tucked the bags near their feet. His hair was mussed and his tie askew, but other than a smudge on the knee of his pants, he still looked fabulous. She, on the other hand, was positive she resembled something dear old Phoebe might dig up in the yard.

"You were right," he said, a hint of admiration lacing his tone. "I'm impressed."

"Don't be." She grabbed hold of his wrist and held his watch up so she could read the time. "Bus should be here any minute."

His luscious green eyes narrowed slightly. "And you know this because . . . ?"

She managed a tired smile. "Because I've lived here all my life."

She'd surprised him. She could tell by the lifting of his right eyebrow.

He leaned forward to unzip a side pocket on the garment bag, then reached in and retrieved a small bottle of water. "Ladies first," he said, twisting off the cap for her.

She took the bottle. "Thanks," she said, then took a nice long drink. The water was lukewarm, but she didn't care. Wet was wet, no matter the temperature.

After she swiped her mouth with the back of her hand, she handed him the bottle and asked, "Now, would you mind telling me exactly who the hell you are?"

CHAPTER 4

Noah didn't know which surprised him more—the overwhelming urge to tell Alyssa the truth, or how easily he could've disregarded a direct order. He didn't break rules. Ever. He followed them, to the letter. His job was to enforce the rules and bring those who broke them to justice. A job that suited his personality to perfection.

As for telling Alyssa the truth, he suspected that impulse came from the fact that he was inherently honest. One reason why he'd never make it as an undercover operative. His conscience would kill him.

Stalling for time, he took a long pull on the lukewarm bottle of water, then offered it to her again. "More?"

She kept looking at him, waiting, her big blue eyes filled with questions she hadn't yet asked. "Thanks, I'm good," she said. "You haven't answered my question."

He tucked the water bottle back into the zippered compartment in his garment bag. "Yeah, about that—"

"Oh, good." she interrupted and stood. "Here's our ride."

Saved by the exhaust fumes, he thought, as the large Rapid Transit District bus rolled to a stop in front of them. Lugging both of their bags, he followed her on board and paid the fare. He was so thoroughly distracted by the sway of her hips as she walked in front of him down the center aisle, he lost his footing and tripped. He mumbled an apology to the owner of excessively large gym shoes, a lanky teenager with a buzz cut, wearing a California State University at Long Beach T-shirt.

Alyssa took a seat halfway down the bus and scooted close to the window to give him room to sit beside her. He slid in next to her and settled their bags at their feet, but not before he gave the floor a quick inspection for gum or the sticky remnants of some kid's lost piece of candy.

"We should've gotten a rental car," he said quietly.

He hadn't used public transportation in years, not since he'd gotten his driver's license at the age of sixteen. He'd hated it then and now, fourteen years later, his opinion hadn't changed.

"The closest rental car office is about ten miles away," she told him. "We're good. I promise, we'll be on the beach before sunset."

Sunset? That was over five hours away. If they rented a vehicle, he suspected they could be there in a lot less time. "Picking us up is part of the service, you know."

She looked at him as if he'd lost his mind. He was beginning to think she might be on to something. In fact, he knew the exact moment he had lost his mind—the instant he'd grabbed Alyssa's hand and practically dragged her from the airport. From that moment on, his testosterone levels were rising at a rate that made him ache—for her.

Nothing was making sense to him. For a guy who liked order in all things, the chaos must be making him edgy. Or maybe that was his libido at work. All he knew was that Alyssa made him want to say screw the rules and jump in with both feet. Lifelong experience told him that just wasn't a good idea.

"And where would you have them do that?" She lifted her eyebrows, still giving him that "God, you're so obtuse," expression that made him want to kiss her, of all things.

"I know. The next bus stop," she said, humor lacing her

voice. "Or better yet, how about in the middle of Shirley Higgins's vegetable garden, right there in her prized sugar beets that you trampled?"

"I thought they were weeds," he said in his own defense. His lips twitched. He couldn't help smiling at her. "But I get your point."

She leaned closer, blindsiding his senses when he caught a whiff of her sweet scent. A contradictory mixture of bold, exotic spice and soft floral perfume, mingled with something uniquely Alyssa—a little sunshiny and a lot womanly.

Her half-smile faded and her expression turned serious. "Those guys found out where I live, right?" she asked in a hushed tone. "Do you think they could access my credit card records, too?"

"They seem pretty resourceful," he said by way of an admission. Too much so, he thought. They'd tracked down her home address in record time. The men paying them were indeed powerful. He couldn't help wondering what other information might be accessible to them.

"I think it's safer if we keep it on the down low as much as possible," she told him.

He nodded solemnly, struggling not to crack a smile. She watched way too much television.

A tired-looking woman across the aisle watched them curiously. They weren't exactly off-the-grid types, he realized, and probably drew more attention than not. If questioned, the woman would be able to easily identify them, which could pose a problem, depending on who was doing the interrogating.

Maintain the status quo. That had been his order from his immediate superior, Supervisory Special Agent Dane Abbott. Which he took to mean his job was to keep everyone around him believing he was Charles Rolston, while Rolston was elsewhere, wherever that might be. If Rolston wasn't in FBI custody, the U.S. Marshal's office could have him in theirs since the all-important Witness Protection Program fell under their purview. Which could mean Rolston had caught wind of the SEC investigation. Quite possibly, he could've made a deal. In exchange for his continued cooperation and testimony at trial, he might have demanded witness protective services. Dropping the insider trading violations would only sweeten the deal.

Granted that was all a whole lot of conjecture on his part, but it was the only theory that made sense to him. If he was right, then why hadn't he been told about it? He'd been in on the SEC's investigation from the beginning. He'd done the legwork, followed up leads and spent hours poring over documents and spreadsheets until they were a blur. What was the point of keeping him in the dark at this stage of the game?

If Rolston *had* made a deal, and Noah highly suspected that was the case, then his job was essentially over, wasn't it? If so, then shouldn't he be on the next flight back to FBI headquarters in Quantico, Virginia? But no. Instead, he was subjected to public transportation with a make-believe bodyguard, whose life was now in danger because someone wanted Rolston silenced—for good.

He didn't like not having answers. He didn't like not knowing what questions to ask. And right now, he had an overabundance of both.

As Alyssa had promised, they had indeed reached the beach before sunset. A good four hours before sunset, too, an event she'd indicated they could enjoy from the balcony of the third story at The Beach Inn once they were settled in their room.

The seaside inn was unlike any hotel Noah had ever seen. The narrow, three-story structure teetered on the edge of being called a crumbling relic. In his opinion, the place was more elaborate beach house than actual hotel. The inn was built in the art deco style, and its faded pink paint seemed more at home in Miami than Manhattan Beach, California.

The front of the weatherbeaten inn faced the Pacific Ocean and, Noah had to admit, the view was a stunner. The interior, decorated in a combination of old Hollywood glamour and tropical beach house, actually worked. Surprisingly, each piece fit the overall style.

Their room was no different. Sturdy, light-colored fifties retro furnishings filled the modest room, while a bold mixture of pastel and jewel-toned accessories offered up an unusual, but informal décor. How relaxed he'd be sharing a room with Alyssa, Noah was afraid to hazard a guess.

He hung up his garment bag and set Alyssa's bag on the suitcase stand inside the closet. She'd disappeared into the bathroom, giving him a few moments alone to figure out their next move. He had no idea how long they'd be staying. Until he received orders indicating otherwise. Or until someone else took a potshot at them. And then where would they go?

For the moment his orders were clear. Which meant he had to continue the pretense of being a pharmaceutical company whistleblower until advised otherwise. Keep pretending to be a man he wasn't.

He was beginning to seriously dislike Rolston.

Frustrated, he shrugged out of his jacket and tossed it over the back of one of the sapphire-blue velveteen chairs positioned in the corner. He walked over to the nightstand next to the king-sized bed and removed his shoulder holster before emptying his pockets.

He frowned. A bed he'd be sharing with Alyssa. He'd never get any sleep. Not when the words *bed* and *Alyssa* conjured up images of late nights, tangled sheets, and sweat-covered bodies.

Loosening his tie so he could breathe, he then unfastened

the top two buttons of his white dress shirt. Sharing a room had been her idea. At the time, he'd actually agreed with her so he could keep her safe. He understood the pragmatism of such a plan, but he seriously questioned the wisdom.

Alyssa was hot, no doubt about it. She was sweet, sassy, and she made him smile. But a physical relationship would be the extent of any personal association he could have with her. They were opposites in every sense of the word. He lived on the East Coast; she on the West. He lived by the rules; she thought they were suggestions. He imagined he would be employed by the Bureau until he retired. She'd had more jobs than anyone he knew. On paper nothing worked. In reality, he wanted her, even if they might say good-bye at any moment.

He dropped to the edge of the bed and toed off his black wingtips. God, he was tired. He checked his watch. Four o'clock. His body was still on Eastern Daylight Time. He wondered if he'd ever recover, not only from the crazy obstacle course Alyssa had led him through, but from the jet lag caused by the three-hour time difference.

He scooped his BlackBerry from the nightstand. He needed a different kind of distraction, so he decided to check in with his SSA to update him on his whereabouts. He couldn't exactly call with Alyssa around, so he had no other choice but to text or e-mail. Text would probably garner him the fastest reply. With any luck at all, he might even receive some concrete information in return. That whole "maintain the status quo" bullshit wasn't working for him.

The bathroom door opened a crack. "I'm going to take a shower," Alyssa called out to him.

He powered up his BlackBerry. "Okay," he said, not sure what she expected him to say.

"You'll be all right?"

"I'll be fine," he told her, struggling to keep the amusement out of his tone. He got it. She thought she was doing her job protecting him, but really, enough was enough. He could take care of himself, and her. That was *his* job.

The thought of Alyssa taking her clothes off little more than ten feet away from him invaded his mind. He tried not to think of her naked and wet. He needed to concentrate on work, on doing his job, on keeping them alive.

Fat lot of good it did him. The minute he heard the tap turn on, all he could imagine was hot, steamy water sluicing over her slender curves. Scented suds sliding, gliding over her skin, over those lush breasts, down her back and over the curve of her sweet ass.

His dick throbbed painfully in his pants. Damn. He wanted her. Badly.

Before he did something really stupid, such as suggest he join her in the shower, he fired off a text to Abbott, bringing the SSA up to speed and asking about Rolston's current status. When his BlackBerry dinged a couple of minutes later, Noah stifled a curse.

ACKNOWLEDGED.

Acknowledged?

"What the fuck," he muttered. Dammit. He was hoping for more. He was hoping for an explanation. Like how long was he supposed to keep up the Rolston ruse?

He had more questions, too, but they were of a much more personal nature. Like what exactly was he supposed to do about Alyssa? There wasn't any sense in denying he was physically attracted to her. Every time he looked at her, he thought about sex. A whole lot of sex.

And he wasn't alone on that score. Not that he was vain, but he'd seen the heat simmering in her eyes, the way she looked at him, as if she wanted to devour him in one sitting.

Feeling even more frustrated, he stood and walked to the sliding glass door. Maybe some fresh air would help, he thought as he pushed the slider open, then stepped out onto the sun-drenched balcony. Using the ledge for support, he leaned forward, resting his forearms on the concrete railing. Maybe he'd catch some of that sunset Alyssa kept promising him.

Problem was, he wasn't all that interested in the sunset. He needed food, sleep and sex, and not necessarily in that order, either.

He was restless, he realized. Hell, he probably needed a vacation, too. He couldn't remember the last time he'd taken time off work. His buds were planning a rafting trip on the White River sometime in the next couple of weeks. He probably should take them up on their offer and make arrangements to go with them. Enjoy the fresh air, do a little communing with nature and sleep under the stars. Nothing wrong with wanting to take it easy for a change. What was wrong with wanting to kick back with friends and catch a buzz while lazing around the campfire every night for a week?

Not a damned thing.

"Hey, Chuckles?"

Noah, dammit. His name was Noah.

He shoved off the balcony ledge and walked back inside the room. "Yeah?" he called out as he slid the screen door closed and latched it. Not that he expected anyone to scale the building to get into their room three floors up, but old habits died hard.

Noah turned around and practically swallowed his tongue. Standing in the space between the mirrored closet doors and the bathroom stood Alyssa, steam billowing out behind her. He blinked, and couldn't help being stunned into silence. The sight of Alyssa wearing nothing but a stark white towel and a smile nearly drove him to his knees. She looked ethereal, like a mirage. A very tempting, sexy mirage that had him moving sex up to the top of his list of immediate needs.

*   *   *

Alyssa might not be an expert at much of anything, especially the bodyguard business, but she knew the look of a
man when he wanted a woman. And the heat blazing in
Chas's eyes had her reading him loud and clear. He wanted
her.

Talk about arousing. Endless possibilities ran though her
mind with lightning speed, each one more erotic than the
last, making her breasts tingle and her inner thighs grow
damp in anticipation. Need awakened inside her with a
vengeance, demanding to be quenched. Denial was not an
option.

The words she'd been about to speak upon exiting the
bathroom evaporated into the thin, humid air surrounding
her. When she opened her mouth, no sound came out, no
protest, no acknowledgment of her body's answering call to
his. She couldn't even manage a sigh. She just stood there
staring at him, wondering where he'd been all her life.

She knew the answer. Up until eight hours ago, he'd been
busy living his own life three thousand miles away. His life
was on the other side of the country; hers was here, in Los
Angeles. She didn't believe in long-distance relationships. In
her opinion they were a waste of time and money because in
the end, they were rarely successful.

What the hell was she thinking? She'd only just met the
man and she was already hot for him. The word *slut* hung
on the fringes of her consciousness, but she pushed that annoying bitch aside and concentrated on Chas and the sexual
awareness radiating from both of them. For the space of a
half a dozen heartbeats, she didn't care that he'd just
walked into her life. In those few brief seconds, she was
blissfully conscious of a variety of intense sensations rippling over her skin, and not a one of them unpleasant.

With agonizing slowness, he walked toward her. Never in
her life had she been so wholly aware of another human

being as she was this man. She didn't understand it. She wasn't sure she wanted to. A blushing virgin she was not, and she'd been to the rodeo a time or two. But this was different. Exactly how she knew that, she couldn't say, but she knew. Deep inside, she just knew.

He stopped in front of her and slid his hand along her jaw, settling it at the back of her neck. He must've taken up all the oxygen in the room, because all of a sudden she couldn't breathe.

His green eyes simmered with desire, making her body ache—for him. He dipped his head and skimmed his mouth along her jaw to her ear. "I'm going to kiss you," he said, his voice all husky and hot.

She melted. Her vocal cords continued to fail her, so she nodded. *Yes,* she thought. *Kiss me. Kiss me now.*

Bless his heart, he did, gently at first, with a soft, tentative brush of his lips against hers. But then he moved his tongue along the seam of her lips, changing the tempo. She opened her mouth and he swept his tongue inside to tangle with hers.

Her world spun out of control. Without an ounce of hesitation she wreathed her arms around his neck and hung on for dear life. With her body pressed up against his, the knot from the towel she'd tied at her breasts dug into her tender flesh, but she didn't exactly care. All that concerned her was that Chas keep kissing her.

He shifted and urged her even closer. She had no trouble discerning exactly how aroused he was, either. That was no gun pressing against her. She knew because she'd spied the holstered weapon slung over the back of the chair when she'd first come out of the bathroom and couldn't find him.

Immediately, she'd thought the worst, that the bad guys had tracked them to the hotel, snuck in and taken him while she'd been in the shower. Panic had gripped her. She'd feared for his safety, and that had shaken her composure.

She didn't even know him, yet the thought of losing him had rattled her enough to traipse around in nothing but a towel without a thought for the consequences.

Now she was kissing him. Letting him kiss her. God, what was she thinking? Yes, there was definite chemistry between them, but he was a client, and a rat. No, a man with a conscience, she amended. And one with a very talented tongue.

She toyed with the hair at the nape of his neck, the thick, short strands silky against her fingertips. Before long, she was threading her fingers through his sable hair.

His big body was warm and hard and nudged against her in all the right places. He even smelled good. Intoxicating. All masculine with the barest hint of some faint, woodsy scented aftershave added to the mix. And she wanted more. A lot more. If the dizzying sensations of being held and kissed by him continued, she'd never want him to stop.

Who was she kidding? She didn't want him to stop. Ever. Because it had been too long since she'd had sex. Because he was hot and ready, and based on the rather impressive erection straining against his pants, more than willing.

His hand cupped the back of her head while his thumb traced lazy circles on the side of her neck. Good heavens, the man could kiss. She'd known she was attracted to him from the minute she'd laid eyes on him, but nothing could've prepared her for the acute sense of abandon bubbling up inside her.

He shifted their positions, walking her backward until her bottom brushed up against the dresser. Deepening the kiss, her tongue mated with his in a scorching, ardent dance, emulating exactly what she wanted him to do to her. She moaned and allowed her barriers to fall momentarily, giving herself permission to become lost in the delicious, sizzling heat building up inside her.

Not that she really believed she had any choice in the

matter. Her breasts were tingling, her nipples tight and hard and begging for attention. They rubbed against the soft terry cloth, but she didn't want to feel fabric against her skin, regardless of the high thread count. She wanted his hands on her, his mouth. She wanted Chas, hot and hard and naked.

She ended the kiss long enough to pull her arms from around his neck. Tugging at his shirt, she freed the tails from his pants. Thank goodness he took over the unbuttoning process, because she kept fumbling the job and was half a second away from popping the damned things.

He shrugged out of his shirt and tossed it aside before yanking his T-shirt over his head. Slipping her arms around him, she smoothed her palms over his torso. Her fingers kneaded the firm flesh and she marveled in the sheer pleasure of touching him, of exploring the hills and valleys of his sculpted and toned body.

He was masculine perfection to the nth degree.

She wanted more.

He grabbed a handful of her still wet hair and gently tugged, tilting her head back. He trailed delightful little kisses and nips that he soothed with his tongue down her throat to her chest to the slope of her breast. When his tongue dipped into her cleavage, she arched her back and let out a low, slow moan of pleasure.

He leaned back and she stared in curiosity at the mirror reflection of her own desire in his gaze. Sweet Mary, how was it possible to be so completely enraptured by a man she'd only just met? She didn't want to consider what that said about her.

She couldn't worry about what would come next. If he left tomorrow, so be it. Where was the risk? She hadn't exactly known him long enough for him to break her heart. Still, the thought of his leaving threatened to fill her with sadness.

No, she thought. With a firm dose of determination, she refused to let that possibility weigh her down in misery. This was not the time for sorrow or melancholy or wondering how many times they could make love between now and the time he did leave. She'd made herself a promise a long time ago to always live in the moment, and dammit, that's exactly what she planned to do.

Slowly, she reached for the knot holding her towel in place. The green in Chas's eyes deepened to a rich emerald color, encouraging her. She untied the knot and held the ends of the towel slightly open, just enough to give him a tempting glimpse. With what she hoped was her most seductive smile on her lips, she glanced pointedly at his pants.

"I'll show you mine, if you show me yours."

CHAPTER 5

Noah swallowed. Hard. He summoned every ounce of control available to him to keep from pushing Alyssa's hands away and letting the towel fall so he could look his fill. The brief glimpse of her silky-looking flesh, of her full breasts and flat, tanned stomach, was nothing short of sweet torment and nowhere near enough.

He wanted more. He wanted her. Need, deep and primal, clawed at his insides. He wanted to taste, to touch, to feel her body moving against his.

He was out of his pants in record time. Standing before her in just his boxer-briefs, he knew he'd never walk away from her now, a decision that defied every ounce of his common sense.

"I can't resist you," he blurted honestly. They were strangers, thrown together by bizarre circumstances, but even that knowledge failed to lessen his need to have her.

"Do you hear me saying no?"

Heat surged through his veins at her sexy admission. He moved closer, her fresh scent wrapping around him. Dipping his head, he tasted the tender flesh below her ear with his tongue, knowing this was only the beginning and wouldn't be nearly enough. He wanted so much more from her.

She tilted her head, giving him better access. With a low growl, he dragged his mouth along her jaw, then kissed her deeply. When she returned his kiss with equal hunger, she slipped her arms around his neck, allowing the towel to fall. He wasted no time in touching her, skimming his hand down her spine to rest on her bottom, where he gently kneaded her firm flesh with his fingers. Her skin was softer, silkier than he'd imagined.

Without breaking the kiss, he carefully lifted her. She wrapped her legs around his waist and held on tight. His dick throbbed painfully in answer to the nearness of her sex pressed enticingly against him. Heaven help him, he couldn't remember the last time he'd wanted a woman as much as he did Alyssa.

How was it possible that one woman, one he hardly knew, could wield that much power over him? She had his insides twisted in knots he didn't think he'd ever unravel. He set her atop the dresser, then broke the kiss long enough to take a step back. If he didn't regain his control, *now*, he'd ended up embarrassing himself.

The smile curving her lush mouth nearly drove him to his knees. Sweet, sassy and sexy all rolled into one intoxicating curve of her lips.

"So beautiful," he murmured, his voice barely above a whisper. She was exquisite. Dressed, she was fun and flirty with curves in all the right places. Bare-assed naked, she was smoking hot and sexy as hell.

She took hold of his hands and brought them to her lips. Pressing kisses against each of his palms, she held his gaze. "Touch me," she demanded, then moved his hands to her breasts.

He palmed her fullness, testing the weight of each globe against his hands. When he scraped his thumbs lightly across her tight, pink nipples, she moaned and closed her eyes. Letting her head fall back, she arched her spine, thrusting her breasts more firmly into his hands.

He'd never known a woman so genuinely confident and comfortable in her own skin. Every inch of her was exposed for his pleasure and she didn't attempt to hide herself from him. She stole his breath and made him forget everything but her.

She braced her hands behind her on the dresser and opened her legs. "More," she whispered in sexy demand.

He grinned. "Not a problem." Moving closer, he kissed her again, long and slow and deep, before he moved on to her breasts. When he took one nipple into his mouth, she released a sigh that had his libido soaring even higher. Smoothing his hand down her stomach, he let his fingers brush against the honey-blond curls at the juncture of her thighs. She rolled her hips in response, silently begging for an even more intimate exploration.

He wasn't about to disappoint her.

She let out a slow hiss of breath as he dipped his fingers deeper into her curls, opening her slick folds, exposing her. She was so hot, so wet, she had him rock hard and aching and struggling to keep his control in place.

He dragged his mouth from one breast to the next, where he caught the tight bud between his lips and suckled her. And still he wanted more. He wanted her on her back, her legs spread wide. He wanted to make her come with his mouth. He wanted the taste of her on his tongue as she cried out his name. He kissed her then, a hungry, scorching kiss. God, would he ever get enough of her? He didn't think it possible.

Using the pad of his thumb, he applied a slight degree of pressure. He stroked her, teased her already swollen and throbbing clit. She moaned a sexy little whimper into his mouth and thrust her hips against his hand.

There was nothing gentle or tender about the way she kissed him. She demanded and took and that was just fine by him. She was primed and ready and had his entire body burning up with white-hot need.

When she shifted her body, opening her legs even wider and exposing her core, he slid his finger inside her. She gave a deep groan of pleasure and he nearly came right then. She was so tight, so damned hot.

Needing a distraction, he tore his mouth from hers. "Look at me," he demanded, his voice hoarse. He continued to stroke her, easing two fingers inside her slick heat.

She opened her eyes for him, her irises the color of dark sapphires, highlighted by tiny flecks of gold, her lids heavy. "Don't stop," she whispered to him before she bit her lip and groaned her pleasure again. With her hands braced on the dresser behind her for support, she lifted her hips to meet the long, slow thrusts of his fingers.

She held him spellbound with the intensity of her gaze. No way was he going anywhere. "Never," he answered as he slipped his free hand around to her bottom, supporting her weight in his hand.

Her lips parted slightly and he was struck by an urgent desire to see her take his cock into her mouth, to watch her pink swollen lips slide over the length of him. The image haunted him and fueled the passion burning him up inside until he couldn't stand it another minute.

He let go of her bottom and wrapped his arm around her waist, gently urging her off the dresser. She made a sound of protest when he turned her so she faced the mirror, her back to him.

He braced her hands on the dresser so she was leaning slightly forward. "Spread your legs for me," he whispered in her ear.

She did, but she closed her eyes. She rubbed her bottom

against his erection. Exquisite pleasure roared through him. She was trying to kill him, he was convinced of it.

From behind, he eased his fingers inside her again and pumped, going deep. The low keening moan that escaped her lips was nearly his undoing.

"Watch," he said roughly when her eyes remained closed. The mirror rested low enough on the dresser, giving them a perfect view of her riding his hand, of her parted lips, of her breasts, her nipples tight buds, begging for his mouth.

When she opened her eyes, he reached around with his other hand and teased her clit. Her moans immediately became sharper, more insistent, escaping with each hard pant of her breath. "I'm going to come," she rasped with urgency, her voice husky and filled with sex.

"Let it go, babe." He pushed her, gliding his finger over her sex until her moans became louder and even more insistent.

"Come on my hand," he whispered in her ear.

Her body tensed around him seconds before she let out a sharp cry of pleasure. She pressed down and rode his hand, her hips thrusting forcefully with the strength of her orgasm.

He held her close while the aftershocks of her climax shook her. Once her breathing returned somewhat to normal, he scooped her into his arms and carried her to the bed, where he gently laid her upon the mattress. He dropped to his knees and carefully positioned her bottom on the edge of the bed, then settled her legs over his shoulders.

He parted her dewy folds and drew his finger over her throbbing clit with agonizing slowness. He leaned over her, kissing her mound, the satiny smooth flesh of her inner thighs. Taking care in her overly sensitive state, he tenderly lapped her.

Her breath exhaled on a long, slow hiss when he circled her clit with his tongue. As he eased a finger inside, her cries became more frantic, more needy. Her legs trembled. The climax he drove her to grew closer until finally, he pushed her over the edge and she came in a rush of heat on his tongue. She cried out, unintelligible sounds of pleasure intermingled with a name that wasn't his own.

His passion receded as if she'd tossed a bucket of ice water over his head. Yes, he still wanted her. He didn't think that would ever change. But that was the problem. *He* wanted her. Noah Temple. Not "Chas."

My name is Noah, dammit.

With care and more regret than he'd believed possible, he slowly brought her back down to earth. He ached for her and there was little doubt in his mind he would've had sex with her, but hearing another man's name on her lips was simply wrong.

She believed he was someone else. The lie he'd perpetrated went against everything *he* believed in, and now he regretted what he'd done.

When she learned the truth, she'd hate him. Period. He knew enough about women to know that much. Women didn't take too kindly to being deceived, especially when it came to intimacy. She'd kick him to the curb for sure, which would be no less than he deserved.

He kissed her inner thigh, then rose up and leaned over her to place a kiss on her abdomen. He ran his hands up her legs and over her hips, hating himself. His job required him to continue the ruse, to keep pretending he was the pharmaceutical company whistleblower. "Fidelity. Bravery. Integrity." The FBI's motto. What he wanted to know was where was the *integrity* in lying to Alyssa?

He couldn't blame his job for the lies he was letting her believe. But his job hadn't given him permission to have sex with her; he'd chosen to do that himself. As far as she knew,

Noah Temple hadn't been kissing her, Charles Rolston had—and it pissed him the hell off.

Regret ran deep when he stood and walked away from Alyssa. He grabbed up his pants and stepped back into them, then scooped up his shirt off the floor.

He didn't want to look at her, but when she sat up, he found himself watching her. She looked uncomfortable, awkward and he hated himself for putting her in this situation.

"Where are you going?" she asked him. Her tone held a combination of caution and concern, and added to the guilt already eating away at him.

He shrugged into his shirt, then grabbed the towel off the dresser to hand to her. "I need some air," he said because he didn't have a better answer for her.

He shoved his hand through his hair. *What the hell have I done?*

She stood and fastened the towel back in place. "Chas? Is everything okay?"

No. Everything was far from okay, and judging by the hurt look on her face, she knew it, too. But he refused to tell her another lie, so he avoided the subject altogether. "Look, why don't you get dressed and we'll go grab a bite to eat," he suggested. He swiped his BlackBerry from the nightstand, then walked out onto the balcony to give her some privacy while she dressed.

His body continued to ache for her, but he ignored his need for her and powered up his BlackBerry instead. Within a minute, he had a signal and found several text messages waiting for him. He quickly scrolled through them, and felt a surge of relief when he spied one from his SSA: MAINTAIN STATUS QUO. PRECAUTION ONLY GIVEN CIRCUMSTANCES. SUBJECT TESTIFIES TOMORROW. IN USM CUSTODY.

Not what he wanted to hear, but at least he did have some answers and an end game. Too bad his exit strategy was nonexistent. Still, as he'd suspected, Rolston was indeed in the custody of the U.S. Marshals, which more than likely meant the weasel had made a deal.

Dammit.

He'd spent weeks investigating and building a strong case against Rolston based on the SEC's allegations of insider trading. And now the bastard was going to walk? It hardly seemed fair, but then he did understand the federal prosecutor had much bigger fish to fry by bringing criminal negligence charges against the men in charge at Bastian Pharmaceuticals.

Like any law enforcement officer, his job was to protect and serve. And if that meant letting a smoking hot mess of a bodyguard believe she was doing her job, then that's exactly what he would do.

Even if it killed him.

CHAPTER 6

Alyssa didn't know whether to laugh, cry or throw something—directly at Chas's stupid head. She also didn't know what she'd done to make him walk away from her right in the middle of having sex.

Almost having sex, she amended. But what they'd been doing up to that point had been pretty damned fantastic.

At least the rat bastard had satisfied her, quite nicely, too, thank you very much. A couple of times, in fact, before he'd gotten cold feet, turned chicken or just lost his ever-lovin' mind.

Whatever his reason for *abrupto interruptus*, it had better be good. He'd just given her the best orgasm—ever—and she'd been more than anxious to return the favor. Who the hell walked away from that?

Oh, yeah. Chas did.

Her second time around in the shower, she took a cool one, then dressed quickly in a pair of jeans and a lightweight, gauzy ruffled yellow tank. Surprisingly, she did have an appetite—strictly for food, however. No way was she putting herself out there like that again only to have him reject her the way he'd done.

"Who does that?" she asked her reflection as she applied a swipe of mascara over her lashes.

Maybe the question she should be asking was *why* he'd

suddenly changed his mind. Had she done something wrong? She really didn't have a clue. What switch on his libido had she inadvertently flipped?

After she twisted her hair up and secured it with a claw-clip, she applied a little more mascara and some lip gloss. The latter she did for her own wounded ego and not for the jerk who'd left her wanting more.

"Idiot," she muttered as she slipped her feet into a sturdier pair of huarache sandals rather than her usual flip-flops in case they had to make a run for it again.

Okay, so he really wasn't an idiot. Not much of one, anyway. He'd just . . . disappointed her. A lot. Plus, he'd hurt her feelings. In her book, that entitled her to at least a little bitchiness. Under the circumstances, she decided she could damn well have herself a proper snit if she wanted to.

She left the bathroom and decided he was also right—they should go eat. At the very least, she thought she deserved some chocolate to soothe her wounded pride. Or alcohol. Alcohol worked for her, too. Maybe she'd have both in the form of a chocolate martini. Or three.

She walked over to the balcony door and quietly slid it open. Chas sat in one of the two deck-type chairs, looking out over the Pacific, his BlackBerry grasped loosely in his big hand. A hand that had brought her such exquisite pleasure.

She let out a quiet sigh. The sun had set low on the horizon, moments from disappearing from sight, and cast an orange-ish glow on the water. "It's beautiful, isn't it?" Not even she could stay mad when there was a gorgeous sunset to enjoy.

"It is," he said, not looking at her. "You don't get this on the East Coast."

He'd buttoned up his shirt. Good. If she caught another look at that gorgeous male chest, she just might do something stupid—like drool.

"You must have some pretty awesome sunrises, then," she said, feeling more than a little awkward. She just didn't get this guy. One minute he was driving her absolutely insane and giving her world-class orgasms, and the next he was almost cold, and definitely distant. Maybe she should throw something at his stupid head, after all.

Finally he looked at her. Desire flared in his gaze. "They're not bad."

She stared at him, wishing he'd stand up and kiss her stupid all over again. Two orgasms weren't nearly enough. She'd take him now, right there on the balcony if she wasn't afraid he'd reject her again. She wasn't super chick. She didn't own a cape with special powers to shield her heart. She was merely mortal, and her pride could only take so much abuse in one day.

"I'm ready if you are," she said, wondering if she really was talking about food.

The regret she'd spied earlier when he'd first backed away from her had returned to his beautiful green eyes. Damn if her already wounded pride didn't take another direct hit. When had she become such a glutton for punishment?

The minute he'd reached for her in the airport that morning, that's when. He made her feel vulnerable, and that she hated. If she was anything it was self-sufficient. She didn't need a man to make her feel safe.

"To go eat." Because she sure as hell wasn't about to put herself out there again. "Dinner," she added in a firm tone, just in case she wasn't clear.

He nodded, then rose. "Give me a minute," he said, and disappeared into their room.

Frowning, she crossed her arms and rested her backside against the balcony's wall. Give him a minute? For what? To find another way to insult her, to make her feel as if she was some lesser being?

Her frown deepened. Given the circumstances, she suspected she was feeling more than a little irrational, but dammit, he'd made her feel like crap about herself. Worse, she'd essentially given him permission to make her feel bad, and that really pissed her off, regardless of how illogical it might be.

And with that thought, she pushed off the wall and stormed back into their room. "What gives, Chas?" she blurted.

He stopped in the middle of tucking his shirt back into his pants and looked at her, his expression wary. "What are you talking about?"

She folded her arms again. "Oh, I think we both know what I'm talking about." If he didn't, then she'd have to adjust her previous position on his idiot status.

Regret filled his eyes. "Look, I'm sorry—"

"Sorry?" She let out a huff of impatient breath. "You're sorry? Do you even know what you're sorry for?"

"For . . . you know," he admitted before he finished tucking in his shirt.

"Because you left me . . . I dunno . . . hanging?" She refused to make this easy for him.

A deep frown suddenly marred his forehead as he zipped up his pants. "I did no such thing."

She *almost* cared that he sounded defensive, and maybe a little irritated with her. Almost. He'd stopped—what was sure to be the best sex of her life—for reasons only he knew. Screw him. Her bitchiness trumped his irritation.

"Let's just say you didn't finish the *job*," she told him. "I'd like to know why."

His jaw tightened and his eyes turned glacial. "It's not important."

She made a sound that could've been a bark of laughter. But she was too ticked off at him right now to find humor in the situation. "Says you. My pride has a different take on the subject. Wanna hear it?"

He buckled his belt. "Not especially," he mumbled, but she was close enough that she'd heard him loud and clear. "I thought we were going to dinner."

She stalked up to him. He must've sensed danger because he backed away a few steps until he came in contact with the wall. He looked cornered, and more than a bit wary, which only fueled the fire burning inside her.

She narrowed her eyes and drilled his chest with her index finger. "*I* changed *my* mind," she said, knowing she was being completely irrational, but unable to stop herself. He made her crazy with wanting him, dammit. "Something you know all about."

He grabbed her hand before she did any real damage to that wonderful, wide chest of his. "You're not being fair."

She attempted to tug her hand free, but he held on tight. The light in his green eyes held a warning she was too annoyed to heed. "I really don't give a rat's ass," she said grumpily. "I want to know what the hell I did to turn you off."

Surprise suddenly lit his gaze. "Is that what you think?"

His surprise only increased her annoyance. What the hell else was she supposed to think? "You're not leaving me much choice here."

He stood there, his back to the wall, in more ways than one, staring at her. The air crackled around them. Her body responded to being so near to him.

"What was it?" she taunted him. "Too loud for you? Didn't talk dirty? Cellulite?"

"Cellu . . . no," he said with a shake of his head. "You're beautiful."

"Not into girls?" she asked as if she hadn't heard the compliment.

Something flared in his eyes, something dark and danger-ous, and damn if it wasn't a total turn-on. Whether chal-lenge or anger, she didn't have time to decipher because he grabbed hold of her shoulders and spun *her* around so her back was up against the wall.

"I want you," he said roughly, surrounding her with his body, with his heat. His hands skimmed down her bare arms to her hands, where his fingers twined with hers. Sud-denly, he lifted her arms over her head and before she could catch her breath, he leaned in and kissed her. Hard. Hot. And demanding.

She was lost. God help her, she wanted him to kiss her. She wanted him to pull her into his arms and kiss her stu-pid. Dammit, she wanted him to make love to her.

He used his tongue, his body, his hands, and she kissed him back. He pressed up against her and she felt the hard ridge of his erection. Her thighs tingled and already her panties were damp.

His lips left hers and he trailed a burning path down her throat to her breasts. "I want nothing more than to make love to you."

"Then fucking do it," she whispered against his ear in hot demand.

She didn't know who was naked first, but she'd reached for his belt at the same time he'd grabbed the front of her jeans and unfastened them, then pushed them down over her hips. She toed off her shoes and yanked at his shirt. He tore her filmy top over her head and dropped his briefs. Be-fore she could blink, they were naked and he had her ass in his hands and was lifting her. Using the wall to support her-self, she wrapped her legs around his waist. He rubbed her sex with the head of his penis and she knew in that moment there'd be no turning back this time.

He didn't give her time to breathe as he entered her in one thrust, going deep. She took all of him and marveled at the incredible sense of completion. Her nerve endings came instantly and vibrantly alive, going off as if they were a series of firecrackers, each one burning her, setting her on fire. She hung on as he stroked her body with his, the tension building, climbing until she rode the wave toward another orgasm. Sensation after sensation crashed into her hard. She cried out and slumped against him, her body humming in absolute pleasure.

But he wasn't ready to stop now that they'd started and he continued to pump his hips, pushing her back to the edge where she followed him over this time. They came together in a rush of heat and passion and exquisite fulfillment.

And they did it all without a condom.

Never. Not once in her life had she ever had sex without the benefit of protection.

Never.

She rested her forehead against his and struggled for breath. Her heart beat too fast and she couldn't blame all of it on sexual satisfaction. Fear was partially responsible.

"That was—" He paused to take a much needed breath. . . .

"Incredibly stupid," she finished. "Let me down."

He kissed her, quick, hard. "Not a chance," he said with a stupid grin on his too-handsome-for-his-own-good face. He carried her to the bed, their bodies still joined. "I'm not through with you yet."

"Seriously?" She let out a gasp as he went down on the mattress, cushioning the fall with his body. He rolled and had her on her back before she could manage even a half-hearted protest. As much as she'd love nothing more than to stay in bed with him until they were forced to come up for air, she really needed to think.

She started to run through the dates in her head, trying to figure out if she could possibly be ovulating. She really wasn't all that regular, so she couldn't state with any degree of certainty exactly where she might be in her cycle.

Okay, this was bad.

As if the safety aspect weren't bad enough, if his little swimmers were overly ambitious, they could very well be attempting to wiggle their way into an egg at this very moment. *Oh, please. Don't let me be one of those really fertile women. Please.*

He kissed her and she lost her train of thought. Her body was too busy glowing for her to think straight anyway.

She was screwed.

Mommy, how did you meet my daddy?

Well, you see, sweetheart, I met your daddy and five minutes later we were naked. What can I say? It happens.

She really needed to stop, but damn, he was just too good at the whole kissing thing. The whole sex thing was right up there, too, because heaven help her, the man was hard again and already moving against her, slowly stroking her.

Her body responded to his, so she gave up worrying about the future for the time being. She clung to him, making love slow and easy this time, but no less satisfying.

And that, she suspected, was only the beginning of her problems.

CHAPTER 7

Noah still hadn't figured out how to tell Alyssa the truth, and it was eating him up inside. Now that they'd had sex, he didn't want to think about the emotional ramifications of his deception. If he'd thought she was mad at him before, she'd likely kill him when he finally told her she'd just had sex with someone she didn't actually know.

Yeah, that was a conversation he couldn't wait to have.

God, he was screwed. She'd never forgive him, because to her, everything about him would be a lie. If the situation were reversed, he doubted he'd be so quick to forgive, either.

Sunset had come and gone hours ago. After a quiet dinner at a local hole-in-the-wall Mexican restaurant and a couple of margaritas a little too heavy on the tequila, Alyssa had suggested they walk back to their hotel via the beach. He'd agreed, hoping the salt air would sharpen the dull edge caused by the tequila. And while he was wishfully thinking, maybe he'd find a magic cure to alleviate the sting still on his tongue from the hottest freaking salsa he'd ever encountered. The spicy dip had been served as an appetizer with warmed, homemade corn tortilla chips. She'd devoured the dish as if it were nothing, but two hours later, his chest and mouth were both on fire. So much so that he'd made a quick stop at a corner drugstore for a bottle of antacids. Alyssa had tossed a box of condoms on the counter. A little late, he'd thought, but when she'd said, "No sense adding dumb to stupid," he'd kept his mouth shut and paid the bill.

Now he sat with his ass on the sand, his feet bare and his pants rolled up to his calves, courtesy of Alyssa, who'd insisted they chill for a while and listen to the waves. He was all for communing with nature, but not when they were the potential target of a couple of hired guns he'd bet were still trying to track them down. Still, he hadn't been able to deny her when she'd smiled and batted those baby blues at him. As a bodyguard, she sucked at the job. As a woman, slowly but surely, she was wrapping him around her little finger.

And he wasn't minding all that much.

She sat between his legs with his arms wrapped around her. Her back rested against his chest, her head nestled just below his shoulder. Her shoes were parked next to his and her miniscule purse was tucked inside his suit jacket, which he'd placed over her shoulders when she'd shivered in his arms.

"I love the sound of the surf," she said. Leaning to the side and looking up at him, she smiled. "Nice, huh?"

His heart rate picked up a notch at the affection shining in her eyes, compounding his guilt tenfold. For the flash of an instant, he saw them sharing many moments like this one. But then he remembered he was a liar and she'd probably never speak to him again once she found out, so he quelled that thought.

Yet, he couldn't shake the words of caution he'd heard his father speak so often to him and his brothers. Beware the woman who captures your imagination, because she too shall capture your heart. Or some such wisdom, usually spoken after one of them had caught his mom and dad being playful with each other.

He pushed that thought aside and gave the fingers of

Alyssa's left hand, entwined with his, a light squeeze. "Yeah, it is," he agreed. "A fire pit would be nice, though." Maybe it was his East Coast blood protesting, but June on the beach was chilly once the sun went down, even in Southern California.

She let out a sigh and pulled his arms tighter around her. "We should probably talk about earlier."

"Which part?" he asked cautiously. They should probably talk about a lot more than that, but until he received word to the contrary from his supervisor, coming clean was out of the question. He'd make it up to her, he vowed. Somehow.

"The part where we had sex—twice—without a condom."

"Ah. That."

"Yeah. That. Doing the deed without protection was incredibly dumb. I'm clean, but you could be a man-whore for all I know."

He laughed. "Not even close." He wasn't exactly a monk, not by any stretch of the imagination, but as a rule, he didn't go in for casual sex. Respect for women had been instilled in him by both parents, and the lessons had stuck.

"My last relationship ended over a year ago," he admitted. "I haven't been with anyone since."

"That's good to know," she said. "But I haven't been in a relationship in a while, so I'm not on birth control. There just wasn't any need."

"Oh, shit."

"That's one way to put it," she said dryly. "Especially since I think I might be ovulating."

Good thing he had his ass parked on the sand, because he'd swear he'd suddenly gone all lightheaded. Christ, he hadn't even thought about *that*. The lack of a condom and the health issues were bad enough, but he could've knocked her up.

Oh, shit.

What did that say about him? What he'd done was not only stupid and immature, but damned irresponsible. He'd put not only his own health in jeopardy, but hers, as well.

She could be pregnant. With his child. Despite the coolness of the sea breeze blowing in from the ocean, he broke out in a sweat.

Fidelity. Bravery. Integrity.

So much for the Bureau's motto being his own personal credo. He'd managed to fuck up all three in less than twelve hours all because he couldn't keep his dick in his pants. One very careless moment could very well change both of their lives forever.

He tightened his arms around her. "If you are pregnant, I *will* be around to help out."

"Gee, free babysitting." She laughed. "How lucky can a girl get?"

He frowned. "I don't think it's funny, Alyssa."

Something in his tone must've caught her attention because she scooted forward slightly and looked at him over her shoulder. A frown drew her eyebrows sharply together. "Sorry. The sarcasm was apparently lost on you." The fear and uncertainty in her eyes belied her blasé tone.

He cupped her cheek and dragged his thumb over her lower lip. "Anyone ever tell you, you have a smart mouth?"

"My mom," she murmured, then kissed his thumb. "Every day. Got me into more trouble, too."

She shifted in his arms until she was facing him. "Look, I don't know your religious affiliation or where you stand on the woman's right to choose issue, but you should know that if I am pregnant, I will be keeping the baby."

"You don't have to do it alone," he told her. How exactly he planned to manage that when he lived on the East Coast and she was in California, he wasn't sure. But there was never any question in his mind that he would do the right thing.

"I was raised by a single mom after my father died. My mom was raised by a single mother with no father in sight, either," she said. "But the difference was, my Granny Belle was rejected by her very uptight Southern Baptist family. She left home, moved to California and raised my mom on her own. She did what she had to do to give my mom what she'd needed. Love, support. She waitressed, picked up bit parts and worked as an extra. Whatever it took, she did, so don't worry about me. I come from a long line of strong women."

His own frown deepened. He didn't like where this conversation was heading. "I accept responsibility for my actions."

She stood and dusted sand from her backside. "So do I," she said. "But I might not even be pregnant. And if I am, I'll handle it, thank you very much."

She bent to scoop up her shoes. "I've had enough fresh air." She extended her hand, which he took and pulled himself to his feet.

"You don't have to do anything alone," he said, bending over to pick up his own shoes.

"Look," she said, stuffing her arms into the sleeves of his jacket, "we really don't know each other. We screwed up. In a few weeks, we'll know if I'm pregnant. Let's not compound an already stupid mistake by making promises neither one of us intends to keep. Okay?" She turned away and stalked off toward the hotel.

What the hell? No, it wasn't okay.

He willed his feet to start moving, but all he could do was stand there and stare at Alyssa as she hurried across the sand toward the hotel. What if it turned out she was pregnant with his kid? What would she tell their son or daughter about him? That he was some guy who blew into town, lied to her about who he really was, knocked her up, then hightailed it back to wherever he came from?

Like hell.

Regardless of what she might think of him, he wasn't the kind of man to leave her high and dry. He didn't shirk his responsibilities. End of story. If they had created a child together, then he'd see to it he was a part of his kid's life.

And if he had to get a court order to make it happen, so be it.

That thought finally got him moving. He took off after her, jogging to catch up with her before she reached the hotel.

The situation had changed. He had to tell her the truth. Now. They wouldn't know for at least a couple of weeks whether she was pregnant or not, but that didn't change the fact that she deserved—no, needed—to know the true identity of the man who could very well have fathered a child with her.

"Alyssa, wait!" he called out, but he was too late. She'd skirted around the building and had slipped inside the warmth of the lobby before he could reach her. Fine. He'd tell her as soon as they were in their room. Better to do it where there was no chance of distractions.

He caught up with her just as she was stepping inside the elevator. He slipped in behind her and pushed the button for the third floor. "We're not finished," he said.

She pursed her lips and stuffed her hands into the pockets of his jacket. A half grin suddenly tugged her lips as she pulled out the box of condoms. "I guess we're not."

His dick hardened. Against his better judgment, he grabbed hold of her and hauled her up against him. He urged her head back and caught her lips in a hot, open-mouthed kiss, a kiss meant to possess, to stake a claim where he had no business staking one. At least not until she knew the truth.

Still, that didn't stop him from sweeping his tongue into her mouth. Didn't stop him from pulling her closer so she knew exactly how much he wanted her. And it didn't stop him from coaxing a sexy little moan from her lips.

Using every ounce of willpower available to him, he refrained from hitting the Stop button and taking her right there in the elevator. The car came to a halt and he reluctantly ended the kiss and took a step back. Satisfaction reared up inside him at the dazed look on Alyssa's face.

With a self-satisfied smirk, he grabbed her hand and pulled her out of the elevator. He led the way to their room, with her trotting behind him to keep up. When he reached their door, he tugged her close, backed her up against the door and lowered his head. "I think it'll be a while before we're finished," he whispered against her ear.

They could talk later. Conversation was overrated, anyway, especially when he couldn't stop thinking about all the ways he wanted Alyssa.

"Oh, God," she whispered against his mouth. "I'm wet just thinking about it."

He chuckled. He reached into the inside pocket of his jacket for the room key, intentionally dragging his fingers across her breast.

She sucked in a sharp breath, then glanced up and down the corridor. A wicked gleam in her eyes, she rubbed her hand over his full-blown erection. "I want you in my mouth," she breathed against his lips.

He nearly swallowed his tongue.

He couldn't get them into the room fast enough. Before he had the door closed behind them, clothes were hitting the floor so fast, he couldn't determine what belonged to whom. Not that it mattered. He was naked and so was she, and they couldn't keep their hands off each other. She shoved him up against the wall and settled to her knees in front of him. She took him into her hot, moist mouth, and he could swear he'd died and gone to heaven.

She tortured him with her tongue, using her teeth and mouth to exquisite perfection. When she used her nails to scrape his balls, his knees went weak. The tension built faster than he could handle. He was on the edge and he reached for her, but she pushed his hands away and shoved him mercilessly over the edge. His release came hard and fast, and she took all he had to give.

Once he could see straight again, he reached for her and dragged her up his body. The buzzing in his ears slowly subsided, as did the beating of his heart as he clung to her. "I can't move," he said. His voice sounded rough even to his own ears.

"You will," she said, her tone filled with sassy confidence he thought completely sexy.

A hard knock on the door had them both frowning. "Who is it?" he called out, because he didn't think his legs would carry him to the door to look out the peephole.

"Room service."

"Shit." He tensed, then gently set her away from him. "Get dressed," he quietly told her. They'd just walked into the room and she'd blown him and his mind, but they hadn't ordered room service.

"Just a minute," he called.

She didn't argue. In seconds she had her clothes on, had the closet open and was hauling their bags toward the balcony. He opened the room safe where he'd put his weapon when they'd gone to dinner. "Stall them," he whispered to her.

"We'll be right there," she called out. "Just another second."

He opened the safe and didn't bother with the shoulder

holster. He readied his weapon and released the safety. Then he pulled Alyssa close to whisper in her ear, "The next balcony should be an easy jump. Think you can do it?"

She nodded.

"I'll be right behind you," he whispered, "and we'll figure a way out of this mess." He kissed her quickly, then gave her a shove toward the balcony door. She had the slider open and was tossing their bags across to the next balcony when he heard the ping of a silencer, just before the larger of the two goons who'd chased them earlier came crashing into the room.

Noah leveled his weapon on the creep with the silencer. The guy lifted his own gun and took aim. "I wouldn't do that if I were you," Noah told him.

The second man came into the room. Immediately, he holstered his own weapon and raised his hands in the air. "Take it easy, pal," he said.

Noah didn't know if the guy was talking to him or the thug with the silencer. He looked to the one with the gun still aimed at him. "I suggest you do as you're told," he said, "so we can both walk away. Otherwise, one of us gets hurt, and it isn't going to be me."

"Do as he says," the second man ordered. "He's not our guy."

Without taking his eyes off Noah, the guy lowered his gun, then tossed it on the bed to Noah's left. Noah motioned for the second guy to hand over his weapon, and he immediately pulled it from his holster, checked the safety and tossed it on the bed as well.

"Who hired you?" Noah asked them, not that he expected either of them to give him a truthful answer. "Was it someone from Bastian Pharmaceuticals?"

Keeping both of them in his sights, he snagged his Black-Berry from his pocket and dialed 911. "Federal agent requires assistance," he said when the 911 operator answered. He answered a few standard questions, then disconnected the call.

"Exactly who the fuck *are* you?" the second guy asked him.

Noah let out a long, weary sigh. "Special Agent Noah Temple. FBI's White-Collar Crimes Unit," he said. "And you're both under arrest for firing on a federal agent."

"What did you say?"

Noah didn't dare turn around, but did catch a quick glimpse of Alyssa in the full-length mirrored doors of the closet. And she looked like she wanted to tear him apart with her bare hands.

CHAPTER 8

Going against everything she knew about herself, Alyssa
sat in absolute stillness. And waited.

Perched on the edge of the blue velvet chair, quietly ab-
sorbing the activity around her, she impressed the hell out
of herself. Waiting was, as a rule, not something she did
well. Patience never had been her strong suit.

The two big, scary bad guys, Milo Simms and Gordon
French, had been taken away by a pair of uniformed offi-
cers with the Manhattan Beach Police Department. Turned
out they never were the hired guns of Bastian Pharmaceuticals. Instead, they were private investigators, licensed to
carry firearms, who'd been retained by the federal prosecutor, Kyle Houston, to keep tabs on Charles Rolston. When
she and the guy she'd believed to be Charles Rolston had
run, Simms and French had wrongly assumed they were trying to give them the slip in order to avoid testifying at the
criminal trial.

She'd overheard the detective from MBPD say Simms
would be free to go, but there was still the issue of French
firing on a federal agent. French claimed said federal agent
had fired first, but she knew that was a line of crap. Even if
she'd bothered to open her mouth on the subject, she still
had a feeling the charges against French would eventually
be dropped.

Still, if the big lug hadn't fired at them in the first place, they might have discovered much sooner that they were essentially on the same team. But then nothing about the last eighteen hours had gone as it should have, starting with her assuming sexier-than-sin Special Agent Noah Temple was Rolston.

She should've trusted her instincts. She'd known he didn't look like a Charles. He wasn't a Chas or a Chuck either. He was Noah Temple, a special agent from the FBI's White-Collar Crimes Unit based in Quantico, Virginia.

And he was the worst kind of liar.

Too bad for him, she now hated the name Noah, too.

With their small hotel room packed to the gills with law enforcement personnel, she hadn't had a chance to tell him what she really thought of him. But she could wait.

From what she'd gleaned from the various conversations going on around her, she might be waiting until God knew when to give the man a piece of her mind because the situation was a jurisdictional nightmare. There were two Los Angeles County Sheriff's investigators, a detective from the Manhattan Beach Police Department, along with three uniforms and one sergeant from his department. A supervisory agent from the FBI's Los Angeles Field Office had been called in, as had someone from the federal prosecutor's office. In addition, the local FBI had notified Homeland Security.

In her opinion, the whole mess was nothing more than a macho pissing match that she wanted no part of. In fact, the sooner she got the hell out of there, the happier she'd be. Sort of. Only problem was, she wasn't going anywhere until she had a word or two with *Whatshisname.*

She didn't care if she was pregnant. After she ripped him a new one, she never wanted to see *Whatshisname* again. In fact, never again would be too soon for her.

She hurt. Her heart hurt and during the ensuing chaos,

she'd had moments when her chest ached so much she couldn't draw her next breath. Telling herself the pain would eventually subside did little to alleviate her hurt, or the anger simmering inside her. With him. With herself. With whatever Fate had thrown them together.

The women in her family were destined to be alone. Her Granny Belle had been shunned by her family after she'd discovered she was pregnant, two days after she'd received word that her fiancé had died in the Pacific during World War II. Her own mother, who'd died from leukemia when Alyssa was only ten years old, had never recovered emotionally after her husband had been killed by a drunk driver not two months after they'd been married. And now, here she sat in a blue velvet chair, with a pain in her chest that had nothing to do with heart disease, wondering if she was destined to follow in the footsteps of prior generations.

Her pride had taken a hit. A bad one. But that's all it could be because she sure as hell wasn't in love with a man she didn't even know. Her mother and grandmother had both believed in love at first sight and what had it gotten them? Nothing but a broken heart.

She looked up at the rat bastard in question and for just one moment she wished he'd been honest with her. She didn't like feeling this way. Didn't like feeling—lost.

Another person entered the room, this one a hotel employee carrying their bags, which she'd thrown over to the balcony next to theirs when she'd thought they would be running for their lives. He set the bags next to the dresser and left without waiting for a tip.

She considered picking up her bag and quietly slipping from the room, escaping down to the lobby where she'd have the night clerk call her a cab. It could be hours before she'd have any time alone with *Whatshisname*.

What good would reading him the riot act do anyway? All she'd end up doing was maybe leave him with a few choice words to choke on, and then she'd be on her way. Home. Alone. To nurse—what? A broken heart?

Hardly.

In order to have a broken heart, she'd have to have feelings for him. She hadn't known him long enough to care. She hadn't known him long enough to have sex with him, either, but that hadn't stopped her. One sultry glance from his get-lost-in-me green eyes and she'd spread her legs like a cat in heat. She was hopeless.

She looked around the room and found him with his back to her, talking to the other FBI agent. Just as quietly as she'd been sitting in the chair for the past two hours, she picked up her bag and exited the room.

She made it to the elevator undetected. She even stood in the lobby for a full fifteen minutes undisturbed. And then she slipped into the backseat of a taxi, gave the driver her address, and never once looked back.

Noah had resisted the urge to panic once he'd noticed that Alyssa had left. He'd been in a heated conversation with the federal prosecutor, essentially telling the guy he was a jackass and should be disbarred for hiring a couple of gun-toting henchmen. The supervisory agent from the L.A. field office had stepped in and Noah had walked away, disgusted by the entire mess. It had taken him half a minute to realize Alyssa was decidedly absent. He didn't need to be a rocket scientist to figure out she'd probably gone home.

The taxi he'd taken from the hotel pulled up in front of her white stucco duplex. He should probably wait until a decent hour before he knocked on her door, but he had a flight to catch in less than six hours and didn't have time to waste. He'd wasted enough at the hotel and then at MBPD straightening out the mess that had become the Rolston case.

Rolston had indeed been in the custody of the U.S. Marshals; he had made a deal. In exchange for the government dropping the pending insider trading charges against him, he would testify at the Bastard Pharm criminal trial, provided he was placed in the witness protection program. The parties involved believed his testimony was strong enough that they'd granted Rolston the protection he sought.

At noon, Noah would board the plane back to Virginia and Rolston would have already testified. The whistleblower would be safely in protective custody, learning to become a plumber or landscaper or in some other non-accounting-related job training program for his new life.

Noah really could care less. He was just glad the ordeal was behind him. Except for one last loose end.

He exited the taxi and paid the driver. For half a second he considered asking the driver to wait, just in case she wasn't home, but he knew that wasn't true. He was in that place in between insane and insecure and he didn't like it one bit. He'd never done well with uncertainty, but that was exactly what he was facing now.

The taxi took off, leaving him no choice but to face Alyssa or stand there on the sidewalk in front of her house looking like a stalker. He walked up the driveway to the side door.

A light was on over the sink, giving him hope that she might be awake. He opened the screen, knocked on the door and waited.

He lifted his hand to knock again a few seconds later, but the curtain lifted and there she was—glaring at him.

"Go away."

He frowned and knocked again.

"Are you deaf?" she shouted from inside the house. "Go. The hell. Away."

He didn't bother knocking again. Instead, he twisted the

knob and was mildly surprised when the door opened. Without waiting for an invitation he knew wouldn't be coming, he walked inside and closed the door behind him.

"Oh. Oh," she stammered when she spun around to face him. "Now that's breaking and entering. You're in so much trouble."

"Not even," he argued, trying hard not to be taken prisoner by the flinty sparkle in her eyes. Damn if she didn't look adorable and cute and sexy as hell when she was all fired up about something. "We need to talk."

She narrowed her eyes. "Go to hell."

He let out a rough sigh and jammed his free hand through his hair. "Alyssa, please."

"Funny how *you* know *my* name when I don't know yours."

She was exaggerating. She knew his name because she'd heard him announce it to the private investigators when he'd placed them under arrest, the 911 operator and every other law-enforcement official who'd entered their hotel room. Still, point taken. "Noah Temple," he said. "Happy?"

She crossed her arms in front of her. "Hardly."

"I *can* explain." If she'd let him. He was beginning to have his doubts.

"You can suck wind, too, for all I care."

He dropped his garment bag on the floor with a thud. His patience was starting to slip. "Would you be rational for one minute, please?"

"Oh? Now *I'm* irrational? You have a hell of a lot of nerve." She stalked out of the kitchen. "Get out of my house," she said, her voice rising. "Better yet, get out of my life. Go back to Quantico, Mr. FBI Man. Your services are no longer needed here."

All right, he knew she was pissed at him, and she had

every right to be. He'd lied to her, but his job had required him to do so. But this wasn't about his job; this was about their having sex under false pretenses.

Not needed? Big difference from not wanted. And in his book, that meant he just might stand a chance.

A chance at what? Forever? Or long enough to know whether or not she was pregnant? How many stolen weekends would they have in a long-distance relationship that had no hope of surviving? But what if they weren't long distance? What if one of them relocated? Was that what he wanted?

He followed her into a dining room that smelled like lemon wax. "What I did was wrong," he admitted. "I should've told you the truth about who I was before we . . ."

"Made love?" she finished for him. Her hands landed on her hips and her chin held a mutinous tilt. "Or had sex?"

The defensiveness was back in her tone and he knew he was screwed. All of a sudden, he felt cornered, trapped in an emotional minefield of his own making. No matter which way he stepped, which answer he gave, he suspected it'd be the wrong one.

"We had sex, Alyssa," he said in an even tone. "We made a mistake and had unprotected sex. I'm sorry for that, too."

The spark in her eyes was extinguished and in that instant, his world suddenly became a very dark place. He'd hurt her, and he regretted that. But really, wasn't it better to put a stop to whatever this thing was between them before they dragged it out for weeks, only to suffer the inevitable tragic ending?

"Thank you for clarifying that for me," she said stiffly, her voice carefully devoid of emotion. "If you wouldn't mind seeing yourself out, I'd appreciate it."

And with that, she walked out of the room without another word. He thought about following her, but why? To prolong the agony? To try to make himself feel better, to assuage his guilty conscience?

Instead, he headed back to the kitchen, picked up his bag and walked out the door. By the time he hit the sidewalk, he knew without a doubt he'd made a mistake, one that couldn't be rectified, no matter how much he wished otherwise.

CHAPTER 9

Eventually the pain that had nearly crippled her when Noah had walked out of her life four months ago had subsided to a dull ache, for which Alyssa remained grateful. She couldn't imagine having to live the rest of her life feeling as if her world were constantly crashing down around her, especially if she had no one around to help her dig out of the rubble.

Once she'd been able to breathe again, she'd made some tough decisions about her life. She'd figured now was as good a time as any to grow up and start behaving like a responsible adult. Her days of trying to find herself were over, so she'd put her expensive education to good use and did what any law school graduate would've done upon graduating—she crammed hard and took the bar exam. She wouldn't know if she'd passed for another few weeks, but come February, she'd have to take it again in her new home state since she'd be clerking for a federal district court judge.

The decision to leave the only home she'd ever known had not been one she'd made lightly. But she had her reasons, and once she'd put the duplex her Granny Belle had left her on the market, everything had fallen into place as if it were meant to be. Despite the horrible real estate market, the duplex sold quickly. Not that she really believed in signs or anything of the sort, but even she had to admit the entire transition was going smoothly without a single glitch.

She really hated to leave Craig and Perry and the other guys at Primo Security Services, but she'd spent the past two weeks training her replacement and felt relatively confident they'd be in competent hands. They'd given her a lovely sendoff, with dinner at one of Venice's newer, trendy restaurants and a small bonus. They'd even had one of their limos booked to take her to the airport in two days.

Despite its being October, a god-awful heat wave had plagued the Southern California coast for the past four days and there was no end in sight. Swiping at the hair clinging to her cheek, she taped up another box marked for Goodwill and carried it to the kitchen to set near the door.

Her back ached from all the packing and sorting she'd been doing. She was nearly finished, though, which was good since the moving van would be arriving tomorrow. She was looking forward to the changes and was anxious to start her new life.

Thirsty and needing a break from packing, she yanked open the fridge for a bottled water. She gulped down the icy cold liquid until a knock at the side door had her screwing the cap back in place before setting the bottle on the counter.

"You're early," she said as she approached the screen door. But instead of opening it for the Goodwill driver she'd been expecting, she came to a halt. Stunned, she stared into a pair of get-lost-in-me green eyes.

"Hello, Alyssa."

The sound of his deep, velvety voice sent a shiver racing down her spine. He was the last man she'd ever expected to see on her doorstep today. She didn't know what to think, and quite frankly, she wasn't sure she wanted to know. She'd spent too many nights crying herself to sleep, too many days trying to shut herself off from the agony of her broken heart.

She couldn't help herself. Pathetic or not, she was convinced she was predestined to fall hopelessly in love, at first sight no less, only for it to end horribly. She was like those women in the Sandra Bullock movie where the men who loved them all died in some bizarre circumstance, only she had no deathwatch beetle to signal the impending tragic end. She was on her own.

"Noah." She'd stopped calling his *Whatshisname* three months ago.

She did not want to see him. Not like this. She'd imagined their first meeting a hundred different ways, and caught off guard and vulnerable was not how she'd envisioned it.

"I wanted to see you."

Sure he did, she thought skeptically. He wanted to see if she was pregnant, wanted to assure himself that her silence wasn't because he'd knocked her up and walked away with her heart in his pocket, whether he'd asked for it or not. He wanted to either confirm his suspicions or alleviate the uncertainty, nothing more.

"Then you should come in," she said, careful to keep her emotions in check. The last time she'd seen him, she'd been an emotional, irrational mess. But not today. Today she had a plan, a set of solid blueprints for her future. And she would confront that future on her terms.

She unhooked the latch and swung the door open for him. She caught him looking, trying to determine if she was indeed carrying his child, but she hiked her eyebrow upward in challenge and he had the decency to at least give the appearance of being embarrassed.

He didn't look good, and that made her heart catch. Partly in satisfaction, but mostly because she cared about him. Damn, but it pained her to admit that, even if it was only to herself.

"Would you like something to drink?" she asked. "All I have left is bottled water."

"Water would be fine."

The stilted politeness was all a little too civilized for her. She might be starting a fancy new job as law clerk for a federal court judge, but deep down she was still a rough-and-tumble kind of girl who wore her heart on her sleeve and said whatever was on her mind. And right now, she couldn't decide if she wanted to throw the bottle or herself at him.

The bottle she decided, because dammit, she was still angry. At him for walking away. At herself for caring so much about him. And hindsight being twenty/twenty, at the circumstances that had brought them together and the pride that had eventually separated them.

"Would you like to sit down?" There she went, being all polite again. "There's some space left in the living room," she said and led the way.

He followed her, then took a seat on the muted blue-and-yellow plaid sofa. "You're moving."

She sat primly on the edge of the light tan side chair. "Yeah," she said. "New job."

The beginning of a smile curved his mouth. "Doing what this time?"

She tried not to take offense. In fact, she couldn't do much of anything since she'd looked at his mouth except relive every deliciously wicked moment those lips had spent on her body. "I'm actually putting my education to good use this time."

"That's right," he said. "UCLA. What did you study, again?"

Sneaky, because she'd never told him her field of study. "Law."

His jaw fell slack and she resisted the urge to smack it back in place. "Don't look so surprised."

"I'm sorry," he said, shaking his head as if to clear it from the shock she'd just given him. "I just assumed you had some sort of liberal arts education."

"A totally useless degree for a totally useless woman, is that it?" she asked without an ounce of animosity. "It's okay. Actually, my really useless degree is in art history from Long Beach State. I went to UCLA for law school."

"I didn't know."

"It wasn't something I broadcasted."

"Then why all the . . ."

"Menial jobs? I wanted to be sure practicing law was what I really wanted to do. All those jobs allowed me to have a small taste of many different fields."

He glanced at her stomach, at the loose-fitting, button-down shirt. "But something made you decide it was time to start practicing law?"

"We all have to grow up sometime," she said with a careless shrug. "And I'm not practicing law yet. I'm clerking while I wait for the bar results."

"And you're moving."

"And you're observant. Look, Noah. I don't know why you're here, or what you want, but I have a lot of work to do before the movers get here tomorrow, so you'll—"

"I wanted to know how you're doing."

She issued a short bark of laughter. "Nice try. You want to know if I'm pregnant."

His hand tightened on the water bottle he hadn't bothered to open. "Are you?"

So that *was* the reason he'd flown across the country. "What do you care?" She didn't give a rip if she came off snappish. He was rude.

"I've missed you."

Oh, God. Just like that, she melted. She couldn't survive him. Not again. "I've missed you, too," she admitted, "but that doesn't cha—"

He sprang up off the sofa and started to pace. "I can't remember the last time I had a decent night's sleep."

"I hear they have a pill for that." Not that she'd taken anything for her insomnia.

He stopped to crouch in front of her. He looked miserable and she wanted to be smug, but he was already chipping away at the wall she'd worked so hard to build around her heart, and all he'd done was show up and tell her he'd missed her.

He slipped a curl behind her ear. "I can't stop thinking about you."

That made two of them, because she'd never fully managed to evict him from her mind. Or her heart.

"It doesn't make any sense."

She smoothed her hand over his jaw. "I don't think it's supposed to."

"I love you, Alyssa."

"I know," she said, but her smile was sad because it didn't make a difference if he loved her or not. "I love you, too. I shouldn't. I should hate you for what you've put me though, but I just haven't been able to manage it."

He held her face between his palms and kissed her, slow and tender and filled with emotions that made her nervous. "Quit your job," he said when he ended the kiss. "The one you haven't started yet. Come back to Virginia with me. I have a condo close enough to D.C. You'll find work there. Between D.C. and Virginia, there must be a million law firms where you could find a job."

"But I've sold this place and already bought another one."

"So sell that one, too. Come with me, sweetheart. Come live with me in Virginia."

Her heart took a nosedive. "I can't, Noah. I can't live with you. Not like that." She'd made mistakes when it came to Noah, and though she couldn't help loving him, she had to draw the line somewhere. What remaining self-respect she'd managed to hang on to was a good place to start.

He frowned, but took hold of her hand. "Yes, you can."

"No," she said with a shake of her head. "I'm sorry, Noah. I won't."

"Then marry me."

He *had* lost his ever-lovin' mind. "Get serious."

"I am serious," he said, his voice filled with confidence. "I told you, I love you."

"It was a rhetorical comment." She still loved him, but nothing had changed. They still didn't know each other. "Is that what you want? Is that why you really came all the way out here? To ask me to marry you?"

He took both of her hands in his. "I came here to convince you that I love you, that we belong together."

"But you didn't plan on proposing."

He leaned in and kissed her. Hard. "I planned to use whatever means necessary to get you to give me . . . give us a chance."

She didn't know what to say to that.

"Look," he said when she remained silent, "I know we didn't have a relationship, not in the traditional sense."

"No, we had some pretty amazing sex and an interesting twenty-four hours," she said with a nervous laugh. "Not exactly the kind of foundation on which to build a lifetime together."

"Why not?" he argued. "What about the last four months? All I've thought about is you. All I've wanted is you. Let me love you, Alyssa. Be mine. Be my wife."

"You'd really marry me?"

"Hell, yes. Right now. We'll rent a car and drive to Vegas."

She was tempted. Very tempted. "What about your family? They'll be disappointed if you eloped with some girl they've never met."

"If I love you, they'll love you."

She wouldn't be calling a bookie to place a bet anytime soon.

"Marry me, Alyssa."

She was cursed and she knew it. Preordained to fall helplessly, hopelessly in love with a man who set her on fire with just one look. *Kerpow.* That's what her mom had said she'd felt the first time she'd looked at her future husband. Same with her Granny Belle. Who was she to think she was any different?

She looped her arms around his neck and kissed him soundly. It took him all of a nanosecond to have her toes curling and her panties damp. "I will marry you. But first you have to listen to what I have to say."

He rested his forehead against hers. "I swear, sweetheart, I'll never lie to you. Ever."

"I know," she told him, and meant it. "I was a little freaked out by the whole situation. I might have overreacted a little."

"A lot," he said, his tone teasing.

"Okay. A lot," she conceded, unable to stop smiling. "Now are you going to listen to what I have to say?"

He stood and tugged her hand, pulling her to her feet, then stole her chair, only to compensate by pulling her into his lap. "I'm listening."

"The house I bought is in Arlington. As in Virginia."

"I'm still listening."

Yeah, and he was grinning like a fool, too. But he was her fool, so it didn't much matter.

She laced her fingers with his. "I have a job clerking for a federal district judge. I start in two weeks. Probably not nine to five in the strictest sense, but close enough for now," she told him. "But I will have to cram for the Virginia bar exam in February, so I'll be a little swamped for the first few months."

"It's your career," he said solemnly. "I'll never stand in your way."

"I appreciate that." She pulled in a deep breath and let it out slowly. "Because I'd really like to try being a working mom. At least for a while. If it doesn't fit, then I'll quit and stay home with the kid, or kids."

Caution, along with a fat dose of optimism, filled his gaze. "Any idea when the kid thing might happen?"

"Yeah, about that." She drew his hand to her stomach and flattened his palm against her abdomen. "Does five months work for you?"

He laughed, the sound even more joyful than she'd been fantasizing about ever since she'd gotten the results of the pregnancy test. She explained to him that her life had been a whirlwind of activity since she'd found out about the baby. At first, she'd been stunned, but she'd made the decision to relocate to Virginia so her son or daughter would at least have a fighting chance at having a caring father in his or her life.

Although she wasn't one to believe in signs, she'd tried to look at the situation in a positive light, especially when every step of her plan had fallen so perfectly in place.

Noah held her close and kissed her senseless. Granted, they barely knew each other, but they'd known enough to have fallen crazy in love. The way she figured it, they had the rest of their lives to work out the rest of it.

Acapulco Heat

ELISABETH NAUGHTON

For Becky,
Lover of books and all things adventure-related.
This one's for you.

CHAPTER 1

His luck was in the crapper. And judging by the sexy show in full swing in front of him, it didn't look to be improving anytime soon.

Finn Tierney's eyes narrowed on the photo shoot across the white sand beach. No, sexy wasn't the right word for what he was being subjected to watching. Pornographic was more appropriate.

He worked to keep his shoulders relaxed as he stood in the tropical Acapulco heat, the light breeze ruffling his shirt. He was a guy. Normally, he'd be all over watching this kind of thing, but after the string of bad luck dogging him like a curse, Finn was rethinking everything he'd once enjoyed.

And if the asshole with the wandering hand moved his fingers even an inch lower on that white bikini bottom, Finn was going to unleash his unique brand of bad luck on the dickwad directly in his line of sight.

"Javier," the photographer to Finn's left said, "spread your fingers and move your hand just a little lower, like you're drawing her in."

Finn clenched his jaw to keep from wrapping his hands around the photographer's neck and wringing the life out of her. The woman seemed to know every one of Finn's twisted that-better-not-happen thoughts and then put them in motion.

As the greased-up male model followed instructions, the photographer shifted. "Good. Now, Lauren, lift up on your toes and slide your arm around Javier's neck. Perfect. Tilt your face up." The photographer looked through her camera lens and clicked the shutter release in rapid fire.

Behind the duo, blue-green water lapped at the sandy shore and a soft breeze blew at the perfectly placed light hoods. Around the perimeter, tourists gathered to watch the shoot, and every second Finn stood here party to this carefully choreographed porn show, his blood pressure amped up another notch.

He reminded himself it could be worse. He could be babysitting a spoiled-ass prince in the Arabian Desert, looking for an heiress lost on safari in the Serengeti or dodging Guatemalan drug lords in Central America. He'd spent more than his fair share of time in shit-hole backwater countries during his years with the Irish Army Ranger Wing, Ireland's special ops unit, baking in heat strong enough to melt a man's brain while being surrounded by morons he'd rather shoot than rescue. And over the past five years as an operative for Aegis Ltd., the elite security firm he worked for now, he'd always been able to maintain that professional distance and those high standards required by his employer. This assignment though? This time not so much.

The sunlight accentuated supermodel Lauren Kauffman's high cheekbones and pouty lips. She shot Finn a wicked look before moving in closer to Javier Santiago's body. So close the tips of her breasts grazed the male model's chest. One side of her mouth curled as she continued to stare at Finn, yards away across the beach. She lifted her face, leaving her succulent mouth only centimeters from the brainless model who was about to lose his hands if he dropped them any lower on her ass. Then she giggled. Like she knew some wicked secret and wasn't about to let anyone else in on the dirt.

Finn flexed and released his right hand. Had visions of whipping out his gun and plugging Santiago right between the eyes. And that's when Finn realized what should have been obvious hours ago. The little vixen was playing him. And she was doing a damn good job of it, too.

That realization should have cooled him out, but instead, the muscles in Finn's back tightened as he watched Santiago's fingers twitch against Lauren's barely-there white bikini bottom.

"No laughing," the photographer barked as she moved in and clicked photo after photo. "Think about sex. Heat. Yes, good. You can't keep your hands off each other. You're all alone. You're ready to jump each other's bones. Perfect. Hold that right there."

Lauren's smile died. She looked up at Santiago, closed her eyes and took a deep whiff, as if drawing him into her lungs and heart and soul. The muscles in her arms and shoulders flexed, her face took on a look of pure ecstasy. When she tipped her head to the side and the sun hit her just right, Finn was almost sure he heard her moan of pleasure. The same one he'd heard last night in his dreams.

"Yes, yes, perfect!" the photographer exclaimed. "Lauren, now open your mouth and ease up like you're going to taste him. Wonderful."

Santiago's mouth opened and his fingers dug into Lauren's hips. He pulled her tight against his groin. Her gasp of surprise was enough to kill the replay of Finn's X-rated dream. He zeroed in on Santiago holding her too tight, too close, caught the way Lauren was trying to push the model away. Training kicked in. Finn's body shifted in automatic response. His hand slid to his back where his Beretta was nestled against the base of his spine as he took a step forward in the sand.

"Wonderful," the photographer said again, standing abruptly and lowering the camera. "I think we finally have what we need."

Santiago let go of Lauren. She dropped down to her bare feet, eased away from the model. As she reached for a towel from her assistant, she shot the photographer a scathing look. Then her gaze landed on Finn, yards away, and she froze.

Ever so slowly, her shoulders relaxed and her lips curled in a sexy, Cheshire *I dare you to do something about that* grin that supercharged Finn's blood all over again.

His skin tightened, and that X-rated dream popped back into his head, only this time they weren't in a bed. She was bent over and he was behind her, thrusting hard, his body and hands and mouth drawing endless moans of pleasure straight from her succulent kiss-me lips.

"Shit," he muttered to himself, trying like hell to dampen the arousal searing his veins in the sweltering heat. "She's playing you, you bloody moron. She's not real. She's a *model*, for shit's sake."

The assistant handed Lauren a cold bottle of water and another did the same for Santiago. Around the perimeter of the photo shoot, the spectators who'd wandered out from their hotels clapped as if someone had just won a marathon. Three spring breakers, clad in nothing but swim trunks and sunburns, hollered at Lauren from the edge of the boundary.

She turned, shot them her famous sexy smirk and waved. Then she did the stupidest thing Finn could imagine. She brushed off her assistant and headed their way across the blistering sand.

"You've got to be fucking kidding me." Finn's jaw clenched; his muscles tightened in response. The woman didn't listen to a damn thing he told her—but why the hell was that a surprise? So far this week she hadn't done a single thing he'd expected.

She stopped near the three college punks, perched one hand on her slim hip and tipped the water bottle from side to side with her other hand. All three losers laughed at something she said, then they stepped around her, boxing her in. The long-haired one, with muscles straight out of a steroid bottle, reached out to touch Lauren's arm.

"Wrong move, dickhead." Finn was across the beach in seconds, dropped the moron to the sand face-first in one move and swiveled back to see if the other two were stupid enough to jump to their friend's assistance. Nope, they weren't. As he secured the kid's arms behind his back, both took a giant step away and held out their hands in surrender.

"Hey, man," the tall one said. "Whoa."

"Tierney!" Lauren grabbed him by the arm. "What the hell do you think you're doing?"

Finn ignored Lauren's protest and wrenched the kid's arm up higher on his back. Long-hair grunted in pain. "I think you boys have had yer fun for the day. This party's over."

"Tierney, you idiot," Lauren said, this time whacking him in the arm with her water bottle. "He was just asking for an autograph. Let him go."

Finn glared at Lauren, his frustration with this crappy assignment, the Latin model with the wandering hands, the asinine photographer, and most of all, *her,* reaching a crescendo. Those shithead Guatemalan drug lords were looking more appealing by the minute.

He glanced around, realized he had an audience and finally let the stupid college kid go. The boy rolled to his side and spit out a mouthful of sand, but at least he had the brains not to mouth off. He pushed up on his hands and knees. Coughed. When Lauren reached down to try to help him, he choked out, "No. No. That's okay. I'm fine."

"I am so sorry," Lauren said as the boy stood and rubbed his arm. "Where are you staying? The least I can do is pay for your dinner tonight. I'll have my driver take you wherever you want to go."

Long hair fell over the kid's right eye. He glanced at Lauren warily, then shifted his gaze to Finn. And yeah, Finn was right, the kid was smart. He caught the warning in two seconds flat. "No, that's not necessary. I'm fine. See?" He lifted his arm, still not looking away from Finn, and waved it in the air. "No harm, no foul." He turned to his friends. "C'mon, guys. Let's make tracks."

The three took off across the sand before Lauren could say something to stop them. *Good riddance*, Finn thought, watching them go. Though in his current mood, pounding the shit-for-brains threesome was still damn tempting.

Lauren turned to face him, perched both hands on her hips and glared. Hard. "If you ever do that again, you're fired."

Finn cut his gaze from the beach to her. To her skimpy bikini that hid nothing from view, to her flat stomach, high breasts and perfect magazine-cover face. She didn't have a clue what those three yahoos had been thinking when they'd boxed her in. Autographs? Like hell. Those three saw what every other guy on this beach with a dick saw. They saw sex on a stick, dangled out in front of them like candy in front of a baby.

He wanted to lay into her, to point out the obvious, but something held him back. He was her bodyguard, not her boyfriend or her brother or even someone she had any kind of relationship with other than professional. And though she didn't have to take his advice, she did have to listen to him when it came to her security.

He ground his teeth and worked to stay professional.

Which, dammit, normally came easy, except around her. Nothing was ever easy around her. "Yer not my boss, Ms. Kauffman. If you have a problem with my performance, call my employer."

Fire flashed in her baby blues before he turned and spotted Mick Hedley, his partner on this shitty assignment, standing on the steps leading up to the Hotel Copacabana's packed pool. Hedley was decked out in jeans and a stupid-looking tropical print buttondown, the ever present toothpick in the country boy's mouth. He waved his typical *way to go, dumbass* salute, but Finn barely cared. He was done for the day. Way past done.

He left Lauren standing in the sun, glaring at his back, no doubt. Technically, his shift had ended an hour ago. He wasn't even supposed to be out here, but he'd told Mick not to relieve him until the shoot had broken for the day. What a mistake that had been.

Dammit, why couldn't he keep his temper in check for ten damn minutes around the woman? After the show he'd just put on, he was pretty sure she'd be on the phone to Aegis within the hour, bitching about his ass. While it was true she hadn't hired security for this shoot, her brother, antiquities dealer Peter Kauffman, had. No one much cared if she liked him or not so long as he got the job done and she got home in one piece. So what was the big fucking deal?

The deal was, he never should have agreed to this job. He'd met the woman numerous times at her brother's gallery and each and every time she'd damn near scrambled his gray matter. He was thirty-five years old, for shit's sake. He wasn't supposed to get worked up over a woman, a model, *a client*, for crying out loud. He was a highly trained professional.

Professional dumbass.

"Thought that surfer dude was gonna cry," Mick said as Finn drew close.

Finn shook off his stupid conscience. "Woulda fucking made my day."

"Boy looked like he was a good sandwich short of a picnic from here." Mick's Australian accent always seemed thicker at the end of the day, but then that happened with Finn's Irish one, too.

The Aussie looked past Finn and sighed. As Aegis recruited from the most elite organizations around the world, that meant Finn's counterparts came from just about everywhere. "Queen Bee's heading in. Looks like I gotta bloody go. You catching dinner out tonight? Heard there's a great seafood place downtown."

Heading out into the nightlife of Acapulco's never-ending party scene held about as much appeal as bashing his brains against a wall right now. "Not on your life. I'll eat something in the pub. Then I want sleep. Fucking photographer's dragging us to some stupid waterfall tomorrow."

Mick smiled, shifted the toothpick in his mouth to the other side. "That's why I like you, Tierney. Always got that glass-is-half-full attitude. Catch ya on the flip side."

Mick sauntered off toward the hotel and Lauren's suite on the seventh floor. Knowing he needed to cool down, Finn shoved his hands in his pockets and stayed where he was as the crew packed up the remainder of the equipment and disappeared as well. The sun dropped low over the beach, casting warm shades of pink and red and gold across the sand. Tourists walked by and the water lapped at the sandy shore with a swish and sway that should have been relaxing but wasn't.

He took a deep draw of the salty air, blew it out. His glass would be half full when this assignment was over. They'd been here five days already. One more and they were booked on a flight back to the States.

One more day. He could survive one more day with the sexy supermodel without losing his ever-loving mind. All he had to do was focus on staying in control and not toasting his temper.

Minutes passed. His cell vibrated. He pulled it from his pocket with a frown. The message from Mick dropped his spirits one more measly fucking notch: LOOKS LIKE THE PUB'S ON HOLD, IRELAND. CHANGE OF PLANS. THE QUEEN BEE WANTS TO SEE YOU. PRONTO.

Finn clenched his jaw. The way his crappy luck was heading, that glass would be empty before the night was over.

Lauren stood under the warm shower spray and let the water wash away the last of her frustration. Clarisse Bidwell might be one of the most sought-after photographers in the biz, but Lauren was pretty sure she had horns growing under all that badly tinted hair of hers.

"Perfect" wasn't a word the woman used because she was happy; it was her signature *you're a fucking moron* phrase, and if Lauren had to hear it one more time today she was seriously going to throw something. What should have been a three-hour shoot had dragged on to nearly eight and now all she wanted to do was drop into bed and sleep for the next three days.

Of course, that wasn't about to happen. They were off to some hidden waterfall tomorrow to—with any luck—finish the shoot, and if trekking into the jungle in sweltering heat wasn't enough to push her mood to the dark side, she still had Tierney to deal with. Who the hell did he think he was, anyway?

Temper back to bubbling, Lauren lifted her face to the spray, tried to cool down all over again. She didn't need a bodyguard, dammit. She'd been on hundreds of shoots without one before, and she'd never gotten more than a scratch as a result. The only reason she had one now was because her brother Pete had turned into some overprotective brute when he'd heard she'd agreed to this spread for

Sports Monthly magazine and the shoot location of Acapulco. The news reports of drug-related gang violence in the area tossed his rational side right out the window. He'd ranted. She'd had no choice but to close her mouth and accept. The clincher to the whole thing, though, was that he'd chosen Finn Tierney to be the one to tag along with her on this gig.

Finn Tierney. God, Almighty. Her skin grew hot beneath the spray as the name revolved in her mind. If her brother had any idea how many times over the last few months she'd fantasized about the sexy Irishman—and just *what* she'd fantasized—he'd have made sure the man didn't come within a continent's reach of her.

She took a deep breath, let it out. Tonight was the night. While her plan hadn't exactly panned out like she'd wanted, all wasn't lost. She was getting to him. The looks, the oil, the rubbing, the heat . . . he didn't like seeing her with someone else. He didn't like it at all.

The wild attraction they'd been flirting with, fighting, or just plain ignoring the past week—the past few months, really—had gone unchecked way too long. The shoot was almost over. After tomorrow she didn't know when she might see him again. If she didn't make a move now, she might never have the chance.

She flipped off the water, opened the glass door and reached for the hotel's fuzzy white towel while her stomach jumped around like she was thirteen again, anticipating her first middle school dance. After drying off, she slipped into a white silk robe, used the towel to shake the water from her hair and rubbed moisturizer onto her face.

Gazing at her reflection, she took a deep breath. She wasn't stupid. He wanted her just as much as she wanted him. This wasn't a mistake. It was . . . inevitable. The key was getting him to admit it. Or, rather, to act.

A rap sounded at the door. Her heart jumped as she whipped around.

"Open up," Tierney called in that sexy Irish voice that did insane things to her libido.

Seductive, she reminded herself as she took one more deep breath. Keep it smooth. Make it *hot.*

She barely had the door open before he pushed his way inside. "Where the hell is Hedley? He's supposed to be outside your door."

Lauren stepped back as he turned and cast her a withering glare. He was still wearing the same clothes he'd had on down at the beach—black tee stretched across an impressive set of pecs, faded Levi's, white at the stress points, and Doc Marten boots he had to be sweating in. And he didn't look the least bit happy with her summons.

His masculine eyebrows were pulled tight across his forehead, his mouth set in a grim line, his eyes as dark as she'd ever seen them. Finn Tierney would never be considered classically handsome, she realized as she studied him. Not with that angled scar near his left eyebrow and another across his chin. His features were too chiseled, his mood too intense. But he was definitely striking. And he commandeered all attention when he walked into a room. Especially hers.

"I sent him with Moira to check out the location for tomorrow," she said, closing the door.

"You did *what?*"

That Irish accent was really gonna do her in. And when he was pissed—like now—it came out even thicker. A tingle ran down her spine, her stomach tightened. Shards of heat ricocheted through her body. "Clarisse might think the waterfall location is hunky-dory, but I want my camp to give it the thumbs-up before I head all the way out there. I'm not breaking my neck for a stupid magazine. And I wasn't about to send Moira out there alone."

He eyed her as if he didn't like her calling the shots, but on this she wouldn't budge. Wicked attraction aside, this was her domain, and he didn't tell her how to run the show.

His jaw muscles clenched and unclenched. "Fine. I'll wait outside until they get back." He glanced at his watch. "How long have they been gone?"

Her heart skipped a beat, knowing she had him all to herself. It was now or never. She took a step toward him, and tried to calm her racing pulse. "Actually, I was thinking about dinner. Room service here is pretty good."

His eyes slowly lifted from his wrist and a skeptical look passed over his hard features. "Who's joining you?"

"No one. I mean, well, no one but you."

His eyebrows drew together, deepening the scar on the left side of his forehead. "Did the sun bake yer brain or something?"

One corner of Lauren's mouth curled up, but the lack of humor in his expression had perspiration dotting her spine. Those nerves came back full force. What would he say if she confessed that this was the first time she'd had to make the first move in, well, years? She hated the fact men fell all over her, and the ones who finally got up the nerve to ask her out in the end only wanted a piece of her fame or celebrity or ass. Finn hadn't once fawned over her, hadn't flirted or cajoled or made even one suggestive comment. And her sixth sense told her he gave a rip about celebrity status. But that only made him more appealing. That and the fact he was the hottest thing she'd seen in months made him irresistible.

"I just thought maybe we could have dinner together."

When he didn't answer, just looked at her with that skeptical expression and those impossible-to-read eyes, she took a deep breath.

Now or never.

She eased forward, closing the gap between them to a mere six inches. Warmth radiated from his skin, infusing her body and giving her the courage she needed. "I've seen how you watch me."

"It's my job to watch you."

He didn't step back, and she took that as a sign to keep going. "There's watching and then there's *watching*. I've seen you do the first at my brother's gallery." She glanced at his bicep, as thick as her thigh, and was reminded how strong he was and just what his job entailed. "Nothing gets by you, I'll give you that. But that's not the kind of watching you do when I'm around. The watching you do with me, the second kind, it's different. There's heat there. Smoldering heat."

She looked up into his eyes, into black pools of obsidian as dark as night, and felt her blood warm like it did every time they were close. "Erotic heat I can feel all the way across a room. The kind that needs just the slightest spark to turn into a full-blown blaze."

He didn't answer, but he didn't look away, and the pulse in his neck picked up, beating like wildfire beneath his skin, matching her own. No, he wouldn't make the first move because she was his job and he was a man who followed duty and service to the letter. If she wanted this, she had to be the one to take the lead.

"I'd like you to stay and have dinner with me tonight, Finn." She reached out, pressed her hand against his rock-hard chest. Warmth gathered beneath her fingers. He tensed, but she didn't let that deter her. Easing up on her toes, she brought her mouth close to his, loving the way he felt against her hand, her body, anywhere she touched him. "And after—or before—perhaps a little more."

The tips of her breasts brushed his chest, sending tingling sensations straight to her center. As far as seductions went, she knew she wasn't a pro. Sure, she looked good on film, but this was real life and she was way out of practice. But she didn't let that dissuade her. Slowly, carefully, she brushed her lips against his, once, twice, as light as a feather.

He sucked in a breath, but didn't move. Didn't kiss her back. He just stood there, frozen.

A thread of anxiety pressed in. "Kiss me, Finn."

Her lips brushed his again. He continued to stand as still as stone. He didn't push away, but didn't join in. Feeling like an idiot, Lauren eased down to her feet, tried to read the reaction in his eyes but couldn't. He stared at her as if she had three heads.

Her confidence wavered. She sensed the conflict in him. He wanted her, dammit. He just wasn't sure what to do about it. It was time to pull out the big guns.

Now or never.

Her hand dropped to the sash on her robe. She tugged until the knot came free and the edges fell open, exposing a long naked line down the center of her chest to her abdomen and lower. "Maybe we should move right to dessert first."

"Don't." His hand closed around hers like a vise. "Don't go where yer about to go, Ms. Kauffman."

Ms. Kauffman. Not Lauren, like she wanted. Not even *babe* or *sweetheart* or *dollface* like some men she'd dated had called her. She'd always hated those generic nicknames. Now, desperate as she was for even a shred of affection from him, she'd take even that.

"I know you're interested," she said. "You want me."

"Yer not my type."

His words pinched something in her chest, but she ignored it. The way he was watching her, the way he couldn't seem to look away, that belied whatever excuse he wanted to throw at her. *That* was what she needed to focus on.

She drew a deep whiff, pulled his scent into her lungs.

God, he smelled good. Like musk and citrus and something spicy that set off an ache low in her belly. She moved a half step closer. "This isn't about type. You're not my usual type either, but I still want you."

His eyes hardened, and his grip tightened until a slice of pain shot up her fingers. "I'm not yer latest boy toy, Ms. Kauffman. But even if I was, yer too skinny for my taste. I like my women to look like women, not teenaged boys."

Her head snapped back, almost as if he'd hit her. He couldn't know it, but he'd just touched on her biggest insecurity.

She told herself not to lose her cool. He was interested. She hadn't misread the signs. For whatever reason, he wanted her to think he wasn't. Maybe because she'd yelled at him out on the beach. Macho tough guys never much liked it when a woman had brains and attitude and didn't put up with their crap.

Her temper resurfaced. "Fine. If we're not staying in, then I'm going out. Seeing as how you're my *bodyguard*, I suppose that means you'll be tagging along."

She turned away and headed back toward the bathroom, reaching for her cell phone on the table as she moved. She resisted the urge to pull her robe tight. Let him see what he was missing. She might be thin, but she had a body worth millions. And if he was too afraid to take a chance with her . . . well, two could suffer just as easily as one. "Be ready to go in an hour, Tierney."

She didn't wait for his response. She flipped the phone open, dialed, lifted it to her ear and said, "Javier? My headache mysteriously disappeared. Yeah, Palladium sounds fabulous."

CHAPTER 2

The pounding bass gave Finn a fucking headache. The pulsing strobe lights messed with his equilibrium. But it was the woman out on Palladium's dance floor, bumping and grinding and flirting with every shithead in the overcrowded club that grated on Finn's last nerve.

Spring break was in full swing in Acapulco and the college crowd was packed to the rafters in the trendy nightclub perched high on a hill over the raging Pacific. Finn stayed on the edge of the dance floor, close enough to make a grab for Lauren if he had to, but far enough in the background to blend in. She was a celebrity in a meat market. Guys circled her like vultures. And every minute that passed—every elbow he took to the ribs and every steroid-enhanced moron who stepped on his feet—only jacked his badass mood higher.

Man, he was way too damn old for this scene.

Lauren threw her head back and laughed at something Santiago said. The dickwad grabbed her hand, pulled her close and dipped her on the dance floor. From his spot, Finn watched her golden hair flare out around her shoulders, her teeth sparkle and her eyes dance with mischief. He remembered the way she'd looked in her hotel suite earlier. The proposition that had been in her sweet baby blues. As Santiago's arm slid around her waist and she rubbed up against him, Finn clenched his jaw and told himself enough was enough. This wasn't about what had *almost* happened between them. It was about doing his job and keeping her fucking safe.

He crossed the dance floor, muscling his way between sweaty bodies. He should be nursing a beer in the hotel bar, kicked back watching *SportsCenter* and blowing off steam from the shitty day. Better yet, he should be sound asleep in his room, locked away from temptation and the really bad move he was about to make.

The song ended. Lauren laughed again, eased back from Santiago. As her arm came down, Finn reached in and snagged her by the wrist.

"Hey! What do you—?"

"I need to talk to you."

He gave her points for resisting his tug, but the three-inch heels and the damn miniskirt that showed way too much leg for his taste made it impossible for her to resist for long. He dragged her across the room, through the grinding bodies to a hallway that led to a series of bathrooms. The music wasn't quite as loud here, but the walls still vibrated and bodies littered the corridor in groups of twos and threes.

This wasn't going to work.

He looked right and left, picked out a darkened door that looked like access to a set of stairs. Pushing it open with his shoulder, he pulled Lauren through with him. The door snapped shut behind them, muffling the music and pulsing bass. Stairs curved up and out of sight. He dragged Lauren in that direction, out of the chaos and up to the first landing, where he pushed her back against the wall, trapping her between himself and the cool stones.

"What gives you the right to—?"

"Are you trying to get yourself raped?"

Fire flashed in her eyes. "What the hell kind of question is that?"

"What the hell kind of dancing was that?"

"It's not your job to critique my dancing." She pushed a hand against his chest. Shoved hard. Didn't come close to budging him. "Your job is simply to stand on the sidelines and watch, like a good little boy."

"I know exactly what my job is." The woman was like a tick that he just couldn't get rid of. He should really step back. He was way too close to the edge and there was something about her that set him off. But instead he shifted forward, pressing into her hand and closing the gap between them. "My job is to stay close to you, *Ms*. Kauffman. That's what I'm doing."

Her long fingers and slim palm pushed against his chest again, which didn't do anything but warm the skin beneath his black rayon buttondown. "I don't want you close to me."

"That's not what you said a few hours ago."

"A few hours ago I was obviously delirious from the sun, as you oh-so eloquently pointed out. Now back off."

"Why? So you can go back out there and rub up against some other guy? I don't think so." He moved even closer, until the heat from her hot little body joined with the floral scent of her shampoo or perfume or whatever the hell it was to make him lightheaded.

She lifted her chin, but the tough-girl shield wavered. Her blue eyes settled on his, dropped to his lips. Those long fingers of hers curled into his shirt to tangle tight in the fabric. "I don't like being pushed around."

"That makes two of us," he said. "And I've had enough of you flaunting your assets for every dick in this bar."

"That's not what I'm doing."

"Bullshit." Common sense told him he was heading into no-man's-land where only bad things happened. But instead of listening to those good ol' instincts that had kept him alive for thirty-five years, he braced a hand against the wall and leaned toward her mouth. "You want to get felt up in the middle of a club? Fine. We'll do it right here."

Her eyes shot back to his. "You wouldn't dare."

"Wouldn't I? This is what you said you wanted, isn't it? In yer suite? So come on with it. Let's get busy. I'm ready right now."

She drew two quick breaths, a woman not quite as confident as she'd been moments before, which was just what he wanted. "I—I changed my mind."

He stared at her lips, millimeters from his own, and debated. Thanks to her little proposition earlier in the day, he now knew how soft and lush and perfect those lips were. How they felt against his. What kind of fire brewed inside her. And now—as it had been then—it was all he could do not to dive in and let go.

But he wouldn't. Because he was smart enough to know one taste wouldn't be enough. Not with her. Before he could change his mind, he moved back an inch. "I thought so."

Challenge flared in her eyes a split second before her hand shifted from his chest to the back of his neck. She pulled hard. Before he realized what she was doing, her mouth was on his.

Something snapped in his brain, pushed all rational thought to the wayside. Instead of pulling back, instead of telling her the night was over and driving her back to her hotel, he let her kiss him. He let her pull him into her touch, let her slide her tongue into his mouth. Let her take whatever she wanted.

Hot damn, she was on fire. Her taste seared deep, a hint of the fruity alcoholic drink she'd been sipping sliding from her tongue to his. Her mouth was wet and warm and so damn inviting his groin tightened and his pulse pounded in his veins. But it wasn't until she moaned that he lost all control.

The dream—the X-rated one that had left him hot and

sweaty with a massive boner the last few nights—spiraled to the front of his gray matter. Urgency pressed in. Took over. Demanded more. He kissed her deeper, stroked her tongue faster, pushed his hips into hers, pinning her against the wall so he could feel every inch of her supermodel curves against his own.

He'd kissed a lot of women. Had been kissed by just as many. And when done properly, he considered kissing an art form. With Lauren Kauffman, though, it wasn't art. It was a frantic race to the finish. To see who would break first. Instead of one taste satisfying his curiosity, he wanted more. More of her mouth, more of her skin, more of everything. He wanted to possess her on a level he'd never experienced.

His hand dropped from the wall to her waist. The other tangled in her long, silky hair to tug her head back so he could show her with his tongue what he wanted to do to her body. As his mouth moved to her ear, then her neck, sampling her delectable skin, her fingers gripped his shoulders, slid down his sides, landed on his hips and tugged him close so his erection pressed into her belly.

"Tierney . . . oh, God."

His pulse picked up speed. He pressed into her. Sucked on her neck. Pressed again. She moaned her approval, pushed against him, gripped his head in both hands and brought his mouth back to hers. One long, luscious, bare leg lifted around the outside of his thigh to rub against his jeans, easing his cock down into the vee created by her body.

Oh, man, she was hot. Fire gathered in his groin, turned his blood to a roar in his ears. His hand dropped to her bare thigh, slid beneath her skirt to grip her tight ass. She moaned into his mouth, wrapped her arms around his shoulders and lifted herself higher, granting him access. His fingers found only skin, juicing his need. His hand slid lower, searching. When he grazed the thin strip of cotton that was her thong, he followed it until his fingers pressed against her swollen center.

"Tierney . . ."

He wanted to touch her skin, needed to know if she was . . .

"Fuck, you're wet," he said as his fingers slid under her panties and into her slick folds.

She groaned as he stroked her, pulled his mouth back to hers again and kissed him deep. He wanted to unzip his pants, lift her around the waist and slide inside her, but hearing her moan, watching her writhe, feeling her hips moving against his hand was too damned erotic. He pushed his thigh between hers, continued to kiss her like a man starved, stroked her faster and slid his other hand across her chest to graze her nipples.

Her entire body tightened. She pulled free of his mouth, closed her eyes and tipped her head back on a long moan. Knowing she was about to peak, he latched on to her ear-lobe with his mouth and let her ride his hand until she came, the sound of her release pushing him from crazed to out of control in the breadth of a heartbeat.

He let go of her leg, reached for the button on his jeans. The rasp of the door at the base of the stairs opening and closing froze his hand against his waistband.

Lauren went still, too, but her chest continued to rise and fall with her rapid breaths as she peered over his shoulder into the dark. No one came up the stairs. No one said a word. Whoever had pushed the door open had obviously changed his mind.

Lauren released a long breath. In the little bit of light shining down from above, Finn saw her kiss-me lips curve in a seductive smile seconds before she wrapped her arms around his shoulders and leaned into him. "Where were we?"

About to make one monumental mistake.

Perspiration dotted Finn's forehead. What the hell was he doing? He pushed back from Lauren, his cock still at rock-hard attention but his brain now firing, at least on a few measly cylinders.

Lauren's hands dropped to her side. "What's wrong?"

He turned away, wiped a hand down his face. "That was . . . shit. That was not what I planned."

Silence met his ears. Followed by the click of her heels against the concrete floor. "Me either, but I'm not complaining."

He turned to look at her as reality slammed into him full force. She was a supermodel, he was her bodyguard. Yeah, there was an attraction there, but in the end he was nothing more than another conquest for her. He'd protected celebrities before. Knew how spoiled they were and how they expected everyone to be at their beck and call. And that wasn't him, not by a long shot, not anymore. As hot as she was, she wasn't worth that kind of humiliation. No woman was. Not ever again.

"Yer done for the night, Ms. Kauffman. I suggest you go out there and tell Santiago yer heading back to yer suite."

"With you?" she asked with just enough eagerness to waver his resolve.

"No." He moved back out of her reach so she couldn't tempt him again with those wicked fingers or that smokin' body. "Alone."

"But . . . but I thought—"

"By the time we get to the hotel, Hedley should be back from his scouting trip with Moira. You have a photo shoot in the morning." His gaze roamed over her features and even in the dark he could see her hair was a wild tangle around her face, her lipstick smeared. She looked wanton and hot and ready to be fucked, and it took all his strength to take another step away from her. "I think it's safe to say you need your beauty sleep."

She pushed away from the wall, her features tightening in the dim light. "You know what you are, Tierney? You're a coward."

"Why?" he asked as she pushed by him, knowing she was good and pissed now. "Because I changed my mind?"

"No." She turned to face him. "Because you're afraid. I don't fit into a nice, neat box and that's driving you nuts. You want to label me, but every time we're together you can't figure out how to act, what to say, so you resort to snide comments and a pissy attitude to turn me off. Well, you know what, buddy? Your plan finally worked. I don't need this kind of aggravation, especially from you."

She headed for the stairs. There was just enough truth in what she'd said to reignite his temper. He caught her before she reached the bottom step. "Hold up."

She whipped back, swatted his arm away in a move that was a little bit self-defense, a little bit kung fu and a whole lotta surprise. "Don't touch me. I'm going out to tell Javier I'm done for the night. But not because you *ordered* me to. I'm doing it because I want to go back to my room so I can get as far away from you as possible."

Finn let her go, following as she headed back out into the writhing bodies and swirling lights of the club and made her way to Santiago, who was talking with a duo of women. As Finn stood in the shadows watching Santiago slip his arms around Lauren's neck and whisper something in her ear, he realized he should have felt relief—he'd gotten exactly what he'd wanted, in a roundabout sorta way—only all he felt was . . . more pissed off than he'd been before.

She was wrong. This wasn't about his fear, it was about his job. He'd made the mistake of falling for a principal once before. When he'd been young and stupid and new on the job. Then he hadn't just lost his heart, he'd lost his self-respect. And he'd almost lost a gig he was actually pretty damn good at. He wasn't about to go down that road again. Not for her. Not for anyone.

One more day. He could make it through one more day on this shitty assignment. Then he was on a plane back to the States and as far away from Lauren Kauffman as was humanly possible.

Movement to his left drew his attention. His gaze shifted that way to where a group of local police stepped out of the crowd on the far side of the dance floor. His instincts went on high alert. Cops in a bar were never good, but something about this group struck him as totally out of place.

They were all in their early to mid-twenties. And the way they held themselves—arrogant, as if they owned the place—and the gang-style tattoos on their forearms didn't jibe with the uniforms. Finn shifted to find Lauren. He wanted her out of the club before the shit started flying.

He pushed his way through the mass of bodies. Strobes pulsed shards of light over skin and leather and hair. He made it only two yards before a shout echoed to his left and some kind of commotion erupted. He looked that way just as the sea of bodies parted, leaving Javier Santiago and his circle of women in clear view of the newcomers.

Shit. Finn pushed harder through the crowd. "God-dammit. Move!"

The two women Santiago had been talking with scurried off. Santiago looked up, locked eyes on the group of men and barked something in Spanish. His big hand landed on Lauren's shoulder. He shoved her behind him. Lauren yelped. She slammed into a man at her back, ricocheted off his chest and hit the ground on her ass just as the cop at the font of the group whipped out a semi-automatic and un-loaded into the crowd.

Finn's heart lurched into his throat. Screams erupted in

the club and bodies rushed from the center of the dance floor in mass exodus. He pulled the weapon from the holster beneath his shirt and fought against the flow of bodies like a salmon swimming upstream. Through the crowd he saw Santiago sail backwards, crash into a high table and slump to the floor. Tables and chairs toppled with a loud crash. For a split second, time stood still as Finn took in the blood spray, the other bodies down behind Santiago, and Lauren laid out on the ground feet away, covered in red.

God, no . . .

The blood drained from his face. His chest squeezed so hard, he couldn't breathe. Just when he was sure he'd fucked up for good, her head came up, her eyes grew wide and she screamed, shifting to her side to push herself up.

Relief released the freeze in his muscles and Finn sprang into action. He darted across the floor. Other cops in the group of assailants screamed orders at the club inhabitants, waving their guns over their heads in a show of force. Bodies darted in every direction. The music died, but the lights continued to pulse in an eerie glow, rippling over bodies and limbs and terror-filled faces. Finn counted six, eight, ten terrorists, not including the shooter. Four he could probably take down, but not the rest, not alone. And his first priority was Lauren.

He reached her in seconds that felt like a lifetime. She was on her hands and knees crawling toward Santiago. Wrapping one arm around her waist, he pulled her back behind an overturned table. "Stay down!"

"Javier! Oh, my God, Finn. Javier!"

She fought his hold but he gripped her tightly, his mind spinning with exit options. "Hold still, dammit."

The terrorists shouted orders in Spanish that echoed off the walls. Women cried; men stood frozen in fear. As Lauren quieted in his arms, Finn glanced toward the darkened hallway they'd just come from. It was ten feet away, the distance littered with downed tables and chairs. But there was no exit. The hallway ended with bathrooms. The narrow stairs went only up, not down. He peered over the table blocking their view of the horror now strewn across the dance floor. The leader stood over Javier's lifeless body, muttering something in Spanish. Finn might not be able to understand the words, but he knew the intent.

Shit. This was no random shooting. That guy knew Santiago. Finn would bet his left arm on it.

"Lauren Kauffman!" The leader's voice rang out strong and heavily accented. He turned away from Santiago and looked toward the crowd. "Which one of you bitches is Lauren Kauffman?"

Every one of Finn's muscles went tight and rigid. In his arms, Lauren stilled and sucked in a breath.

"Don't you fucking answer," he whispered in her ear.

She swallowed hard, her eyes as wide as saucers.

"Lauren Kauffman," the leader said again, his shoes clicking across the floor as he advanced on a group of women huddled near the far wall. "We have business, you and I. Come out and no one else shall be hurt."

Lauren's fear-filled eyes shot to Finn's. He didn't know what the hell was going on, but he was sure if Lauren showed herself, she'd wind up just like Santiago, and he wasn't about to let that happen.

Finn saw only one way out of this.

"Are you hit?" he whispered.

She shook her head.

"Can you crawl?"

She hesitated, then nodded.

"Go slow, on your belly, behind those tables over there." He pointed toward the hallway. "It's dark enough to cover you. Can you do that?"

She looked, nodded again. He had to give her points. She wasn't hysterical like a lot of the women around them. She was scared, but she didn't look ready to lose it. At least not yet.

"*Las luces, rapido.*"

Finn knew just enough Spanish to know they were about to lose their one shot to make it out of here alive. He let go of Lauren, pushed her forward. "They're about to turn the lights on. Hurry. I'll cover you."

She flipped over onto her stomach and didn't look back before belly crawling toward the first table, three feet away.

There was trust there. Regardless of how pissed she'd been a few minutes before, she trusted him to keep her safe.

Finn's anxiety ratcheted up as she inched away from him. From his hiding space behind the table, he trained his gun on the closest thug, the man's profile outlined by the throbbing lights. Lucky for the idiot, he didn't turn their way, didn't even notice Lauren crawl just feet to his right and disappear behind another table.

Relief rushed back, hard and fast. Finn shifted to his stomach and followed her path. Together they made their way to the hall.

When he reached the darkened threshold, Lauren was waiting for him in the shadows. He pulled himself to his feet and stepped around the corner into the stairwell just as the lights in the club flipped on behind them.

"Go," he whispered, pushing her up the stairs. "Fast."

Lauren's face was famous. In the light it wouldn't take the thugs long to figure out she'd escaped. As she gripped the banister with one hand and skipped stairs in those sky-high heels, Finn pressed one hand at the small of her back, both to steady and urge her on.

A heavy metal door blocked their exit. Finn brushed past Lauren, pushed against the waist-high bar with his hip. The door stuck. He pushed again, his anxiety amping up. With a long groan, the door finally gave and he stumbled out on the roof of the club, pulling Lauren with him.

The lights of the hotel district twinkled far below the Las Brisas hillside. To the right, the blackness that was Acapulco Bay was littered here and there with ship lights. Finn dragged Lauren to the edge of the roof and looked down. At least three stories below and another twenty vertical feet, cars whizzed by on the busy street. Even if they could get down there, chances of being seen were pretty good, and he bet the terrorists had the front of the club covered. That left the back of the building and the hillside jungle behind. He turned and looked over the roof. Triangular glass skylights, vents and what appeared to be an air-conditioning unit filled the flat space.

Lauren peered over the edge. "How are we going to get down?"

One hand wrapped around hers, the other holding his gun, Finn looked right and left. "I don't know." He spotted a curved metal arch on the opposite side. "Look. That could be a ladder."

Lauren turned to look just as voices echoed in the stairwell behind them.

"Shit. Go!" Finn pushed Lauren toward what he hoped was indeed a ladder. Because if it wasn't, they were fucked. And definitely not in the way he'd been thinking of earlier.

CHAPTER 3

The Givenchys were the first thing to go.

Lauren stumbled, would have gone down but Finn's death grip on her arm prevented her from slamming face-first into the hard surface. He pulled up, shooting pain down her shoulder. "Come on!"

"Wait!" She pulled back.

He gave her just enough time to slip out of her three-inch heels, pick them up by the straps and start running again.

They reached the curved white metal Finn had spotted earlier, which was—thank God—a ladder that disappeared over the edge and hugged the side of the building.

Finn pushed her forward. "Go."

She hooked her shoes over her fingers, turned and put her first foot on the top rung. Across the roof, the door to the stairwell flew open and two men—two really big-ass, threatening men Lauren had seen downstairs in the club—spilled out of the space.

"Go!" Finn ducked behind a venting unit with his gun gripped in both hands.

Lauren's heart rate shot into the triple digits. Shouts exploded from the opposite side of the roof. Gunfire lit up the night sky. She ducked out of the way, her hands shaking as she grasped the metal rails and lowered her foot to the next rung. Holy shit, what the hell was going on? What did these men want? It was as if she'd stumbled into a scene straight out of a James Bond movie, only this wasn't fiction, it was real life.

Sweat broke out over her palms, making the bars hard to grip. She lowered herself down another rung, said a prayer she wouldn't slip and kill herself. Just before she cleared the roof, she caught movement as a man charged Finn's hiding spot.

Her adrenaline surged. "Finn!"

Finn ducked back behind the metal vent and shifted to the other side. From his vantage she knew he couldn't see the gunman. Reacting without thought, she pushed back up on the ladder and chucked one beaded strappy Givenchy heel his way. It hit him in the face with a *thwack*. Dazed, the man stumbled, righted himself, shouted something in Spanish Lauren didn't understand. She hurled the second shoe and yelled, "Finn!"

Finn was on his feet in a split second. His fist plowed into the gangster's chin, knocking the man back and down. The gun sailed from the man's hand. A blur caught Lauren's attention. Fear closed her throat. Before she could even scream, Finn lifted his gun, whirled and fired toward the second man, charging from the other direction. The bullet struck the man in the shoulder, the impact jerking him off his feet.

The guy on the ground scrambled to his feet, hollered in Spanish, then surged forward, slamming into Finn, taking them both to the ground hard. Finn's gun flew from his fingers. The two reached for the weapon at the same time, wrestling for control.

Lauren cringed as fist met bone. Cracks and grunts resounded. Finn and the terrorist rolled across the roof. Finn landed on his back. From above, the guy slammed his fist into Finn's jaw. Finn's head smacked back against the roof. The man shouted in Spanish again, his arm sweeping out, searching for his gun. Just as his fingers closed around the grip, Finn threw a right hook that landed square in the other man's nose. A loud crack resounded. Blood spurted in every direction.

"*Mi nariz!*" the man shrieked.

Finn wriggled out from under the man's weight, kicked him in the ribs. "Yer damn nose is the least of your problems, asshole."

Across the roof, the second man, dazed and bleeding, found his balance. The gun in his hand glinted in the moonlight.

Panic nearly stole Lauren's breath. Indecision froze her mind. Words clogged in her throat. "Gun! Turn! Tierney . . . oh, *shit*!"

Finn looked up and saw the threat. In a blur, he jerked the other terrorist against his body, wrapping his arm around the man's throat. His right hand closed over the man's gun hand. He lifted and fired. Gunshots echoed and sparks lit up the darkness.

A scream caught in Lauren's throat. Before she could make a sound, the man on the other side of the roof dropped to his knees. The gun fell from his hand. Finn let go of the limp terrorist in his arms, blood seeping from the wound in his chest, and stepped over the body at his feet.

Too stunned to believe what she'd just witnessed, Lauren stared at the carnage. Footsteps echoed somewhere close. She looked up and into Finn's tight face, mired in blood and dirt and fresh bruises. "What the hell are you waiting for? Get off this fucking roof! There'll be more coming."

His voice shocked her back to reality. She didn't argue, didn't question. She picked her way down the ladder on her bare feet, her sweaty hands slipping on the rungs while her heart raced. When she reached out with her foot and felt nothing but air, her gaze shot down. The ladder had ended and she was still eight feet above the ground.

Oh, shit. "Tierney!"

From three feet above, Finn stopped climbing, glanced down. "Shit. Can't one damn thing go right tonight?"

She knew he saw exactly what she did. No bushes, no trees, nothing but hard, packed dirt that ran all along the back of the building. "You'll have to jump."

"I'll break my leg!"

"It's either that or get shot. Hurry it up, Slim. It's not gonna take them long to figure out the two yahoos they sent up to the roof are dead."

Images of what she'd witnessed in the club assailed her, followed by the leader shouting her name and what Finn had just done on that roof.

She took a deep breath, eased down as far as she could. On a gasp, her legs sailed free, swinging from side to side. She yelped, but Finn was right there above her, urging her on in a voice that was oddly gentle compared to the fury he'd just unleashed. "This is a piece of cake. You got it. That's it, Slim. Okay, now, just drop."

Her pulse roared in her ears. *Just drop?* He made it sound so easy. She hated heights, always had. With one quick prayer she let go of the ladder and was airborne for only a split second before her feet slammed into the hard earth, jarring her legs. Her knees buckled, went out from under her. She landed with a crack on her ass. Pain spiraled up her spine.

"You okay?" he called.

She winced, wiped the dirt off her hands. "Great. Never better. I'm—"

He was at her side in a flash, pulling up on her arm. "We have to keep moving."

"Hold on a minute, would you? I—"

Voices echoed on the roof. Instead of heading around the side of the building toward where her driver was parked,

Finn dragged her up the hillside and into the dark trees and thick underbrush.

"Wait," she said. "We—"

"We're not taking any chances." He didn't slow even a second to let her breathe. Vines and twigs scraped at her arms and legs. "This hill drops over into a residential area."

"How do you know?"

"Because I pay attention."

She pulled on his arm, stopping him, dirt and twigs and things she couldn't see digging into the soles of her feet. "I'm not wearing any shoes!"

He stopped, glanced down at her bare feet, then swore just before grabbing her around the waist and tossing her over his shoulder.

"Tierney!"

"Keep it down, Slim. We'll move faster this way."

"But the car—"

"Is either not there or filled with people I'm pretty sure you don't want to meet up close and personal. Now stop wiggling."

She didn't like this situation—not with her ass sticking straight up in the air, barely covered by the miniskirt she'd worn tonight—but he was right. They did move faster. Before she knew it they were at the top of the hill, thick with palms and deciduous trees she couldn't name, and he was already traversing the other side. Far below she could see the lights of Acapulco Bay. When she pushed her hands against his back and eased up to look in front of them, she saw the dark hillside indeed dropped into what looked like a heavily treed residential area.

He put distance between them and the club faster than seemed possible. He was a man who didn't notice he should need a machete to get through this damn forest. Lauren couldn't tell if anyone was following them. All she could hear was Finn's heavy breathing, the scrape of vines and tree limbs against skin and clothing, and her racing pulse.

He dropped her to her feet in the shadows of several large palms. Soft dirt squished between her toes, moonlight filtered from the sky. Across an expanse of grass, a dark shape that looked like a Mediterranean-style house sat silent in the warm night.

"What are we—?"

"There," he whispered, pointing past the end of the house. "Yeah, that'll work."

She didn't have a clue to what he'd spotted. Couldn't see anything more than large, looming shapes. And the way he kept cutting her off before she could finish a thought was really grating on her nerves.

His hand wrapped around hers and he pulled her into the yard. They made it halfway across the grass when voices echoed from the trees where they'd just been.

"Shit," Finn muttered. "Hustle."

He pulled hard on her arm. Her heart rate kicked up again. Seconds later, he tugged her to a stop on the other side of the garage next to what she now realized was an old rusted-out Jeep.

He tried the door. It swung open. With a muttered "yes," he dropped into the seat, leaned down and reached under the steering column, pulling out a handful of wires from under the dashboard.

"Oh, my God," Lauren whispered, his intent registering. "You're going to steal this thing, aren't you?"

Finn didn't answer. Instead, he used his fingernails to strip the wires, tapped them together until a spark lit up the darkness and the engine roared to life.

A ruckus of noise echoed near the edge of the trees. Lights flipped on in the house and a dog barked. Finn bolted out of the front seat, pushed her into the vehicle and hopped back in, forcing her to slide across to the passenger side.

Shouts and voices erupted from everywhere and nowhere all at the same time. Finn shoved the car into reverse, backed out of the drive and tore down the gravel road.

"Holy crap." Lauren braced her hand against the dash. "We just committed grand theft auto." Her gaze swung his way. "You just stole a car!"

"*That's* what you're worried about?"

"That's a major felony! I've never committed a crime in my life! I don't even talk on my cell phone when I'm driving!"

"You've gotta be kidding me," he mumbled, glancing in the rearview mirror, his features tense and focused in the light from the dashboard. He made a quick turn, then another, which jolted Lauren in her seat. "We didn't steal it, Slim, we borrowed it. And in case you weren't paying attention, it was either that or get chummy with your friends back there in the club."

"I don't know them! I don't know what the hell is going on or what they want from me!" The scene in the club flashed in front of her eyes, and her stomach rolled when she remembered Javier lying motionless on the dance floor. Her hand darted to her stomach. "Oh, God."

Finn glanced her way, made another turn. "Stay with me here."

She was trying. God knew she was trying, but . . .

Finn shifted, pulled the fancy satellite phone that his boss made them all carry from his pants pocket and flipped it open. He pushed a button, shoved the phone to his ear and muttered, "Come on, Hedley. Pick up."

Dark houses, trees, shapes and lights Lauren could barely focus on whizzed by her window. Javier. They'd killed Javier. Right there in the club. He hadn't done a single thing to them. All he'd done was shout—

"Mick," Finn said in a frantic voice from across the car. "We had an incident. No, wait. What?"

The alarm in Finn's voice brought Lauren's attention around. She gripped the door with one hand, the dashboard with the other, trying like hell to keep the contents of her stomach from lurching up her throat.

"Fuck," Finn muttered after listening for a second. "No, shit, we can't. How the hell—"

Lauren didn't like the sound of this. The hair on her neck stood up.

"Mick, no, listen—"

A loud *pop* echoed from Finn's phone. He yanked it away from his ear, stared at the cell in his hand and pressed it back to his ear with more urgency. "Hedley? Hedley!" Another series of popping sounds echoed across the line before it went silent.

"Fuck," Finn yelled, slamming the phone against the steering wheel. "Fuck!"

Lauren's anxiety went through the roof. "What happened?"

His jaw clenched with controlled fury. He glanced in the rearview again and made a sharp turn. "We gotta get off this damn road."

He wasn't answering her. That was an even worse sign. Fear mixed with the anxiety to send heat prickling her skin. "Tierney, what the hell happened?"

"I don't know. Hedley told me not to come back to the hotel. Said the cops were there, looking for you."

"For *me*?" Lauren's brows drew together. "Why?"

"I don't know. Before I could ask him . . ."

"Before you could ask him, what?"

Finn's jaw clenched like he didn't want to answer. "Someone fired."

Lauren's heart lurched into her throat. The popping

sound had been gunfire. "Oh, God." She sat back in her seat, breathing slowly as she tried to make sense of everything in her head. Javier was dead. Mick was probably dead as well. Her staff . . . Oh, God, Moira. Her stomach churned again. All those people in the club . . .

Dear God, what the hell is going on?

"I don't know," Finn said, taking twists and turns in a road Lauren barely saw. She didn't even realize she'd voiced her question out loud until he added, "But I'm going to find out."

His intense gaze shot her way. In the dim light from the dash, she saw worry, anxiety and a whole lot of pissed off. "What the hell are you wrapped up in? You'd better spill the damn truth right now or I swear—"

Her eyes flew wide. "Me? You think I did this?"

"They were looking for you. They called yer damn name back there!"

Anger replaced the fear and guilt. "I've never seen those men in my life. I don't have a clue what they want with me! And who the hell are you to say I'm wrapped up in anything? You've been with me all week. Do I look like someone who would have anything to do with a group of terrorists?"

His mouth slammed shut. He glanced from her to the road and back again. She could practically see the wheels turning in his head, replaying everything that had happened. While she was pissed he'd immediately suspected her, part of her couldn't blame him. His partner was either injured or dead, and everything did seem to be pointing her way.

She closed her eyes, the guilt rushing back in over everyone who'd been hurt or killed tonight because of her. "I don't know what they want with me," she said softer. "I don't . . ."

Words caught in her throat.

"I had to know," he said, his voice softer, too. "If yer honest with me, I'll be honest with you."

Her eyes flicked open. "I am being honest, Tierney. I'm as clueless as you are right now and this whole thing is pissing me off."

"That makes two of us," he mumbled.

He made another turn, and his gaze shot to her again. In the dim light she saw his dark eyes had softened considerably. "I'm going to keep you safe. Whatever's happening . . . I'll get you out of it. You trust me, don't you?"

Lauren swallowed hard, felt a wave of emotion she couldn't define sweep over her. Finn Tierney was a man who made things happen. Regardless of what had or hadn't gone on between them, she knew he meant every word he said. The key was getting her to believe them as well.

In the darkness of a night that had turned into a nightmare, she couldn't bring herself to answer. The best she could do was nod.

CHAPTER 4

They ditched the Jeep in an empty lot miles from where they'd started. When Lauren threw another fit about the stolen car, Finn dug around in the glove box until he found some kind of registration, jotted down the name and address of the unsuspecting owners and promised they'd make it worth their loss when this was over. That seemed to appease Lauren for a few minutes, until he told her they needed to hoof it a mile or so till they could find another means of transportation.

Standing beside the rusted Jeep, Lauren's eyes blazed as hot as the ruby-red pendant dangling from a chain around her neck. A pendant he didn't remember seeing before. "I'm not wearing any shoes, in case you didn't notice."

He glanced at her bare feet, surrounded by rocks and dirt. "What did you do with yer damn shoes?"

He was pretty sure she'd had them on when they'd been in that stairwell. Vaguely remembered the sound of her heels clicking against the concrete floor. Then had a visual flash of her in that stairwell wearing those fuck-me heels on her slim little feet and her bare thigh wrapped around his hip.

A rush of heat slammed into him out of nowhere, lighting up his groin and pissing him off all at the same time.

"I threw them at that idiot on the roof when he came after you with that gun."

His mind raced back to the scene. He'd heard her scream his name when all hell had broken loose, had wanted to smack her for coming back up the ladder when he'd told her to go down. He realized now she'd pretty much saved his skin. A little of his anger eased. "Did you really think throwing yer shoe was going to do any good?"

"It gave you the chance you needed, didn't it?"

"Maybe." He couldn't stop wondering when she was going to freak out and lose it over the way he'd killed those two men. "But I'd have been just fine without yer help. And at least then you'd still have shoes."

"You son of a bitch. That's the thanks I get for saving your life?"

Pissed, he told himself, was better than a melted puddle. Safer still than turned on like she'd been in that hallway. He was still awed by the way she'd rallied when he'd turned on her in the car. He'd had terrorists crack under the weight of his stare more easily than Lauren had under his interrogation. The woman was tougher than he'd given her credit for being. But she was still a woman, and they were all the same.

His gaze swept her moonlit body. Her cheeks were flushed, her hair a wild tangle, her eyes as intense as he'd ever seen. Right now she looked sexier than any photo, hotter than she had in that skimpy bikini on the beach. And staring at her in the middle of the vacant lot, he realized, hell, yeah, he wanted to thank her. Thank her with his mouth and hands and body and finish what they'd started in that damn stairwell.

He took a deep breath, glanced around the empty lot, tried to shove the memory of her riding his hand to a blistering climax out of his mind for good. "We need to get going."

"I can't walk without—"

He swooped her up in his arms. She pressed a hand against his chest, glared at him again, but didn't fight his hold. He ignored the feel of her silky skin against his arms, the heat from her body infusing his own. But when her lips turned down in a sexy little pout, it was all he could do not to kiss it from her face.

"Do you even know how much those shoes cost?" she asked. "They were my favorite pair."

He cut across the lot, headed for the little fishing village nearby. "You can buy another pair when you get home."

They needed to regroup. He needed to call Jake and figure out what the hell was going on, and Lauren needed to rest. Okay, so she hadn't yet cracked, but she would. All women did sooner or later.

"Not those shoes," she said, softly. "They were ten years old."

"They're just shoes."

"Those weren't *just* shoes. They had sentimental value. Not something I'd ever expect you to understand."

There was enough hurt in her voice to tell him she was serious. Though why someone like her would hang on to a pair of outdated heels when she could buy a new pair any day she wanted was anyone's guess.

They moved in silence across the street, staying in the shadows. The sidewalk was cracked and overgrown with weeds. At this hour there was barely a soul around, with most of the businesses shut down for the night. Half a mile ahead, Finn spotted what he hoped was a motel, its flashing neon sign burned out in two places. He headed in that direction.

He dropped Lauren to her feet outside the door of the two-story structure. "Stay close to me."

She didn't answer, but at least now she was following directions. As he pushed the lobby door open, she stepped in after him and stayed by his side while he headed for the chipped tile counter and rang the bell.

Not the Ritz. The lobby held a couple of cracked plastic chairs, a fake plant and a TV in the corner of the room that flickered with a late-night Spanish soap opera. A chair scraped the floor in the back room. Then a middle-aged man with black hair and dark skin rounded the corner and approached with wary eyes.

"*Sí, Señor. En que puedo servirle?*"

"Um . . ." Finn held up one finger, ran through his crappy Spanish. "*¿Un cuarto?*"

The man's eyes narrowed. "*¿Tu hablas español?*"

"Not very well," Finn muttered.

"What you need?" the man asked in English, his voice heavily accented.

Finn reached for his wallet. "Just a room for the night."

The man looked over the counter at Lauren, glanced at her bare feet. His curious gaze slid back to Finn. "Thirty dollars. U.S."

Finn pulled cash from his wallet, slapped it on the counter. "We'd like a first-floor room if you've got it." He added another twenty, hesitating before handing the bill directly to the man. "We don't want to be disturbed. By anyone. If you know what I mean."

The man glanced at Lauren again, nodded in a knowing way, then turned, grabbed a key from a hook and pointed toward the door. "Last room. Numero eleven. No disturbance."

"One more thing," Finn said as Lauren turned for the door.

"*¿Sí?*"

"You wouldn't happen to know where we could rent a car, would you?"

The man's eyes lit up. He stepped back from the counter, motioned with his hand. "Come, come. You see."

Finn sized the man up, didn't sense any danger. He turned to Lauren. "Stay put."

He followed the man around the corner into a small office. The man moved to the window on the far side of the room, pulled the curtain back and pointed through the glass.

Finn stepped closed and peered out. What seemed to be a blue, beat-up seventies Chevy pickup sat parked behind the office. "You want to rent me that?"

"You buy," the man said. "I make you good deal."

Like Finn had never heard that before. "Does it even run?"

"*Sí, sí.* Runs good." The man reached for a key on the desk, held it up. "You buy."

It looked pretty old, but the condition of the tires, the fresh bugs on the grille and the dust outlining only the edge of the windshield all indicated it had recently been driven. Finn wasn't above roughing it. And they did need wheels. Ones that weren't stolen. He just didn't have time to take it for a test drive. "How much?"

"How much you give me?"

Finn reached for his wallet again. "I've got a hundred bucks."

"Is yours." The man handed him the key.

If only all auto purchases were that easy.

Finn took the key, headed back out into the lobby. When he reached Lauren, he said, "*Gracias,*" to the man, then steered Lauren toward the door.

"What was that all about?" She stumbled when they reached the sidewalk, and cringed.

He caught her by the arm before she went down. "Got us a car."

"Does it run?"

"We'll find out soon enough."

She didn't say anything else, and he figured her meltdown

was imminent. She was taking longer to break down than most women, which just told him when she did finally crumble, it'd be a whopper.

The room held a double bed, a chipped nightstand with a lamp and rotary phone, and a scarred desk and chair. No TV, no DVD, none of life's creature comforts. The door snapped closed behind them. Finn pushed the bathroom door open, swept a look through the hole-of-a-room, then stepped to the window and looked through the blinds. Lauren stood still in the small entry hall, unmoving. Behind the building, no lights twinkled. From what Finn could see, a barren field ran to jungle and God knew what else beyond.

Lauren took a deep breath. "I'm filthy. I . . . I need a shower."

He turned, pointed toward the door at her left. "Through there."

She stared at him a beat, nodded, then disappeared.

The vulnerable look he'd seen in her eyes stuck with him as the shower was turned on. He should go in there and make sure she was okay. She wasn't used to the seedier side of life. Not like him. She'd grown up with money, assistants and bodyguards waiting on her twenty-four-seven. While her emotional well-being wasn't in his job description, he still didn't like the idea of her melting into a puddle on the dingy bathroom floor.

Indecision brewed inside him. There were more pressing matters than Lauren's mental stability. Before he could change his mind, he whipped his cell from his pocket and dialed.

Jake Ryder, CEO and founder of Aegis, picked up on the first ring. "Does bad luck just follow you or what, Tierney? I've been waiting for your damn call. You secure?"

Finn let out a breath. Jake had already heard the news. Finn hoped that meant things weren't as bad as they seemed. "Yeah. We're good. Did you talk to Hedley? Is he okay?"

"Hedley's fine. Took a bullet to the shoulder, but it's nothing the sonofabitch can't handle. He's at the ER now getting patched up. The shooters weren't cops, though they were dressed like them."

Not cops. Finn's suspicions had been right. "Same ones from the bar?"

"Or linked to them. How's Kauffman?"

Finn glanced toward the bathroom door, felt that tug to go check on her again. "Fine. For now. So far she's shown balls of steel, but it's not gonna last." He looked away, fighting the weird pull she seemed to have on him. "What about the others?"

"No casualties. There was a woman . . . Mierna—"

"Moira." *Shit.* "That's Lauren's assistant."

"Moira. Right. According to Hedley, she got a little banged up in the scuffle. Nothing a few days of R&R won't fix."

Relief pulsed through Finn. But just as quickly anger over the situation pushed in. "What the hell's going on, Jake? The hit on Santiago was professional. And they had a hard-on for Lauren. I almost didn't make it out with her."

"Anything stand out from the shooting?"

Finn thought back to that moment. Images flashed behind his eyes. He saw the group of men step into the bar and Santiago's immediate reaction. He saw Santiago push Lauren to the ground behind him, heard the leader shout something in Spanish. Heard Santiago's bellowed response. And he saw . . .

"Maybe," he said. "They were shouting something that sounded like . . . 'rojo diablo.' *Donde está* . . . '" Crap, he was no good at Spanish. "What . . . who . . . No, where. Where is *el diablo rojo*? That was it."

"You sure that's what they said?'

"Yeah. Why?"

"*Diablo rojo* means red devil," Jake said in a knowing voice.

"Does that mean something to you?" Finn asked.

"Unfortunately, it does." Paper rustled over the line. "Javier Santiago is the son of a Maria Elena Rosarió Vargas and Philippe Leon Santiago Cárdenas. Ring any bells?"

Finn's chest went cold. "No way. Santiago's linked to the Cárdenas drug cartel?"

"Bingo."

"Holy shit." Finn's mind tumbled. The Cárdenas Cartel was one of the largest in this region of Mexico, responsible for numerous killings in the Acapulco area alone. "And Cárdenas's son is a model? How is that even possible?"

"One of his sons." Papers rustled again, and Finn imagined Jake behind the big mahogany desk in the dimly lit office he kept in his monster of a house. "Javier is the youngest of three sons. The older two—Manuel and Philippe, Jr.—followed in good ol' Dad's footsteps, running drugs north for the cartel. From what I can deduce, Javier's been the black sheep of the family for quite some time. He doesn't play by the rules and he makes no bones over the fact he has no interest in joining the family biz. He's a player, a spoiled rich kid. Modeling apparently pisses his old man off, which is why he keeps doing it, but he's small time in the industry. Most of his cash comes from Cárdenas sources, though lately reports have surfaced that he's had intimate contact with the Tijuana Cartel."

"Shit," Finn whispered. "So what was this? An honor killing?"

"Sorta," Jake said. "Though not in the way you think. One of the Cárdenas Cartel's lesser known drugs is Seconal, a barbiturate. Ever heard of it?"

"No."

"Doesn't surprise me. It's also called 'red dillies' or 'red devils.' " It's been around since the twenties, but it fell out of popularity a while back. Word on the street is the Cárdenas Cartel's created a new, more potent form of the drug—bigger highs, longer lasting—really nasty shit, and they were getting ready to start shipping it. They've got several key Mexican politicians in their back pocket, several with ties to the U.S. The influx of these new red devils on the street could turn the drug trade upside down in Mexico and seriously cut into the other cartels' profits."

"God, you're talking about a bloodbath between rival cartels. And Javier knew about this? He was feeding info to the Tijuana Cartel about the new drug?"

"Possibly. No one knows for sure. But it's probable he had access to family documents. Names, dates, shipments . . . maybe even the new drug formula. Tierney, the Cárdenas Cartel put a price on young Javier's head just this morning."

Holy hell. Things were seriously heading straight for the toilet. Finn blew out a breath. "What does all this have to do with Lauren?"

"I don't know. How well does she know Santiago?"

How the hell would Finn know? "Well enough to let him grab her ass in public."

Jake chuckled. "She's a supermodel, Tierney. I imagine a lot of guys get to grab her ass on camera."

No shit. And Finn didn't like it one bit.

He pushed down the frustration. "Javier's been with us at the shoot for the last week. He wasn't at Cárdenas headquarters, spying on the cartel. Why now, all of the sudden, would they take him down, when if what you're saying is true, he could have had the info a week ago?"

"I don't know. But any way you toss this, it doesn't look good. Are you still in Acapulco?"

"No. But within driving distance."

"You got access to a vehicle?"

"I've got something lined up."

"Good. Zane Archer's a couple hours south of you, in the mountains northeast of San Marco." Jake rattled off the GPS coordinates. "I'm going to alert him that you're coming. He can get you two on a chopper out of there, unseen. You can't risk going to the authorities in the area. The Cárdenas Cartel has too much influence over local P.D. in the state of Guerrero, and Kauffman's face is too well known. My guess is all eyes are watching for you, so it won't be easy."

"You sure Archer's up for this?" Zane Archer was a former Aegis operative. Last Finn had heard, the man had taken an extended leave of absence after his principal was killed in a botched rescue attempt. Most of the guys in the agency figured Archer was knee-deep in Therapy 101 with good ol' José Cuervo. But no one knew for sure just what he was up to in Mexico. Or for how long.

"He's up for it. You just worry about getting Kauffman's ass to his compound. Let Archer do the rest."

Finn's mind drifted to Lauren in the bathroom and he looked that way again. "Will do, but she needs an hour or two of rest first."

Jake's sigh said he didn't like the delay. "You sure you're secure where you're at?"

No, but it was the best they had for the moment. Lauren was in no condition to move just yet. "Trust me. It's as good as it's gonna get for the time being."

"Okay," Jake said, his voice growing tight. "Keep your eyes peeled. And Tierney?"

"Yeah?"

"Don't let history repeat itself."

Finn hung up, unsure just what history Jake was referring to. Archer's botched extraction? Or was the warning more personal, regarding Finn's mistake with his own principal?

Telling himself he was reading more into it than he needed, he waited a handful of minutes, then figured enough time had passed for Lauren to wrap up her shower. Screw Jake's warning. He wasn't going to make the same mistake he'd made before. He was just checking to see if she was okay.

He stopped at the bathroom door and listened. The water had been shut off minutes before, but no other sound met his ears. He knocked gently. "Slim?"

"What?"

"Are you okay?"

"Fine. I'll be done in a minute."

Her rushed words amped his already strung-tight nerves. He reached for the door handle. "I'm coming in."

"No, don't. I—"

He pushed the door open. Bright light flooded his eyes. He blinked twice and found her sitting on the edge of the tub facing the door, her blond hair dripping down her bare shoulders. One foot was propped up on her opposite knee, the towel laid out beneath her.

She jerked, and her foot hit the dirty tile floor as she grabbed the ends of the towel and wrapped them up around her breasts. Around her very naked, perfect breasts. But there was no point in covering herself. The image of her bare and glistening from her shower was now alive in his mind.

She shot him an irritated look. "I said don't come in."

He looked from her face to her foot and back again, catching the glint of red in the gem she wore around her neck. The only thing she wore. She didn't look like a woman about to have a mental breakdown. He saw no signs of tears. In fact, the irritation marring her features drew his brows together. "I thought . . . what are you doing?"

Her lips pressed together. She lifted her foot back to her knee. "Trying to get a damn piece of glass out of my foot."

"Glass?"

"I must have stepped on something outside on the sidewalk when you put me down. It's not big, but it hurts like hell. I'd give just about anything for tweezers right now."

"Let me look." He crossed the floor and dropped to his knees in front of her. Pushing her hand away, he inspected the bottom of her foot. The skin was red and irritated near her arch.

She ground her teeth, but didn't fight him. When he ran his finger over the spot to feel for the shard, she sucked in a breath.

He looked up at her face, then reached back for the pocketknife in his pocket. "Okay, hold still. I think I can get it."

Her eyes grew wide as he pulled out the knife, flipped open the blade. But she didn't flinch, not even when he put the tip of the knife against the bottom of her foot and applied just enough pressure to work it under the edge of the shard.

"Oh, *shit*." She drew out the word as he applied more pressure. Her hands hit the edge of the tub and she grabbed on to steady herself.

"Almost have it."

Her body tensed, and then the small shard of green glass popped free and hit the dingy tile with a soft tinkle.

"Oh, my God, that hurt," Lauren breathed.

"Sorry." Finn clicked the knife closed, set it on the ground and reached for a wad of toilet paper, which he held against the bottom of her foot. It wasn't bleeding too badly, but considering everything else she'd been through tonight, he didn't need her passing out from seeing her own blood. He dabbed at the wound. Looked. Dabbed again. Wished they had something to clean it properly.

From the corner of his eye he noticed the towel had dropped to her lap, leaving her beautiful breasts bare in the dim overhead light. His thoughts shifted. Naked with only that red stone against her chest, she looked like a goddess.

His throat grew thick. He tried like hell to keep his eyes on her foot. "It should be okay now."

Lauren let go of the edge of the tub, grasped the towel and pulled it tight again. But he didn't miss the way her cheeks turned pink as she said, "Thanks. My Givenchys might not have been practical while we were running, but they would have deterred glass."

"Your Gi-*what*?"

"Givenchys." Her gaze lifted to his. "My shoes. Famous French designer. You've never heard of him?"

"French?" What the hell was she mumbling about? And why wasn't she still naked? "Ah, no. I'm a guy, remember?"

He sat back on his heels as she shook her head like he was an idiot, took the toilet paper from his hand and dabbed at the bottom of her foot. Her skin was dewy and soft, her blond hair curling around her shoulders as it dried. With her foot still propped on her knee, he could just see the long line of her bare thighs hiding the treasure nestled in the shadow between her legs. The memory of touching her there exploded in his head, followed by her cry of pleasure as she came against his hand.

His blood pulsed, and warmth circulated in his veins, slid down his torso to pool in his groin. *Don't let history repeat itself. . . .*

Okay, he needed to back off. Like . . . now. So why wasn't he moving?

"What?" Lauren asked, looking away from her foot to glance at his face.

"What, 'what'?" he tossed back, startled by her voice. Was he sweating? He reached for the wet washcloth on the edge of the tub and swiped it across his face, wiping away the sweat and dirt and dried blood.

"You're watching me."

He dropped his hand, frowned. "I thought we went through this before. It's my job to watch you."

Her knowing blue eyes held his before glancing back to her foot. "And I thought you set me straight on that kind of watching."

He flashed back to their conversation in her suite earlier in the day, and the proposition she'd offered him then. Warmth turned to white-hot heat. Why the hell had he turned her down? God, had that been only a few hours ago? It seemed like days. Weeks.

He swallowed hard, trying to keep his brain from shorting out. She smelled really good. Fresh. Clean. Like God intended.

"You're watching me again," she said.

He was. He couldn't seem to look away. He tried to change the subject. "Why aren't you freaking out?"

"Should I be?"

He tossed the washcloth into the tub behind her, braced both hands against his thighs. "Considering everything? Yeah."

She dropped her foot to the ground, focused on his eyes. "Will it do any good?"

"No, but . . . most women would be, after everything you've been through tonight."

"You've been through it, too, and you aren't freaking out, are you?"

She had a point, but in his experience women like her behaved one way, and one way only.

She stood up. "You've met my brother, Finn. Freaking out isn't part of the Kauffman doctrine of life."

He picked up the knife, slid it back into his pocket as he stood and carefully studied her eyes. They didn't look wild, didn't look dilated. If anything, they looked normal. In control. "I don't see how that—"

"While I'll admit running from crazy men isn't part of my normal, everyday routine, freaking out about it isn't going to do me any good. We need to figure out what happened and why, who those guys were and why they killed Javier."

Okay, that sounded way too rational. Why wasn't she melting?

"I've seen death before," she said with more confidence than he expected. "Granted, it wasn't like what you did to those guys on the roof, or what happened in the club, but it was still death. I was with my parents the night our car was hit by a drunk driver and they were both killed. I watched the light go out of my father's eyes, saw the gruesome details of my mother's death. I even survived the loss of my grandparents when I was in high school. For a long time it was just me and my brother before he went off to figure out his own life."

"Yeah, but—"

She held one hand out to the side. "*This* is not the product of a pampered upbringing like you and a lot of people think. I fell into this gig in college when they were filming a commercial on campus. One day I'm walking through the quad and the next I'm being offered a modeling contract. When you're thirty thousand dollars in debt, you don't have much of a family to lean on and the job market isn't looking all that promising, sometimes you don't question the whys of things, you just take the opportunity that's being offered."

He couldn't quite keep up with her. "I thought—"

Irritation flashed in her eyes. "You thought what? That because I'm a model I'm some sort of diva? That's your problem, Tierney. You thought wrong." She took a step toward him and jabbed her index finger in his chest. "I'm good in a crisis, in case you haven't noticed. I've got brains, and even when this body's different, I'll still have those brains. I'm not some spoiled princess who needs you to hold her hand."

She turned away, but he snagged her by the wrist, compelled to soothe what he'd just riled. "That's not what I think at all."

She whipped back, fire brewing in her light blue eyes. "Could have fooled me."

"Lauren—"

"Hedley told me what your issue is. He told me about Sylvia."

Finn stilled at the mere name. A name he purposely didn't think of because it reminded him what a schmuck he'd been. The trouble he'd caused. How wrong he'd been about one person who'd had the power to fuck up not only his life but several others' as well.

He let go of her. "I don't know what you're talking ab—"

Instead of stepping back as he expected, she moved forward. "Bullshit. I've met her, you know. The modeling industry isn't all that big. Former models turned model-agency owners aren't that rare, but Sylvia Grace's agency was on the rise. I even considered signing with her at one point. Would it surprise you to know I decided against it because I thought she was a bitch? And that was before all the shit about her little side business hit the papers."

Finn's chest chilled. Sylvia's side-business had been a high-class call-girl ring. She'd been recruiting models that just didn't have that extra spark to make it in the industry, then conned them into working for her.

Her moonlighting had been going fine until one girl wound up dead after a date with a Middle Eastern U.N. ambassador, in New York for a summit meeting. The girl's father had dug around, found out about Sylvia's scam, and threatened her life. Sylvia'd wigged, hired Aegis for security, claiming a former fan was stalking her. And Finn had been assigned to protect her. Of course, he hadn't known what she was doing behind closed doors. Not when he'd started. Not when she'd seduced him. Not when he'd been dumb enough to fall for her looks and charm and fame.

He swallowed back the deep burning humiliation and the guilt for what he'd put Aegis through when he'd found out and walked. "Good thing you decided not to sign with her."

She ignored his smart-ass comment. "Mick told me how she turned on you. How she made trumped-up allegations that you were involved in her prostitution ring, how the publicity jeopardized not only your job, but Aegis's reputation as well. Do you honestly think I'm at all like that woman?"

His skin tingled. No, he didn't think Lauren was a madam in disguise. Earlier he'd been suspicious that she was somehow involved with what had gone down tonight, but in his gut he knew that wasn't possible. The problem was, his gut had been wrong before. And where this woman was concerned, he wasn't sure of anything anymore.

"You're attracted to me, Tierney. We both know it. Only you're too afraid I'm like Sylvia to take a chance on something we both know could be really good. Look at me, Finn. Take a good, long look. And tell me. After everything you've learned about me in the last week, do you honestly think I'm some spoiled heiress who's going to use you and ruin you when I've had my fill?"

His throat grew thick as he stood in the bathroom, studying her eyes, trying to get a handle on the sensations pinging around in his chest. A tiny part of him cursed Hedley for ratting him out, but another part was glad. She'd pinpointed exactly what he was afraid of. Learning the truth about Sylvia hadn't just bruised his pride, it had nearly cost him his job and the trust of a man who wasn't just his boss, but a good friend as well. And taking a chance on yet another client—a model to boot—had bad news branded all over it. He knew better.

Don't let history repeat itself. . . .

And yet . . . everything Lauren had told him tonight suddenly made sense. Everything he'd noticed about her in the last few hours finally gelled. And tonight, right now, she was proving she wasn't at all what he'd originally thought.

Which made her that much more enticing. Intoxicating. Irresistible.

His heart picked up speed. The room suddenly felt hot and cramped. And the fact she was naked beneath that towel was all he could focus on.

As if sensing the struggle within him, she moved closer, the fire from her hot little body swirling until it was all he could do not to reach for her.

"Tell me something," she said softly. "If you weren't my bodyguard, if I weren't a model . . . if we'd just met one day on the beach, or in a club, or even at the coffee counter at the mall, what would you be doing right now?"

He swallowed hard. "I don't drink coffee."

She rolled her eyes. Smiled a sexy little grin that sent the blood singing in his veins. "Frozen yogurt counter then. Focus, Tierney. If we'd met anywhere else, what would you be doing to me right now?"

"Slim, people under extreme duress do things they wouldn't do otherwise. I—"

"Stop stalling, Tierney, and answer the question. What would you be doing now?"

His blood pounded hard in his ears, and his groin tingled with awareness. The look in her eyes said she wouldn't let him go until she squeezed out every ounce of truth left in him. And some small part of him didn't want her to let him go.

The words left his lips before he thought better of it. "I'd be stripping off that towel faster than you could gasp."

"Done." Victory flashed in her eyes a split second before the towel dropped from her hand. It hit the floor at their feet, leaving her naked and wet and his for the taking.

A dim, last warning flashed in his brain. "Lauren—"

She pressed her hands against his chest, jackknifing heat through his torso until she was all he could feel. And then she leaned in, her kiss-me lips millimeters from his, just begging him to take a long, succulent taste. "The next move is yours, Tierney. What are you gonna do now?"

CHAPTER 5

He was too far gone to *think* of what he was going to do next. He simply acted.

Finn's mouth came down on Lauren's, harder than he planned. When she groaned, he eased back, but her hand fisted his hair, her mouth opening to take him in. This time the groan wasn't pain, but pleasure. The sound he'd heard echoing in his dream. A sound he wanted to hear again and again and again.

His tongue slid into her mouth, his arms wrapped around her small waist to tug her close. The long, naked lines of her body pressed up against his, heating his blood to explosive levels. He changed the angle of the kiss, tasted her deeper, pushed her back until she bumped into the sink. He forgot about everything going on outside these walls and focused only on her.

She grabbed on to his shoulders, wrapped her legs around his waist as he lifted her from the floor and set her on the counter. As she kissed him crazy, her hands went to his waistband, tugging the shirt up and over his head.

He broke the kiss, let her tear the garment from his body. Then he pressed his hungry mouth to hers again, sliding his hands up her ribcage to caress her warm, plump breasts while her tongue did nasty things to his mouth. She tasted like sin and seduction, felt like everything he'd been missing. As her fingers found his belt buckle and made quick work of the button and zipper, he tried to slow things down, tried to tell himself not to attack her as soon as she freed him from his jeans, tried to keep some semblance of control.

She pressed her palm against his lower belly and slid it into his boxers to grip his aching shaft. "Mmm," she moaned into his mouth, "I knew you'd be worth waiting for."

That was it, as much as he could take. The taste of her hot little mouth, the feel of her warm hand gripping his length . . . he wasn't going to last much longer if he let her go on like this.

He lifted her off the counter, swung around toward the door. She gasped, her legs clinging tight. "Where are we going?"

"Bed. I've dreamed of this body in a bed. Not in some grungy bathroom."

She laughed as he reached the side of the bed, grabbed the comforter and ripped it back. He dropped her on the cool sheets. She sucked in a breath as he lowered himself and his lips found the soft skin of her earlobe.

"Oh, God, Tierney . . . you dreamed about me? I thought you said I was too skinny."

"I never said that." He trailed his lips down her throat to the indent between her shoulder and neck, ran his finger over the chain of her necklace, kissed the hollow of her throat.

"Yes . . . yeah. I think you did." She swallowed as he brought his hand up to her breast, palmed the heavy mass and skimmed the tip of his finger over her nipple. "You, um . . . you said I was like a teenaged boy."

He drew back, looked down at her glistening skin, her

taut nipples, her narrow waist and the triangle of blond curls that led to what he wanted most. "I had to have been high."

"You said—"

His brows snapped together. "Why the hell would you listen to me? You know I'm full of crap. Yer proving it right now, aren't ya?"

That victorious smile spread across her gorgeous face again, and she reached for him, pulling his mouth back to hers. "You're damn right, I am."

He lost himself in her kiss, in her mouth, in the softness of her body. He trailed his lips down her neck, over the gem at the apex of her cleavage, to her breasts, laving his tongue across one nipple, then the next, drawing each deep in his mouth until she writhed on the bed and begged for more.

His body screamed for release, but he didn't rush things. He loved the sounds she made, wanted to see just how far he could push her before she lost her famed control. She wasn't a melted puddle after everything they'd been through tonight? That was fine. That was great. But he wanted her to melt beneath him just the same.

She tensed when his lips passed over her belly button, moaned when he kissed the top of her mound and groaned long and deep when his tongue finally ran between her folds and he tasted her for the first time.

"Tierney . . ." She lifted her knee, planted her injured foot on the bed, pressed her hips against his mouth, urging him on.

He licked her slow, tasted her deep, flicked his tongue over her tight knot again and again until her whole body tensed and she came in his mouth.

Not nearly as satisfied as her, he sucked the skin between her hip and torso until she groaned, then pushed himself up and wrestled his way out of his jeans. Her eyes were heavy with desire as she looked up at him, her body limp from her release. He climbed over her, took her mouth again and kissed her deep as his naked skin finally came into full contact with hers.

"Finn," she whispered, kissing him back, "oh, yes . . . yes."

Her knees fell open, and he sank into the vee of her body. Heat consumed his pelvis where he pressed against her. The tip of his cock slid into her slippery folds, and she lifted her hips in invitation, groaning again into his mouth. "Oh . . . yeeeeeeesssss."

Common sense had funny timing, but he was thankful it snapped in now. He broke the kiss, eased back and reached for his jeans on the floor.

She pushed up on her elbows, her lips plump from his mouth, her hair wild around her face. "What are you doing?"

He grabbed the wallet from his jeans, pulled out the condom, waving it as he leaned back over her. "Protection."

"You take this gig seriously, I see." She smiled and took it from his fingers, kissed his lips. "Let me."

"I'm a professional, you know." He let her push him over onto his back, stared up at the ceiling as she kissed her way down his torso. And lost all sense of humor when her lips found his hip and her soft fingers wrapped around his erection. She stroked him once, twice, and he closed his eyes, groaning at the feel of her hand sliding along his flesh. But it wasn't until he felt her lips wrap around the tip of his cock that he knew what true heaven really was.

"Lauren . . ."

She ran her tongue along the underside of the flared head, then sucked him deep. His dick swelled in her mouth. He lifted his hips, but she didn't need the help. She knew just how to tease him to drive him mad. Somehow he had the strength to push her back just before he lost it for good. "Lauren . . ."

"I love it when you say my name." That victorious grin was becoming a permanent fixture on her face. She tore open the package, slid the condom down his length. Before he could push up to help her, she was climbing over him, lowering her body to his and claiming his mouth with her own.

"God, you feel good," he whispered against her mouth, wrapping his arms around her waist. Don't repeat history? Shit, nothing and no one could ever compare to this woman. He wasn't repeating history. He was blazing a new, more dangerous trail. "This is a really bad idea."

She lowered her hips until the tip of his cock found her opening and his aching length was pressed up inside her one reaching inch. The red gem of her necklace fell against his chest, warm from her skin. "Not a bad idea, Tierney. The best idea. Let me show you."

He was too far gone to argue with her now. She lowered the rest of the way, took him deep inside her hot little body. Squeezed him so tight he thought he would come right there and then. And then she began to move, riding him hard, taking him deeper with every stroke, drawing him closer to the edge until she was all he could see and feel and touch. Until madmen, gunshots, drug cartels and all the reasons he couldn't have her slipped right out of his mind.

Until, in that last moment before she arched her back and reached the peak, the body and face and woman he'd sworn to protect became the only thing that mattered anymore.

She must have fallen asleep, but how long she was out, Lauren didn't know. When her eyes fluttered open, she was lying on her back, the sheet was pulled up to her chest, and Finn was stretched out beside her on the small bed, leaning on his elbow, watching her in the dim light coming from the bathroom.

"If you weren't my bodyguard," she said with a smile,

turning into his warm, strong chest, "that could come across a little creepy."

Something wary crossed his features, but he got the hint when she slid her hand around the nape of his neck and tugged. He leaned down and kissed her. "Just doing my job, Ms. Kauffman."

The way he said Ms. Kauffman struck her as odd, but she ignored it. With every other guy she'd worried her career and celebrity status would eventually ruin their relationship—which it had. Finn was already hesitant about being involved with her. And so far they didn't even have a relationship—just good sex. Really, hot, sweaty, bone-melting sex. Just the thought of what they'd done earlier sent heat careening through her veins all over again.

She ran her finger over his pec, down his sternum. Wondered how easy it would be to get him to go for round two. "You don't look tired."

"I'm not."

Okay, something was up with him. "How long was I asleep?"

"Not long. An hour." His gaze slid to her throat, and he touched her necklace. "This is pretty. I don't remember you wearing it before tonight."

The mention of the necklace brought memories crashing back in and shattered the serene moment. She saw Javier, the club, the gunmen, heard the shots and screams and horror.

She closed her eyes tight, took a deep breath.

"Hey," Finn said softly. "You okay?"

She managed a pathetic laugh. "You know I said I was good in a crisis, right?"

"Yeah."

"Apparently not so good after."

"Come here." Whatever was bothering him seemed to

disappear. He tugged her close, until the strength of his arms surrounded her and her body pressed into his, her cheek against his warm chest, her legs entwined with his. Okay, this she could get used to. She valued her independence, didn't need anyone to take care of her, but this comfort, this sense of completeness she could definitely use more of. "It's gonna be okay."

"I know. I just . . . why Javier? I don't get it."

"How well did you know him?"

"Not well at all. This was the first time we'd worked together. But he seemed so down to earth. I don't know. I liked him."

He didn't answer, and his silence unnerved her. "What?"

"There was a lot more to Santiago than either of us knew." When she pushed back and looked up at him, he sighed and told her about his conversation with his boss while she'd been in the shower.

Shock rippled through Lauren. "No way."

"That was my first reaction, too."

"And you're saying he ratted his family out? For what? Money?"

"Most likely. That's usually what it comes down to. But this isn't a normal family, Slim. This is the biggest crime organization in all of southwestern Mexico."

Lauren wasn't sure she liked the way he called her *Slim* again. It seemed so . . . impersonal. When they'd made love, when he'd said her name . . . something about the way he'd said it had felt . . . right.

She told herself what he called her was the least of her worries right now. Snuggling back into Finn's chest, she tried to make sense of what had happened. Nothing about what she knew of Javier matched the picture Finn had just painted.

"He gave it to me," she said softly.

"Gave you what?"

"The necklace." When he pushed her back again, she reached down and touched the tear-shaped red gem the size of a quarter. "At Palladium. After I came down from the stairwell with you. Just before"—she swallowed—"just before they killed him. He pulled me aside, slipped the necklace around my throat and asked me to keep it safe for him."

Finn's brow pulled together. "Did he say why?"

She thought back to that last moment with Javier. She'd been so upset over what had happened with Finn in the stairwell, she'd barely paid attention to Javier's ramblings. "No, he just said it was a pain in his ass. The family devil or something like that."

Finn sat up, the low light reflecting the muscular planes of his chest, the dark stubble on his jaw. His face took on a serious look. "Devil? He used the word devil? Are you sure?"

"Yeah," she said, easing up herself, clutching the sheet to her breasts. "What now?"

He fingered the gem. "The new improved drug the Cárdenas Cartel's unveiling used to be called red devils."

She glanced down at the gem nestled just above her cleavage. "Are you saying you think this thing contains—"

"No." He turned it in his fingers. "There's nothing inside this. I took a close look when you were asleep. It's some kind of transparent stone. Could be colored glass, I guess. But . . ."

"But what?"

He shrugged. "I'm no expert, but the way it sparkles, it almost looks . . ."

"What?"

"Real."

Lauren looked down again. "A real ruby? No way. It has to be fake. Costume jewelry. You can get stuff like this at Macy's, for crying out loud. Besides, if it was real, what would Javier have been doing with a ruby this size in Palladium? And what would a ruby have to do with those gunmen or the Cárdenas Cartel?"

"I don't know," Finn answered. "But it's one more piece of this puzzle worth looking in—"

The phone on the bedside table blared. Finn tensed beside her, but leaned over to pick up the receiver. He didn't say hello, but the heavily accented rapid-fire voice on the other end of the line came through loud and clear. Finn glanced Lauren's way as he tossed back the covers and pushed to his feet. Before he could say anything to her, a loud popping sound echoed over the line, and he tore the phone from his ear.

"Sonofabitch." He dropped the phone as if it had burned him. "Get dressed. Right now."

She scrambled from the bed. "What happened?"

Finn was already in his jeans by the time Lauren came back in the room, clothes in hand. He tugged on the shirt she tossed him, checked the magazine on his handgun. "That was the motel owner. They found us."

Fear burst in Lauren's throat. Hands shaking, she dragged on her dirty clothes and hustled across the floor to the window Finn was already prying open. "Come on, Slim. Hustle."

That popping sound had been gunfire. Again. Was the motel owner dead now? Swallowing the bile rising in her throat, Lauren gripped the window ledge with one hand, put the other on Finn's shoulder, bracing herself as he helped her up. Before she could get all the way out the window, gunfire exploded behind them, tearing apart the door to the small motel room.

"Go!"

Finn shoved her out the window. She hit the ground on her shoulder, groaned at the stab of pain and rolled to the side. Seconds later, Finn was beside her, hauling her up by the arm and dragging her across the dirt-strewn back lot. "Run!"

She didn't have any other choice. Pushing her legs as fast as she could, she didn't slow until they reached the old beat-up truck behind the office. Finn cranked the door open, pushed her inside. Shouts echoed behind them. Finn slammed the door, shoved the key in the ignition. "Please, baby. Start."

The truck coughed once, expelling a burst of exhaust, then turned over.

"Yes!" Finn shoved the truck into reverse, slapped his hand on the back of the seat and whipped the truck around. Gunfire echoed behind them. His hand hit her in the head, forcing her to fall across the seat. "Get down!"

Lauren covered her head with her hands and tried to stay on the seat as the truck whipped back and forth on the gravel. They turned toward the road, but just before they reached the pavement, Finn slammed on the brakes. Lauren's body sailed forward into the dash, then dropped to the floorboards.

She squealed, then groaned. Finn didn't seem to notice. He rolled the window down, lifted the gun and aimed.

Gunfire echoed in Lauren's ears. Shouts followed. The truck's tires spun out but finally found pavement. More gunfire exploded behind them, and then all sound faded but the hum of the old engine and the beat of Lauren's racing heart.

She pushed herself up from the floor, crawled back on the seat. "What the hell was that?"

Finn's jaw was a slash of steel beneath his skin as he shook his head. "I don't know how they found us so fast. I shot out their tires, so hopefully they won't be able to follow us."

"Oh, my God," she whispered, sinking back into the seat, staring out at the headlights illuminating the barren road. "The motel owner."

"Don't think about it."

Right. Like that was possible. She fingered the gem at her chest. Was all this really about some stupid necklace?

Finn reached for the phone in his pocket, hit a number and held the phone to his ear. "Jake? They found us. Shit, yeah, we're on the move. No, we're both okay. Wait. I'm gonna put you on speaker."

He hit a button, set the phone on the dashboard. "Lauren's here with me."

Lauren. Why, in the midst of a life-or-death crisis, did the sound of her name on his lips set off butterflies in her stomach?

"Busy night for you, Ms. Kauffman. You doing okay?"

Jake Ryder had a strong, confident voice, one that for some odd reason put Lauren at ease. "I'm still alive. I guess that counts as okay."

A soft chuckle echoed from the phone. "Balls of steel," he muttered. "Tierney, you were wrong."

Lauren had no idea what the man meant by that, but Finn obviously did. "I know," he muttered. "Look, what do you know about a ruby called the Red Devil?"

Silence echoed over the line, followed by the distinct sound of computer keys clicking. "Nothing, but then I'm not big on the gem trade. Why?"

Finn checked the rearview mirror and glanced at Lauren. "Santiago gave Lauren a necklace. A teardrop-shaped gem, looks like a ruby, could be glass but . . . sonofabitch is big. He called it 'the devil.' "

"Lauren," Jake said after a moment's pause. "Describe it for me."

She told him what she could, detailed the shape and

weight and color of the gem, then said, "It can't be real, can it?"

"I don't know," Jake answered. "Let me do some research. I'll call you back."

The phone clicked off. Finn glanced in the rearview again, then turned off on a side road, one Lauren didn't even see in the dark.

"Are we being followed?" Anxiety amping, she twisted in her seat to look behind them.

"No, I'm just being cautious." He looked her way, the lights from the old dash illuminating the contours of his now-familiar face, the bruise across his jaw, the little hickey on his neck she'd given him only hours ago. "You're pretty damn good in a crisis, Slim."

She sat back again, couldn't help feeling warmed by his compliment. Then cooled by that nickname all over again. Fortunately, her heart rate was finally back in the normal range, and she felt she could breathe once more. "You're not so bad yourself." She looked ahead at the dirt and gravel illuminated by the truck's headlights and the thickening jungle on both sides of the makeshift road. "Where to now?"

"Jake has an operative who's got a place down here. He's got a chopper at his ranch. Should be able to fly us out."

"An operative? Way out here?"

"Yeah. He's kind of on a break."

"What kind of break sends a guy out into the sweltering jungle?"

Finn gripped the steering wheel as they bounced over a large pothole. "A pretty big one. Why don't you lie down and get some sleep. We've got a long drive ahead of us."

Alone with Finn in the cab of the truck, surrounded by nothing but darkness, for the first time all night Lauren felt safe. And tired. More tired than she'd been in longer than she could remember. She lifted her bare feet onto the seat, shifted over so she could rest her head on Finn's thigh. He tensed, and for a second she thought he was going to ask her to move over. But then he dropped his right hand and ran it down her hair.

Her eyes slid closed. A sigh slipped from her lips. Yeah, she could totally get used to this. Not the guns and running and scare-the-shit-out-of-her part, but the comfort. These hands. This man. Somehow, before whatever this was was over, she had to convince him he needed to get used to her as well.

CHAPTER 6

"Dammit." Finn pulled the old truck as far off the road as he could before it died.

Lauren pushed herself up from his lap. Blond hair fell over her face as she licked her lips and looked around with eyes sleepy and sexy as hell. "Wh . . . what happened?"

Resisting the urge to reach for her, Finn pushed his door open. "Ran out of gas. We're gonna have to hoof it from here."

Lauren's eyes cleared. Her brows knitted together as she looked out the windshield at the gray morning light seeping in through the thick jungle canopy. "What? How far is it? I still don't have any shoes, remember?"

"No more than three miles." Finn reached under the seat. "And don't worry. I've got you covered. These slid out from under the seat when we turned a corner." He pulled out a filthy pair of dingy orange flip-flops that had obviously seen better days.

Lauren stared at the flip-flops. "You're kidding, right?"

"Come on, Slim. I'm sure these shoes have sentimental value for *someone*."

She frowned, took the flip-flops with restrained enthusiasm and slid them on her feet. "You owe me a pair of Givenchys. I'm not gonna forget this."

He didn't say anything as she slid out of the cab of the

truck, her skirt riding high on her thighs. Told himself he didn't want to take her shopping to pick out that pair of Givenchys. Definitely didn't want to see her slide her sexy feet into those icepick heels and model them just for him, naked.

Sweat broke out on his forehead. He turned away, wiped his brow. Reminded himself about being a class-A schmuck. It was all he'd been able to think about this morning while she'd been asleep with her head nestled on his lap. There wasn't going to be a repeat of last night. He wasn't going down this road again, no matter how smart and unique and sexy she was. Last night had been . . . a reaction. A surge of adrenaline. A rush of hormones. A natural response to a near-death experience. It didn't mean anything.

Keep telling yourself that, buddy.

He pulled in a breath, let it out slowly. Okay, so it had been hotter than hot. More erotic than his X-rated dream. The best sex he'd had in . . . shit, a long-ass time. But that didn't mean it wasn't a monumental mistake. He had a job to do here. He was going to get her to Archer's compound and then get her the hell out of Mexico. And that would be it.

Resigned, he pulled out his satellite phone, checked the GPS coordinates and pointed through the trees. "That way."

They hadn't trudged more than a half mile before he wished he'd had the foresight to stop for water in one of the small towns they'd driven through early that morning. He whipped off his shirt, swiped the sweat off his face and neck, then stuffed the dingy rayon in his back pocket. From the corner of his eye he saw Lauren pulling the skimpy top she wore away from her chest, fanning the fabric to cool herself off.

Images of her succulent breasts popped into his head. Of

her arching her back, offering them to his mouth. He clenched his jaw and tried to force the memories away.

Didn't work.

"Did you hear back from your friend Jake while I was asleep?" she asked.

"Yeah."

"And?"

He'd wanted to avoid this conversation, but at least it kept him from imagining what it would feel like to slide into her naked body from behind. How it would feel to caress her breasts until she screamed his name again like she'd done last night.

He wiped the growing sweat from his brow. Told himself to refocus. The info Jake had passed on changed things dramatically. He stopped on the path so she could catch her breath. "Know much about Aztec mythology?"

"No. Do you?"

"Not much. There are a bunch of gods and goddesses, way too many to remember. All do different stuff. Anyway, this one goddess, Chantico, she's like the goddess of fire. Her symbols are a red serpent and cactus spikes, and she rules over fire, wealth and precious stones within the earth."

Lauren's brow drew together, and he could almost read her mind. She knew where this was going.

He looked at a bird chirping high in the canopy. "When Cortez swept through Mexico, he commandeered more than just Aztec gold. He loaded boats full of Aztec treasures and sent them back to Spain. Including, according to legend, one twenty-five carat, rare red diamond known as 'the red serpent.' The gem of Chantico herself."

Lauren's hand drifted to her throat, but her eyes stayed locked on his. Finn figured she was as speechless as he'd been when Jake told him what he'd found, so he went on.

"The way the story goes, Chantico's got quite a temper,

and she doesn't like thievery, especially when it involves something that belongs in Mexico. Several of those ships went down in hurricanes. Were never seen or heard from again. Treasure hunters have been scavenging sunken Spanish galleons in the Caribbean for decades, with no sign of the diamond. About two years ago, a guy made the find of a lifetime. A rare red diamond. Which historians quickly called the Red Devil.

"It sold at auction for some insane amount—talking millions and millions of dollars here—but before the treasure hunter could collect, he was killed in a car accident. The buyer had plans to take it out of Mexico, but he died in a freak boating accident before he could do that, and his son, who—after several death threats—was convinced the diamond was cursed, loaned it to the National History Museum of Mexico so it would be out of his possession."

"Good Lord."

"It gets better. Three weeks ago, the diamond was stolen from its display box in the museum. No one's seen it since."

Lauren was silent for a second and then said, "You're saying this is a diamond . . . not just a ruby?"

"I'm saying it's possible, yeah."

"And Javier stole it?"

"No. If this is *the* Red Devil from the stories, the Cárdenas Cartel stole it. Which is why they want it back so bad. My guess? Javier stole it from them. Why? Who knows. Maybe he wanted it for himself. Maybe he wanted to piss them off. Maybe he wanted to return it where it belonged. I don't know. Bottom line . . . they killed him because of it."

She looked down at the ground, her fingers still on the stone at her chest. "They knew he was with me. They must have figured he gave it to me."

"Yeah." That was his guess, too.

"My God, this isn't about drugs after all. It's about one cursed necklace."

"Not cursed, Slim. Superstitions may run deep in this country, but that thing's no more cursed than those shoes you're wearing. It's just a stone. Worth a lot of money. I told you before, everything comes down to money."

"Not to me. Money's not nearly as important as people think." Her fingers slid up to the chain around her neck. "I shouldn't be wearing this. I—"

He covered her hands with his own, brought hers down in front of her. "I think it's safest right where it is. You've taken good care of it so far. Let's not rock the boat, okay?"

Her eyes settled on his. "Do I sense a little superstition, Tierney?"

The corner of his mouth curled up. He liked her, dammit. The more time he spent with her, the harder that fact was to deny. "I'm Irish, Slim. A little superstition comes with the blood. But that doesn't mean I think things are doomed."

"I like hearing that," she said, her husky voice just above a whisper. "I really like hearing that."

He looked from the gem to her brilliant blue eyes and had the strangest sensation they weren't talking about the necklace anymore. An image of their bodies tangled in the sheets of last night's bed slid through his mind, lighting up his blood and squeezing his chest so hard it hurt to draw breath.

She looked down the path. "So your friend . . . Archer? He can fly us out of here? Then what?"

Then he needed to get away from her before he did something stupid like forgot about all the rational reasons this thing between them would never work.

He dropped his hand, moved back. "Um . . . then we turn that stone over to the authorities and let them sort out the mess."

She nodded, and he figured telling her the rest of it—that Jake had confirmed young Javier was planning to sell the stone to a rival cartel who believed it would grant them power and protection from the gods—was more than she needed to know. Let her go on thinking her friend had been trying to right a wrong and leave it at that.

They didn't speak as they moved through the overgrown jungle, and Finn was glad. The longer he spent with the sexy supermodel, the more tangled his thoughts became.

He cleared a path as best he could, but vines and twigs snagged their clothing and scratched Lauren's bare legs. The humidity made it hard to breathe. The thick foliage left all but what was directly in front of them hidden from view. What little light filtered down from above showcased vibrant greens, bright oranges, deep reds and golden yellows.

She didn't complain, not about the heat or humidity or even the ridiculous orange flip-flops on her feet. And as they moved, Finn marveled at one more piece of Lauren Kauffman that just didn't fit with her public persona. At this point, Sylvia would have been whining her ass off. The thought stilled his feet. No, by this point Sylvia would have been a blubbering, crying, moaning mess. If, that is, she'd ever been able to get off the roof of Palladium. Which he seriously doubted she ever could have done amid the chaos.

He flashed on Lauren throwing her precious Givenchys at those thugs on the roof. Coming to his rescue and saving his ass. A chuckle slipped from his lips.

"Something funny, Tierney?" Lauren stepped by him, taking the lead on the small path he'd found about a quarter mile back. It wasn't wide, but at least following it meant they didn't have to blaze their own trail.

He watched the sexy sway of her backside as she moved ahead of him, the flex of muscles in her shoulders and back left bare by her halter top. He remembered running his fingers over those ridges and dips, following them with his lips and tongue. God, she was sexy, and so damn beautiful. He couldn't believe she'd actually listened to him when he'd said she was built like a teenaged boy. Didn't she have eyes? Couldn't she see what he did?

She swatted at a bug, reached for a vine and carefully stepped over it, kept on going. And from where he stood, he almost thought he heard her . . . humming.

No, he realized, listening to the soft lilt of her voice. Fame and money and modeling aside, Lauren Kauffman was as different from Sylvia Grace as apples were from, well, crabapples.

Her humming stopped abruptly, her feet stilled on the path. But it was the squeal that slipped from her mouth that shocked Finn back to reality.

He pulled his gun from the small of his back and sprinted to catch up with her, his heart in his throat because he'd spaced out when he should have been paying attention. But when he reached her, he realized she wasn't hurt or scared or in danger. She was smiling. Excitement illuminated her face and brought a sparkle to her eyes.

"Look," she whispered, pointing through the trees toward what he now realized was a small river. She stepped forward.

"Slim, wait."

She took off running, her flip-flops clacking against the soles of her feet. By the time he caught up with her, she was already tearing off her shirt and shimmying out of her skirt.

Holy hell. All he could do was watch as each inch of glowing skin came into view. He'd had his hands on that last night. Had run his fingers over that slim hip, had caressed those luscious breasts, had drawn his tongue over and around that sweet little belly button. His gaze slid lower. He swallowed back a rush of arousal. He'd tasted that . . .

She dropped the garments on the riverbank, kicked off the grimy flip-flops and didn't even look back as she ran into the water and dropped down until all that was left was the tip-top of her golden head.

Common sense finally kicked in. He moved to the edge of the water and waited until she came back up. She emerged on her back, where she floated with her head reclined, water sliding down the curves of her naked flesh, making her skin sparkle like diamonds in the sunlight flittering through the treetops. "Okay, Slim. Get out of the water."

"This feels so good," she said, ignoring him as she let the current carry her downstream. "You should get in, Tierney. Cool off."

No shit, he needed to cool off, but he doubted water was going to do the trick. He picked up her clothes and shoes, followed her down the riverbank so she didn't float away from him. "You don't know what's in that water. There could be snakes, bugs . . . crocodiles." Were there crocodiles in Mexico? Shit, he didn't know.

"At this point I'm willing to take my chances." Her eyes slid closed, and she moaned, the same sort of sound she'd made last night when he'd been deep inside her. "Oh, my God, Finn. This is heavenly."

His blood warmed and his skin grew tight, but he pushed down the desire because what he needed was for her to get out of the damn water. "Slim, Archer's waiting for us. We don't have a lot of time to dick around here."

"Yeah, okay. Just . . . a few more minutes."

He clenched his jaw, stepped over a downed palm tree. The foliage on the edge of the river thickened, so he moved around a clump of mangrove. A crashing sound met his ears. For just a split second she was out of view. A scream cut through the hot, humid air.

Shit.

He raced around the trees and stopped on the edge of the river again, but Lauren had disappeared.

"Lauren!" He dropped her clothes, rushed into the river.

The cool water reached his thighs. Heart in his throat, he pushed his free hand through the murky depths, searching for her. Laughter echoed from somewhere close.

He turned, looked ahead, realized that the river dropped and the crashing he'd heard was actually the rush of water over rocks. He pushed himself through the water toward the sound and stopped at the top of a fifteen-foot waterfall. Lauren looked up at him from the pool below, treading water with a smile on her famous face.

"Now *that* was a rush!" she hollered up at him. "Better than Blizzard Beach! Come on down!"

Holy shit, she was . . . She *had* to be kidding. She wanted him to . . .

He turned before he said something he knew he'd regret. Made it back to shore without losing his cool. Yanking her clothes from the rocks, he headed down the embankment toward the edge of the pool, water squishing in his shoes as he moved, muttering to himself about all the other, more important things he could be doing right now. Like pulling hostages out of a refugee camp, saving orphans from crime lords in South America, guarding a fucking president, for crying out loud.

He pushed through the palm fronds on the edge of the pool and found her floating in the middle of the lagoon, the tips of her breasts visible above the surface. She didn't even seem to care that she'd just scared the shit out of him.

He stomped two feet into the water, worked like hell to keep his voice calm. "Get out of the water now, Slim."

Her head popped up, and she shot a sassy smile his way. "I've still got the necklace, don't worry."

Like he cared about the damn necklace right now? His jaw clenched. "I'm not kid—"

"Oh, come on, Tierney. No one knows we're here. You said yourself we weren't followed. We've got time."

That was true. But it didn't mean they had time for

screwing around. He needed to get her to safety sooner rather than later—if not for her sanity, then for his. "I'm not going to tell you again."

Surprise registered in her baby blues, followed by a look he recognized as a very clear challenge that curled the edge of her mouth in a wicked way. "Why don't you come in here and *not* tell me that again?"

"I swear to God, Lauren, if you don't—"

Her splash cut off his words. She swam toward the rocks, spraying water in her wake. At the base of the waterfall she grasped the rocks and pulled herself up and out. Water cascaded down her model-perfect naked body. She laughed, braced her hands on the rocks above to steady herself. At her back the wall of stone curved in to form the start of a natural cave, this portion of the wide opening protected by the streaming liquid. She let go of the slippery rocks with one hand, ran it over her hair, pushed the wet mass back from her face.

Around her, majestic green ferns and vibrant orchids the color of the gem at her chest framed the falling water. She looked toward him as the cool liquid continued to rush over every inch of her sultry skin. Then she grinned.

"You're not scared, are you, Tierney?" She slid her foot to the right, to the edge of the moss-covered rock and made a face, pretending to lose her balance. "I could slip and hurt myself. Are you sure you don't want to come over here and . . . save me?"

That was it. As much as he could take. It was the same wicked challenge she'd been dangling in front of him all week. The same I-want-you, are-you-man-enough-to-come-and-take-me look that had nearly driven him to insanity. His chest constricted, his jeans grew tight. The blood turned to a roar in his ears, so loud it was the only thing he could hear. She expected him to be a gentleman like he'd been last night. But every man had a breaking point, and she'd finally pushed him to his.

"Yer gonna regret making me come get you," he said in a low voice.

Her eyes flared with victory, and her grin grew wider. "I doubt it."

"You will."

Bugs and snakes and crocodiles forgotten, Finn maneuvered his way out onto the rocks. Lauren shifted so she was on the far side of the waterfall, well out of his reach. Knowing he was getting wet one way or the other, Finn kicked off his wet boots, stripped out of his clothes and dropped them and his gun on the rocks. Then he dove.

When he came up for air beneath her, she was laughing. His hand wrapped around her ankle, and he pulled. Her squeal met his ears just before the crash of her body slapping water. Then he didn't hear anything. He felt and he tasted and he took exactly what he'd wanted since the first moment he'd laid eyes on her.

CHAPTER 7

Maybe teasing the sexy Irishman had been a bad idea. Finn's naked body was as hard as the stone in that waterfall, his mouth blistering hot against her own. Lauren pushed away, needing to reach the surface for a breath, but he held her below the water and kissed her harder, until her eyes flew wide and she thought she would pass out.

Finally, he dragged her to the surface. She gasped for air, but he didn't give her a chance to catch her bearings. He flipped her around so her back was against his chest and the long, lean line of his body was pressed up tight against her own. His arms wrapped around her torso, pinning her in place, his erection pushed against her ass—hard, thick, insistent.

Her heartbeat picked up speed. Desire flooded her veins, mixed with apprehension over this new show of force.

"Is this what you wanted?" he whispered in her ear, his breath hot and sensual sliding over her skin.

"Um—"

His teeth sank into her earlobe, and she moaned, the shot of pain unexpected and at the same time, arousing.

"We seem to have a little trouble in the communication department, Slim. I think it's time you started listening to me." He pulled her toward the waterfall. "Grab that rock."

She did as he said, mostly to keep from drowning. His

hand slipped between her legs, and she gasped as he pushed a finger deep inside her.

"That's right," he said in her ear. "Yer not in control of this anymore. I am. I told you you'd regret making me come after you. Spread your legs."

She gasped when a second finger joined the first and he circled her clit with his thumb. His other hand slid up to palm her breast, and his cock found its way into the valley between her cheeks.

This was not the same slow, easy lover she'd been with last night. This was a man who knew what he wanted and was taking it. The thought superheated her blood and was so erotic she softened in his arms without a thought, giving herself over to his wicked touch and tantalizing mouth.

He sucked her earlobe, stroked her deep as he drove her headlong toward the peak. His other hand grazed her nipples, sent shards of electricity to that spot between her legs.

"That's right, Lauren. Yer gonna come for me. Right here, right now, aren't you?"

The way he said her name . . . oh . . . She moaned, tipped her head, tried to find his mouth, but he avoided her lips. Instead he bit her neck, circling her skin with his hot, wet tongue.

The feel of his hands, the draw of his lips, that hard cock pressed against her ass . . . it was all too much. Bright light exploded behind her eyes and a shockwave of sensation arced outward from her center.

He didn't give her time to ride the high of her release before he was pushing her forward in the water. "Climb up on that rock, Slim."

Arms weak, she reached up. Her foot found the rocky ledge. He lifted her until she got her balance. Her body came three-quarters of the way out of the lagoon as she gripped the rock at her front and pulled. Water cascaded down her skin, bathing her limbs in the cool, clear liquid.

Then he was at her back, easing her toward the boulder, lifting her hips, kicking her legs wider and pressing his body tight against her own.

She realized what he had planned a split second before he thrust. A groan tore from her chest. He didn't ask permission, didn't wait to see if she was ready. She was so wet from her release, he slid in deep. He pulled out and thrust again.

Fire rippled through her body just before all thought slipped from her mind. His guttural moan echoed in her ears. His fingers dug into her hips, pulling her back tight against his hips as he thrust again and again.

"God, Lauren, I love being inside you."

His fingers slipped down between her legs, found her clit. Her eyes drifted closed as she braced herself, pushed back against him, gave herself over to him. Completely. She loved being with him too. So much . . .

His thrusts picked up speed. Electricity spiraled through her body until she felt ready to come out of her skin. She arched her back, reached behind and grabbed his ass, pulling him into her. Deeper. Harder. The sound of skin slapping skin, the thought of what he was doing to her, out here in the open, it was all so hot. Before she could brace herself the orgasm slammed into her, stole her breath, ricocheted through her limbs and tore a cry from her throat. He grew impossibly hard inside her, igniting a second, all-consuming wave of pulsing pleasure that went on and on and on.

He groaned long and deep, thrust once more. Twice. His entire body shuddered, and then he slumped against her back, breathing hard, his pulse racing like wildfire next to her skin.

Minutes passed. Or maybe it was only seconds, she wasn't sure. Time seemed to stop in those moments. He was heavy against her, and she was pretty sure she was going to have bruises from being pinned up against these rocks, but a smile stretched across Lauren's face as she rested her cheek on her hand and breathed deep.

Now that . . . that was what she'd expected from him the first time. Hot. Wild. X-rated. Totally out of control and better than anything she could remember.

Water dripped over her cheek, ran down her lips. She opened her mouth, desperate for the cool, clear liquid to quench her thirst. But it was the man at her back she couldn't get enough of.

"Shit, Lauren," Finn mumbled, pushing away from her. "I'm sorry. I didn't mean to—"

Alarm bells rang. Any pain she felt slipped to the back of her mind. She turned quickly, caught him around the neck before he could get away from her. "Didn't mean to what?"

His eyes widened as he lost his balance. His hands flew out to steady them both, but it was too late. They were already tipping back, falling into the pool below.

Lauren didn't let go. They submerged, and both kicked to the surface. When their heads cleared the water, she pressed her lips against his and pulled back. "You'd better not be sorry for what just happened."

"I didn't plan—"

"So what? That was awesome." She pulled herself tight against him, wrapped her legs around his lean waist so he had no choice but to slide his arms around her ribs to keep them balanced. The gem at her chest rested between them, warmed from their skin. "If we didn't have to be somewhere, I'd find a way to get you to do it again."

"I wasn't thinking, Lauren. I didn't plan . . . *shit*." He took a breath. "I . . ."

His worry and embarrassment registered, and eased the pinch in her chest. *Please let this be his only issue right now.*

She ran her fingers through his dark, thick, dripping hair, desperate to ease his angst. "I've got you covered. Don't worry."

His gaze narrowed. "What—?"

"I'm on Depo. You know, the shots?"

"You—"

Her back came up, just a tad. "I don't get around, if that's what you're thinking. In my profession I can't chance an unplanned pregnancy. It's just safer to be prepared. And I'm clean, in case that's what you're worried about. I know the tabloids make me out to be some hussy, but you're actually the first guy I've been with in quite a while, and I, well . . ."

Her mouth slammed shut when she realized he was staring at her as if she'd sprouted wings. Okay, now she was rambling. And sounding desperate. Dammit, that wasn't the way she wanted to sound right now. Calm, clear, confident, collected . . . any of those would suffice. Heat rushed to her cheeks.

"That's not what I'm worried about," he said softly.

"It's not?"

"No. Though thanks for pointing out one more thing I fucked up on."

"Oh. Then what's wrong?"

"Why aren't you pissed at me?"

Her brow wrinkled. "Should I be?"

Exasperation crossed his rugged features. "Yes, dammit. Especially after everything you just mentioned." He moved an arm's length away from her, slapped the water between them. "I'm supposed to be keeping you safe, not . . ."

"Not what?"

His jaw clenched. "Not fucking you against a rock like an animal, hurting you in the process and putting you in more jeopardy than you were before."

A space in her chest eased. He wasn't rejecting her. Not yet.

"Finn, do I look hurt?" When his skeptical gaze swept over her, she added, "Seriously, do I sound like I'm complaining over here?"

He stared at her, the wrinkle between his brows so damn cute, she ached to kiss it from his forehead. "Why aren't you?"

"Because that was hot. You wanted me so bad you didn't stop to think. That's what every woman wants."

"She does?"

"God, yes." Her lips curled. "To be desired that much? It's the sexiest thing ever."

She moved into him, her breasts grazing his chest, her arms wrapping around his shoulders so he couldn't get away. "And before you go getting all bent out of shape on me, remember this. I happen to know you'd never put me in danger, consciously or subconsciously, whether you agree or not. If I had said no, I know you would have stopped. I trust you, Finn. With my safety, with my body. With every part of me."

He didn't answer. Simply stared at her again, this time like she'd sprouted horns to go with those wings. In the silence her anxiety peaked, and she wondered if he was going to push back. She couldn't read his mind, but she knew what was in hers. She was falling for him, and she had no idea if he felt the same, or if this thing between them was nothing more than sex. If it was only sex . . .

She swallowed hard, hating the thought. And just when she was sure he was going to move away, he sighed and closed his eyes. His arms came around her, drawing her tighter into his embrace and holding her close, as if she was the only thing that mattered.

"Yer gonna be the death of me, you know that?"

"I hope not," she said against his neck, loving the feel of him, the scent of him, loving everything about him. "I kinda like you, Tierney."

Something in her chest squeezed tight as he cradled her in the water, ran his fingertips up and down her spine. She didn't want to push things, didn't want to do anything to scare him away. But their time was ticking down. In a matter of hours, it could be over. If she didn't go after what she wanted now, she might never have the chance. And what she wanted most, she'd realized, was him.

Now or never . . .

She eased back, stared at his tanned face, ran her finger over the scar near his left eyebrow. And swallowed back the fear. The fear that had kept her single for way too long. "Finn, I—"

The wind kicked up, whipped past their faces, ruffled the palms and foliage around them. Lauren's words died as they both looked toward the trees along the edge of the pool. A low rumble sounded above the jungle, growing progressively louder.

"Oh, shit," Finn mumbled.

Lauren's eyes narrowed as she tried to see past the thrashing tree branches. "What is that?"

Before he could answer, the helicopter appeared above the parted canopy. Rushing right toward them.

Finn let go of her, hollered something Lauren couldn't hear over the whir of the blades. The door of the big bird opened, and a man leaned out of the chopper.

They'd been found. Lauren's eyes flew wide. Oh, God . . . they'd been found.

Finn slapped one big hand on her head and pushed. She went down with a gasp. Water filled her mouth and lungs. But the only thing she could focus on was the image she'd seen before plunging beneath the surface. An image she would take to her grave.

The barrel of a machine gun trained on her heart.

CHAPTER 8

Finn wrapped his hand around Lauren's wrist and pulled hard. A muffled grunt came out of her under the water, followed by the slurping thump of bullets cutting through the liquid toward them.

He kicked harder, cursed himself for leaving his gun yards away on the rocks, for putting her in danger like this. Ahead he spotted the cave he'd noticed earlier, the one that started at the waterfall and ran back deep into the limestone rocks.

The water curved in under the protection of an arching ceiling of stone. He pulled Lauren in after him, made sure she was out of sight of that chopper and pushed her up onto the rocky ledge. She gasped for air.

"Are you okay?" he asked. "Are you hit?"

"No." She coughed, braced her hands on the rocks and pushed herself out of the water. "No, I'm"—she hacked up a lungful of water—"I'm okay."

Thank God.

"Stay here, don't move. I'll be back."

She scrambled to grasp his wrist. "You're not going back out there."

"I've gotta get my gun if we're going to have any kind of chance."

Her grip tightened. "Finn. Please don't go out there. Please?"

The fear in her voice cut at him. He put his free hand over hers, tried to reassure her. "I'm like a bad penny, Lauren. I always turn up." He glanced around the dark cave, spotted a ray of light way in the back. "If I'm not back in twenty minutes, look for a way out back there."

"Finn—"

"Archer's ranch is a half mile due east of here. Did you hear that? If I'm not back, Lauren. If something happens . . . get to Archer for help."

She swallowed hard. Squeezed his hand tighter. The intensity of her gaze held his until his chest pinched. "You'd better come back, Tierney. You still owe me those shoes, you know. I'm holding you to that."

She let go of him, moved farther into the shadows until her back was pressed up against the slick rock wall. She drew her knees up to her chest, wrapped her arms around her legs and stared at him.

He'd never thought her vulnerable. Not until this minute. Even before, when they'd been on the run, when these whackos had been chasing them, she'd always seemed able to deal with anything they threw her way. Which had made all of this easier on him, he realized. Now though? Now she looked . . . almost lost.

It wasn't because of him, he told himself. It wasn't because she'd fallen for him. It wasn't because the thought of something happening to him was the one thing that could break that iron strength he'd so come to admire.

He took a deep breath, turned and dove deep. But as he swam, he knew he was feeding himself a line of shit from here to the States. Because if something happened to her now . . . God help him, he wasn't sure he'd be able to handle it.

He kicked hard, pulled with his arms. The thump of bullets hitting the water echoed to his left. His lungs burned as he swam back toward the rocks where he'd left his clothes. A prayer whipped through his mind that he'd be able to reach his gun and that he hadn't just flat-out lied to Lauren right to her face.

His lungs filled with sweet air as soon as he broke the surface. He grasped the rocks and pulled himself out of the water without looking back. Darting behind the waterfall, he peered around the side of the rocks and spotted his clothes lying ten feet away.

His adrenaline surged. The handle of his Beretta stuck out from beneath his black shirt. He glanced up toward the black-and-white striped Huey circling the trees, the gunman leaning out over the open door, searching.

There wasn't time to plan. If they changed their angle, they'd be able to see Lauren in the cave. The Huey circled back around, headed Finn's way. His muscles coiled and he sprang toward his gun. Rocks tore into the skin of his leg as he skidded to a stop, gripped the weapon with both hands and aimed.

His vision zeroed in on the pilot. All he needed was one well-placed shot. The white of the man's helmet was like a blinking target as he unloaded into the cockpit. Glass shattered. Bells and beeping filled the early morning air. The Huey tipped to the side, the gunman hollered, lost his balance. The machine gun fell into the lagoon with a splash. Finn fired again and again until the pilot's head slumped forward and the nose of the bird went down.

Oh, fuck.

Too late he realized the Huey was coming straight for him. His heart lurched into his throat. He grabbed his pants and shirt from the rocks and sprinted into the trees. The chopper struck the rocks feet from where he'd been sitting, nose first, crushing the pilot in a crash that sounded like a detonated bomb. The force knocked Finn off his feet. The blades of the chopper hit the rocks, shattering with deafening *thwacks*. Shards of metal flew in every direction. The fuel tank shot forward and slammed into the cockpit with a boom.

Finn twisted, covered his head with his hands. Sound died down as the back of the big bird settled against the shore of the lagoon with a crunch. Pulse racing, Finn scrambled from the ground, dragged on his pants and stuffed his shirt in his back pocket. Gun gripped in both hands, he inched forward, half expecting a survivor to pop out of the Huey and start firing.

Steam rose from the wreckage. Nothing moved. He hesitated. Sniffed. Caught the unmistakable scent of gasoline.

Fuck. *Fuck!*

Instinct kicked in. He turned and ran. Was fifteen feet back in the trees when the gasoline reached the smoldering motor, igniting the fumes in an explosion that rocked the world right out from under his feet.

His body sailed through the air, crashed into the base of a palm. Pain exploded behind his eyes, raced down his spine. Groaning, he rolled to the side and pushed himself up. His gun was five feet away, lying on a palm frond. The hair on his arms was singed.

Holy shit.

Grabbing his gun, he hobbled toward the lagoon and the cave where he'd left Lauren. He cringed at the pain exploding like fireworks in his head.

When he reached the edge of the water, breath heavy from exertion, he realized the wreckage blocked his path behind the waterfall. That left swimming to reach her. Which could fuck up his gun. He wasn't chancing leaving it on the shore this time. He didn't know who else was out here in this jungle.

He leaned forward to rest his hands against his thighs, sucked in air. Crimson droplets dripped down onto his hands. Swiping a hand across his brow, he realized he was bleeding.

Screw it.

He thought about yelling for Lauren, but didn't want to tip off any other terrorists hiding in the jungle. Then he remembered the light he'd seen in the cave. Moving around the far side of the lagoon, he climbed the hillside until he found what he'd been hoping for. An opening in the rocks. A tunnel that looked like it went through on this side.

He tucked the gun into his pants, braced his hands on the rock walls and picked his way across jagged stones that bit into his bare feet. The tunnel was narrow, but tall enough so he could stand. The rich scents of earth and decay met his nose as he moved. Ahead, the tunnel curved to the left, and the echo of water slapping rocks drifted in.

Relief pulsed through him as he stepped down onto the flat shelf of limestone near the water's edge and saw Lauren standing in the light, staring out at the water. She was nothing but a dark silhouette against the brightness of the morning behind her, but from where he stood she looked like an angel. A sultry, sexy, gorgeous angel who'd been sent from above to watch over his ass.

He breathed deep. "Told ya I always turn up."

She whipped around. Froze. But even in the darkness of the cave he saw her eyes fly wide open. "Finn!"

He caught her in both arms before she knocked him back against the wall. Warmth spread through his chest, condensed around his heart as she grabbed on tight. He pushed the pain in his head to the back of his mind. Her naked skin filled his hands, pressed up against his body, reminding him just what they'd done only minutes ago in that water. What he desperately wanted to do with her again. As soon as they were out of this mess and he could get her alone.

"You son of a bitch!" She smacked his shoulder hard. Then she cringed as if she'd hurt her hand. "I thought you were . . . When I heard the gunfire and that explosion . . ." Her voice hitched. "Dammit, Tierney. You scared the shit out of me."

She eased back but he caught her arms before she could pull away, rubbed the sting from her hand. Her eyes filled with worry as she focused on his face. "You're bleeding." Her hands flew up to touch his forehead. "You're hurt."

He pulled her arms down. "I'm fine. Just a scratch."

"But—"

"I'm okay, Lauren. Trust me. I've been through a lot worse."

Her mouth slid closed but the fear remained. And he knew what she was feeling because he was feeling it, too. He wasn't ready to leave her. He'd thought he would be, thought he could walk away from her when all was said and done, but knew now he couldn't.

"Yer not getting rid of me that easy," he said softly.

Her gaze held his, and tears filled her brilliant eyes. "You're toying with me, Tierney. I may be tough, but I don't know how much more I can take."

He didn't know how much he could take either. His chest was strung tight as a drum as he stood staring at her, but it was nothing compared to what he'd experienced when he'd thought he might lose her.

"Come here." He pulled her into his arms and kissed her. She answered by wrapping her arms around his neck and holding on as if she never wanted to let go.

And he knew in that moment he could easily spend the next hour—the next year if she let him—wrapped in her embrace. But the rational side of his brain said he needed to get her out of here ASAP.

He eased back from her mouth, rubbed his thumb over her bottom lip, marveled at how she'd turned his life on its axis in a mere matter of days. Forget rescuing hostages from South American gangs or protecting presidents. Right here,

right now, this woman . . . *this* was the most important assignment of his life.

Reluctantly, he let her go, pulled the shirt from his back
pocket, then shot her a half-smile he hoped helped calm her
nerves and his as well. "I didn't have a chance to grab yer
orange flip-flops. This'll have to do."

She took the black buttondown from his hands, and
looked at the dirt-strewn rayon. "Now you owe me new
clothes on top of the shoes? Oh, I sense a whole shopping
spree in my near future."

He sensed a lot more in her near future. A lot more of
him. If she'd have him. As she tugged his shirt on and buttoned it, he realized the idea sounded good. It felt right.
And though the realization still scared the shit out of him . . .
it didn't make him want to run screaming for the hills.

He grasped her hand and pulled her away from the water
toward the back of the cave. "Come on. Let's get the hell
out of here."

He led her out the tunnel, careful to go slow over the
sharp rocks so she didn't re-injure the bottom of her foot.
When they reached the sunlight, she squinted at the brightness, glanced around the jungle with a wrinkled brow.
"Half a mile? That's it?"

"At the most." He just hoped like hell there weren't any
more surprises along the way.

They headed east. Found what appeared to be a seldom
used road. The jungle pushed in from both sides but didn't
hide the path. They made it a quarter of a mile before they
heard the whine of an engine somewhere close.

"Finn?"

Finn's adrenaline surged all over again. He pulled his
gun, shoved Lauren into the foliage, far enough back to
hide them both from view. Against his back where she huddled close, her pulse picked up speed to match his own.

He held his breath. Tried not to think about how many

could be out there, what could happen next. He wasn't about to lose her, not now. . . .

As the rumble of the vehicle drew close, he trained his gun on the road and reminded himself that all he needed was one well-placed shot.

"Tierney, you dickhead! If you're out here you'd better fucking answer. I'm not in the mood for a rabbit hunt today!"

In front of her, Finn expelled a long breath. He clicked the safety on his gun, shoved it in the waistband at his lower back and turned Lauren's way. "Thank God for the cavalry."

He grasped her hand and pulled her out of the foliage. On the path he let go of her and looked toward the four-wheeler being swallowed up by the jungle as it headed away from them. "Archer!"

Finn waved his arms. Relief pulsed through Lauren when the four-wheeler skidded to a stop and the man at the controls turned to look their way.

They'd been found. They weren't going to die out here. And yet . . . she glanced around the silent jungle . . . she couldn't shake the strange feeling they were being watched. The same feeling she'd had as soon as they'd come out of that cave.

Finn pulled her toward the four-wheeler. Archer climbed off the machine, tugged off his Ranger ball cap and frowned. "You're missing a few eyebrows there, Tierney. Better be careful or I'll start to believe all that shit about your luck being worse than mine."

The sunlight filtering through the canopy picked out the highlights in Zane Archer's dark blond hair. He was roughly the same size as Finn, but his accent pinned him as a Southern boy. "Saw that ball of fire and just knew it was you. Shit, man. You don't do anything easy, do ya?"

Finn shook Zane's hand. "You know me. Always gotta end things with a bang. Though I'm still not sure how they found us so fast."

"You're in Mexico, Ireland." Archer rested his hands on his hips. "Everybody knows everybody around here and a few pesos grease all the right wheels. The Cárdenas Cartel's got eyes all over this region. Don't you know that?"

"I do now." Finn turned her way. "Archer, this is Lauren Kauffman."

Archer didn't reach out to greet her, but his gaze swept her body from head to toe. His deep blue eyes held a haunted look and told Lauren he'd seen things she couldn't begin to imagine. "She's prettier than the last one."

Okay, she should be ticked the man was talking about her like she wasn't even there, but a small part of her couldn't help being pleased by his comment. She cut him some slack because—obviously—his people skills were lacking from his time away from civilization.

Her gaze shifted to Finn, and their eyes met. Then his softened a touch. Just enough to make her forget all about Archer and whatever the heck was wrong with the man. Finn's lips curled in that soft, seductive smile, the one he'd flashed her in that cave, the one she now knew he kept only for her. And just that fast her insides went all liquid and her heart picked up speed until she was sure both men could hear it pounding in her chest.

"A helluva lot smarter, too," Finn said.

The smile edged her mouth before she could stop it. She stepped forward, grasped Finn's hand as he reached out for her. Didn't even try to act like that wasn't the best compliment he could have given her.

Archer swiped the sweat from his brow, tugged his cap back on and frowned. "Yeehaw. Y'all ready to get the hell out of here or what? Chopper's juiced up and ready to go back at the ranch. Take us about five minutes to get there if ya hurry it up."

"I'm more than ready," Lauren said, ignoring his sarcasm.

Finn motioned her toward the four-wheeler, but a snapping sound off to her right caught her attention.

Before she even looked, the hair on her nape stood straight and the feeling they were being watched rushed over her again. The foliage on both sides of the path rustled. Finn tensed, tried to push her behind him but it was too late. The jungle expelled four native men, all dressed in camouflage with automatic weapons trained right on them.

"Sonofa-fucking-bitch," Archer muttered, hands going up.

Lauren's heart lurched into her throat and fear raced up and down her spine. Finn held up both his hands, and Lauren followed suit, but her gaze darted to the handle of Finn's gun sticking out of the waistband of his jeans. Could she grab for it? Would it do any good?

"No one's leaving," the leader of the group said in a thick, Spanish accent. He looked from Finn to Archer. "Your weapons."

Panic closed Lauren's throat. She knew instinctively if Finn gave up his gun, there was no way they were walking out of this alive.

Archer swore under his breath, pulled the nine millimeter from his shoulder harness, held it out and dropped it on the ground. Finn did the same, and as she watched his gun land in the soft dirt at their bare feet, the last of Lauren's hope evaporated.

The leader's lips curled in a nasty smile, revealing gleaming white teeth. He said something in Spanish to the man at his right. The man picked up both guns, inspected them, then shoved them in his belt. The leader's dark gaze swept over them and landed on Lauren. Her spine stiffened when she recognized him.

He'd been in the club. He'd been the one calling the shots. The one who had killed Javier. Her pulse picked up speed until it was a whir beneath her skin. This close, she saw the similarities in his features and realized he had to be Javier's brother.

"You have created a lot of trouble, Ms. Kauffman." His gaze dropped to the necklace. "The Red Devil belongs to me." He motioned with his gun. "Come."

Finn stepped fully in front of her before she could move. He was careful to keep both hands up, but Lauren felt the panic radiating from him. "She's not going anywhere. Look, you can have the necklace, okay? Just let her walk."

Her heart squeezed hard. Without his weapon, what chance did they stand? If she didn't go with these thugs, they were all dead. If she did as they said, maybe they'd let Finn and Archer go.

Tears burned her eyes. "Finn—"

She reached out for his arm, but he shrugged her off, his voice growing hard. "No. This is bullshit." He refocused on the leader. "Take the fucking necklace but let her go. She's not gonna tell anyone about this, okay? No one will know what happened here. I'm the one you want. I'm the one who shot down that helicopter and killed your men on the roof at Palladium. Take me, instead. Blame the whole fucking thing on me."

He was sacrificing himself for her. The enormity of the moment slammed into Lauren, stole her breath. Yeah, he was her bodyguard, and keeping her safe was his job, but this was more than that. This was his surrendering everything for her. This was personal.

The leader's gaze shifted from her to Finn. And his eyes grew dark and hard. The weapon in his hand moved until the barrel was pointed at Finn's chest. "My brother Manuel was in that helicopter."

No! Lauren's muscles coiled tight as she reached for Finn's arm. A scream echoed in her head but she heard the roar of it outside herself. The leader shifted his finger to the trigger. Around them, the foliage rustled again. As the man's head swiveled to the right, Lauren realized the roar hadn't come from her.

A blur of black flashed from the trees, slammed into the leader and the man next to him. Before they could lift their weapons and shoot, a horrific cry tore out of both men. They hit the ground hard. A snarl echoed, and Lauren's eyes flew wide as she scrambled back from the enormous black jaguar sinking its teeth into the leader's throat.

She was right. They had been watched. Only it hadn't been by a drug cartel as she'd assumed. It'd been by a beast.

The man next to Santiago tried to get up. The jaguar swiped out with its claws, caught him by the throat and chest. Blood spurted in every direction. His body slumped to the ground before he even had time to scream.

"Lauren! Run!"

Tearing her eyes away from the carnage, she saw Archer and Finn struggling with the remaining two thugs. Fists met bone. The terrorists' machine guns lay on the ground at their feet. The man Archer was fighting went down with a crack and didn't move. The jaguar snapped its jaws as it tore into the man, and roared again. Lauren looked down and saw Finn's gun had been knocked free when the beast had attacked.

She reached for the weapon just as the jaguar's head swiveled toward the struggle to her right. Finn's fist slammed into the other thug's jaw. The man hit the ground on his ass. The jaguar roared and abandoned its kill, stepping toward the commotion. Hands shaking, Lauren lifted the gun, pointed.

The man Finn had knocked down whipped toward the sound. His eyes flew wide open when he saw the beast stalking his way. A scream ripped from his chest a split second before he scrambled from the ground and tore off into the jungle.

The jaguar's muscles flexed. Sensing a chase, it bounded across the ground after the man, nothing more than a blur of black that disappeared into the trees as fast as it had appeared. A scream echoed deep in the jungle, followed by a roar. Then nothing but silence filled the humid air.

"Fuck me," Finn said, breathing hard as he turned Lauren's way. "No way that just happened."

Archer leaned over, rested his hands on his thighs and sucked in air. "You're not fucking invited to stay. You got that, Tierney? I've been here six months and haven't seen a damn jaguar. You're here ten minutes and every beast in the goddamn place is coming out of the woodwork for you." He reached down, picked up the semi-automatic weapon. "I swear to God you're cursed."

Heart thundering, Lauren lowered the gun.

Archer swore under his breath as he moved past her toward what was left of the leader. "Man, that's gross."

Lauren didn't look. Her pulse pounded in her ears, her heart raced in her chest, but her gaze stayed locked on Finn. Bloody, bruised and covered in a mixture of dirt and sweat, he was the most beautiful thing she'd ever seen.

"It's over," he said in a low voice.

Relief rippled, but it was short lived. Movement behind him caught her eye. The man on the ground pulled a handgun from somewhere in his shirt and raised his arm, pointing the weapon at the back of Finn's head.

Lauren's adrenaline surged. She lifted her arm, braced the butt of the gun against her other hand and fired. Gunshots echoed. She wasn't sure how many times she pulled the trigger. The man's eyes went wide a split second before his body slumped back and the weapon flew from his fingers to thump against the jungle floor.

In the silence that followed, Finn looked from the body now sprawled across the ground with three holes dead center in the chest to her with surprised eyes. "Where the hell did you learn to shoot like that?"

"The range," she said, staring at what she'd done.

"The range?"

His question pulled her attention. "Why do you think I haven't needed a bodyguard until now? My brother made sure if I went into modeling I'd know how to take care of myself."

Finn stepped toward her and reached for the gun. "Give me that."

"Why?"

He slid the weapon from her fingers, flicked the safety and stuck it in his waistband. "Because you look like yer gonna drop it. And keeping you safe is my job now. Besides, I don't want to give you any reason to think you don't need me around after this."

The reality of what she'd done threatened to consume her, but she focused on his eyes to keep from freaking out. His gorgeous, beautiful eyes. "Do you really mean that?"

He pushed the hair back from her face. "I do. If, that is, you think you can put up with me on a more regular basis."

She threw her arms around his neck. Closed her eyes and held on tight.

He laughed and tugged her body close. "I take it that's a yes."

"No, this is a yes." She pressed her lips to his. He answered by kissing her as though he couldn't get enough of her.

Oh, yeah, she was already used to this. Thank God he'd gotten used to her as well.

He eased back. "Yer not worried I might actually be cursed?"

"Cursed?" she asked, looking up at him. "No. Though I'm starting to wonder if this necklace might be blessed. If that jaguar hadn't shown up when it did, we'd all be dead."

The corner of his mouth curled in that sexy half-smile again. "Why, Ms. Kauffman. Do I sense a little superstition in you?"

"Well, you know, I am part Irish. I guess a sprinkling of superstition's in my blood, too."

His smile widened to brighten his whole face.

Archer coughed. "Um, kids? Far be it for me to rain on your sappy-ass parade, but does the word *jaguar* mean anything to y'all? I'd like to get the hell out of here before that thing comes back and decides it wants dessert."

Lauren slid her hand down to twine her fingers with Finn's. Surrounded by gruesome reminders that nothing in life turned out the way you planned, she knew the road ahead wasn't guaranteed to be smooth. But she was willing to travel it. With him. Because she'd finally found something worth more than her independence, worth more than her career, worth more even than the gem around her neck.

"I'm ready," she said. "How about you?"

Finn's eyes sparked with heat. "Only if I get to watch you."

"In my brand-new Givenchys?"

"And nothing else."

"You're on, Tierney."

Don't miss Dani Harper's sexy debut,
CHANGELING MOON,
out now from Brava!

Freezing rain sliced out of the black sky, turning the wet pavement to glass. Zoey stared out at the freakish weather and groaned aloud. With less than two days left in the month of April, the skies had been clear and bright all afternoon. Trees were budding early and spring had seemed like a sure bet. Now *this*. Local residents said if you didn't like the weather this far north, just wait fifteen minutes. She gave it five, only to watch the rain turn to sleet.

Perhaps she should have asked more questions before taking the job as editor of the *Dunvegan Herald Weekly*. She was getting the peace and quiet she'd wanted, all right, but so far the weather simply sucked. Winter had been in full swing when she'd arrived at the end of October. Wasn't it ever going to end?

Sighing, she buttoned her thin jacket up to her chin and hoisted the camera bag over her shoulder in preparation for the long, cold walk to her truck. All she wanted before bed was a hot shower, her soft flannel pajamas with the little cartoon sheep on them, the TV tuned to *Late Night*, and a cheese and mushroom omelet. Hell, maybe just the omelet. She hadn't eaten since noon, unless the three faded M&Ms she'd found at the bottom of her bag counted as food.

As usual, the council meeting for the Village of Dunvegan had gone on much too long. Who'd have thought that such a small community could have so much business to discuss? It was well past ten when the mayor, the councillors, and the remnants of a long-winded delegation filed out. Zoey had lingered only a few moments to scribble down a couple more notes for her article but it was long enough to make her the last person out of the building.

The heavy glass door automatically locked behind her, the metallic sound echoing ominously. Had she taken longer than she thought? There wasn't a goddamn soul left on the street. Even the hockey arena next door was deserted, although a senior men's play-off game earlier had made parking difficult to find. Now, her truck—a sturdy, old red Bronco that handled the snow much better than her poor little SUV had—was the only vehicle in sight.

The freezing rain made the three-block trek to the truck seem even longer. Not only did the cold wind drive stinging pellets of ice into her face, but her usual businesslike stride had to be shortened to tiny careful steps. Her knee-high leather boots were strictly a fashion accessory—her bedroom slippers would have given her more traction on the ice. If she slipped and broke her ankle out here, would anyone even find her before morning?

The truck glittered strangely as she approached and her heart sank. Thick sheets of ice coated every surface, sealing the doors. Nearly frozen herself, she pounded on the lock with the side of her fist until the ice broke away and she could get her key in. "Come on, dammit, come on!"

Of course, the key refused to turn, while the cold both numbed and hurt her gloveless fingers. She tried the passenger door lock without success, then walked gingerly around to the rear cargo door. No luck there either. She'd have to call a tow—

Except that her cell phone was on the front seat of her truck.

Certain that things couldn't get any worse, she tested each door again. Maybe one of the locks would loosen if she kept trying. If not, she'd probably have to walk all the way home, and wasn't that a cheery prospect?

Suddenly a furtive movement teased at her peripheral vision. Zoey straightened slowly and studied her surroundings. There wasn't much to see. The streetlights were very far apart, just glowing pools of pale gold that punctuated the darkness rather than alleviating it. Few downtown businesses bothered to leave lights on overnight. The whispery hiss of the freezing rain was all she could hear.

A normal person would simply chalk it up to imagination, but she'd been forced to toss *normal* out the window at an early age. Her mother, aunts, and grandmother were all powerful psychics—and the gene had been passed down to Zoey. Or at least a watered-down version of it. The talent was reliable enough when it worked, but it seemed to come and go as it pleased. *Like right now.* Zoey tried hard to focus yet sensed absolutely nothing. It was her own fault perhaps for trying to rid herself of the inconvenient ability.

No extrasensory power was needed, however, to see something large and black glide silently from one shadow to another near the building she'd just left. *What the hell was that?* There was nowhere to go for help. The only two bars in town would still be open, but they were several blocks away, as was the detachment headquarters for the Royal Canadian Mounted Police. There was a run-down trailer park a block and a half from the far side of the arena, but Zoey knew there were no streetlights anywhere along that route.

A dog? Maybe it's just a big dog, she thought. *A really big dog or a runaway cow. After all, this was a rural community. And a northern rural community at that, so maybe it's just a local moose, ha, ha. . . .* She struggled to keep her fear at bay and redoubled her efforts on the door locks, all the while straining to listen over the sound of her own harsh breathing.

The rear door lock was just beginning to show promise when a low, rumbling growl caused her to drop her keys. She spun to see a monstrous shape emerge from the shadows, stiff-legged and head lowered. *A wolf?* It was bigger than any damn wolf had a right to be. *Jesus.* Some primal instinct warned her not to run and not to scream, that the animal would be on her instantly if she did so.

She backed away slowly, trying not to slip, trying to put the truck between herself and the creature. Its eyes glowed green like something out of a horror flick, but this was no movie. Snarling black lips pulled back to expose gleaming ivory teeth. The grizzled gray fur around its neck was bristling. Zoey was minutely aware that the hair on the back of her own neck was standing on end. Her breath came in short shuddering gasps as she blindly felt for the truck behind her with her hands, sliding her feet carefully without lifting them from the pavement.

She made it around the corner of the Bronco. As soon as she was out of the wolf's line of sight, she turned and half skated, half ran for the front of the truck as fast as the glassy pavement would allow. *Don't fall, don't fall!* It was a litany in her brain as she scrambled up the slippery front bumper onto the icy hood. With no hope of outrunning the creature and no safe place in sight, the roof of the truck seemed like her best bet—if she could make it. *Don't fall, don't fall!* Flailing for a handhold, she seized an ice-crusted windshield wiper, only to have the metal frame snap off in her hand. She screamed as she slid back a few inches.

The wolf sprang at once. It scrabbled and clawed, unable to find a purchase on the ice-coated metal. Foam from its snapping jaws sprayed over her as the beast roared its frustration. Finally it slipped back to the ground and began to pace around the truck.

Zoey managed to shimmy up the hood until she was able to put her back against the windshield, and pulled her knees up to her chin. She risked a glance at the roof behind her— she had to get higher. Before she could move, however, the wolf attacked again, scrambling its way up the front bumper. Vicious jaws slashed at her. Without thought, Zoey kicked out at the wolf, knocking one leg out from under it. It slid backward but not before it clamped its teeth on her calf. The enormous weight of the creature dragged at her and she felt herself starting to slide. . . .

One hand still clutched the broken windshield wiper and she used it, whipping the creature's face and muzzle with the frozen blade until she landed a slice across one ungodly glowing eye. The rage-filled snarl became a strangled yelp; the wolf released her leg and slipped from the hood. This time Zoey didn't look, just turned and launched herself up-ward for the roof rack. She came down hard, adrenaline keeping her from feeling the impact of the bruising metal rails. She was conscious only of the desperate need to claw and grasp and cling and pull until she was safely on the very top of the vehicle.

Except she *wasn't* safe. Not by a long shot. *Crap.* She could plainly see that she wasn't high enough. *Crap, crap, crap.* The enraged wolf leapt upward in spite of the fact that its feet could find little traction on the ice-coated pavement. What it couldn't gain in momentum, the wolf made up for in effort, hurling itself repeatedly against the Bronco. Its snapping jaws came so close that Zoey could see the bleed-ing welts across its face, see that one of its hellish eyes was now clouded and half-closed. She slashed at it again, catch-ing its tender nose so it howled in frustration and pain as it dropped to the ground. Snarling, it paced back and forth like a caged lion, watching her. Waiting.

The wind picked up and the freezing rain intensified. Huddled on her knees in the exact center of the icy roof, Zoey's adrenaline began to ebb. She was cold and exhausted, and parts of her were numb. But she wasn't helpless; she wouldn't allow herself to think that way. The thin windshield wiper was badly bent with pieces of it missing, but she'd damn well punch the wolf in the nose with her bare fist if she had to. If she still could. . . .

The wolf sprang again.

Try THE DARKEST SIN by Caroline Richards,
out this month from Brava!

Rowena Woolcott was cold, so very cold.

She dreamed that she was on her horse, flying through the countryside at Montfort, a heavy rain drenching them both to the skin, hooves and mud sailing through the sodden air. Then a sudden stop, Dragon rearing in fright, before a darkness so complete that Rowena knew she had died.

When she awakened, it was to the sound of an anvil echoing in her head and the feeling of bitter fluid sliding down her throat. She kept her eyes closed, shutting out the daggered words in the background.

"Faron will not rest—"

"The Woolcott women—"

"One of his many peculiar fixations . . . they are to suffer . . . and then they are to die."

"Meredith Woolcott believed she could hide forever."

Phrases, lightly accented in French, drifted in and out of Rowena's head, at one moment near and the next far away. Time merged and coalesced, a series of bright lights followed by darkness, then the sharp retort of a pistol shot. And her sister's voice, calling out to her.

The cold permeated her limbs, pulling down her heavy skirts into watery depths. She tried to swim but her arms and legs would not obey, despite the fact that she had learned as a child in the frigid lake at Montfort. She did not sink like a stone, weighted by her corset and shift and riding boots, because it seemed as though strong hands found her and held her aloft, easing her head above the current tried to force water down her throat and into her lungs.

She dreamed of those hands, sliding her into dry, crisp sheets, enveloping her in a seductive combination of softness and strength. She tossed and turned, a fever chafing her blood, her thoughts a jumble of puzzle pieces vying for attention.

Drifting into the fog, she imagined that she heard steps, the door to a room opening, then the warmth of a body shifting beneath the sheets. She felt the heat, *his heat*, like a cauldron, a furnace toward which she turned her cold flesh. Her womb was heavy and her breasts ached as he slid into her slowly, infinitely slowly, the hugeness of him filling the void that was her center.

Was it one night or a lifetime of nights? Or an exquisite, erotic dream. Spooned with her back against his body, Rowena felt him hard and deep within her. She slid her hip against a muscular thigh, aware of him beginning to move within her once again. She savored the wicked mouth against the skin of her neck, pleasured by the slow slide of his lips. Losing herself in his deliberate caress, she reveled in his hands cupping and stroking, his fingers slipping into the shadows and downward to lightly tease her swollen, sensitized flesh.

"Stay here . . . with me," he whispered, breath hot in her ear.

And she did. For one night or a lifetime of nights, she would never know.

Good girls should NEVER CRY WOLF.
But who wants to be good?
Be sure to pick up Cynthia Eden's latest novel,
out next month!

Lucas didn't take the woman back to his house on Bryton Road. The place was probably still crawling with cops and reporters, and he didn't feel like dealing with all that crap.

He called his first in command, Piers Stratus, to let him know that he was out of jail and to tell him that there two unwanted coyotes in town.

The woman—Sarah—didn't speak while he drove. He could feel the waves of tension rolling off her, shaking her body.

She was scared. She'd done a fair job of hiding her fear back at the police station and then at the park, at first anyway. But as the darkness had fallen, he'd seen the fear. Smelled it.

Sarah had known she was being hunted.

He pushed a button on his remote. The wrought-iron gates before him opened and revealed the curving drive that led to his second LA home. In the hills, it gave him a great view of the city below, and that view let know him when company was coming, long before any unexpected guests arrived.

When the gate shut behind him, he saw Sarah sag slightly, settling back into her seat. The scent of her fear finally eased.

Like most of his kind, he usually enjoyed the smell of fear. But he didn't . . . like the scent on her.

He much preferred the softer scent, like vanilla cream, that he could all but taste as it clung to her skin. Perhaps he would get a taste, later.

With a flick of his wrist, he killed the ignition. The house was right in front of them. Two stories, Long, tall windows.

And, he hoped, no more dead bodies.

He eased out of the car, stretching slowly. Then he walked around and opened the door for Sarah. As any man would, Lucas admired the pale flash of thigh when her skirt crept up. And he wondered just what secrets the lovely lady was keeping from him.

"We're going to talk." An order. He wanted to know everything, starting with why the dead human had been at his place.

She gave a quick nod. "Okay, I—"

A wolf bounded out of the house. A flash of black fur. Golden eyes. Teeth.

Shit. It wasn't safe for the kid. Not until he found out what was going on—

The wolf ran to him. Tossed back his head and howled.

Sarah laughed softly.

Laughed.

His stare shot to her just in time to catch the smile on her lips. His hand lifted, and, almost helplessly, he traced that smile with his fingertips.

Her breath caught.

Lucas ignored the tightening in his gut. "Shouldn't you be afraid?" After the coyotes, he'd expected her to flinch away from any other shifters. And Jordan was one big wolf, with claws and teeth that could easily rip a woman like Sarah apart.

She looked back at the wolf who watched them. "He's so young, little more than a kid. One who's glad you're—"

No.

Understanding dawned, fast and brutal in his mind. *I'm more than human.* She'd told him that, he just hadn't understood exactly what she was. Until now.

His hands locked around her arms and Lucas pulled her up against him. Nose to nose, close enough so that he could see the dark gold glimmering in the depths of her eyes. "Jordan, get the hell out of here." He gave the order to his brother without ever looking away from her.

The wolf growled.

"Go!"

The young wolf pushed against his leg—*letting me know he's pissed, cause Jordan hates when I boss his ass*—and then the wolf backed away.

"Now for you, sweetheart." His fingers tightened. "Why don't we just go back to that part about you not being human?"

Her lips parted. She had nice lips—sexy and plump. He shouldn't be noticing them, not then, but he couldn't help himself. He noticed everything about her. The gold hoops in her dainty ears. The streaks of gold buried deep in her dark hair. The lotion she rubbed on her body—that vanilla scent was driving him wild.

He was turned on, achingly hard, for a woman he barely knew. Not normally a big deal. He had a more than a healthy sex drive. Most shifters did. The animal inside liked to play.

But Sarah . . . he didn't trust her, not for a minute, and he didn't usually have sex with women he didn't trust. A man could be vulnerable to attack when he was fucking.

"You know what I am, Lucas," she said and shrugged, the move both careless and fake because he knew that she cared, too much.

"Tell me." Her mouth was so close. He could still taste her. That kiss earlier had just been a tease.